"MRS. CHINDLER," FRANK SAID, SMILING DIFFIDENTLY, "WOULD YOU LIKE TO SEE HOW THE WORLD CAME TO AN END?"

She looked as he had expected her to look, startled. "I mean the Cretaceous extinction," he explained. "That was the time, maybe seventy million years ago, when all the dinosaurs became extinct. I've done a computer simulation of the event for, ah, for a government agency.

"The theory is that a big asteroid hit the earth around then. Its impact threw up so much dust that it darkened the sky for several years. Without light, everything died.

"Anyway, I have a consultancy with this, ah, government program, and they asked me to simulate the theoretical episode, only rewritten to assume that the point of impact was right here in Hawaii."

"Why would they do that?"

He glanced up to shake his head humorously: Why did any government agency do anything?

Terror

FREDERIK POHL

BERKLEY BOOKS, NEW YORK

The institutions described in this novel are quite different from any to be found in the real world of Hawaii. That is because they, like all of the novel's characters, are imaginary and do not represent any existing institutions or persons. The scientific and historical facts on which the novel is based, however, are unfortunately not imaginary at all.

TERROR

A Berkley Book/published by arrangement with the author

PRINTING HISTORY
Berkley edition/August 1986

ISBN: 0-425-09106-6

1

On that lovely October day, with glorious sunshine outside the trapped plane and death inside, Rachel Chindler contemplated the ironies of her life. You tried so hard, to end so badly! You went back to school when you were thirty-five years old, in spite of having a child to support and no husband. You got your bachelor's degree at night school, and then you got your Master of Library Science in a concentrated, full-time race against starvation. You went out into the job market as a skinny, not exceptionally good-looking forty-year-old woman, with no experience and a stagnating economy. Marvelously, you got your job anyway! A good one. Then you got two promotions, and you celebrated making Head Librarian by giving yourself a low-budget, two-week tour of Hawaii. And, my God, how lovely Hawaii looked after St. Louis in the cold weather! And then, on impulse, you stopped in at the local college, and, wonder of wonders, they had a good-sized library, and a Distinguished Professor Emeritus took you to lunch with his weird, ancient grandmother and, maybe because the old lady had taken a liking to you, promised to recommend your name to the Search Committee—

And then you wound up here.

You wound up in an unmoving turboprop airplane at the end of an auxiliary runway at the airport in Hilo, with all the plane's toilets stopped up and awful, and an elderly man crying out loud in his sleep a few seats ahead of you. And across

the aisle was the murdered body of the woman who had been
your roommate on the tour.

It certainly was not fair! Rachel would surely have wept at
the unfairness of it if she could. She couldn't weep anymore,
because she was wept out.

Cautiously she peeped out of the blankets around her head.
At the end of the aisle the hijacker with the solid green ski
mask leaned sleepily against the first-class partition. She took
the chance and peered out the window at the sunny Hawaiian
airport scene. Far across the field she could see the four police
cars, overhead lights flashing. Beyond them were clusters of
people. Most of them had been there for two days now,
fascinated with the spectacle, waiting to see some action.
David Yanami, the old Hawaiian professor who had taken her
to lunch, was probably there, along with, no doubt, every
newsperson in the islands. Out of the window on the far side
of the plane the airport perimeter fence was nearby, with the
empty road behind it that the Hilo city police had blocked off
on the hijackers' demand. Rachel didn't look that way. She
didn't want to see Esther's body, even though somebody had
thrown a blanket over it. The blanket was not enough.
Although it was hard to tell with all the other stenches that
filled the plane's interior, Rachel was sickly sure that Esther
was beginning to smell.

She caught a glimpse of movement at the front of the plane
and craned her neck to see.

That was a mistake. The biggest of the four hijackers was
stepping gracefully down the aisle, huge head turning from
side to side as the black eyes behind the ski mask searched for
trouble. Rachel froze. She wasn't about to make any trouble.
No one was, anymore. Esther had tried that at the very beginning, ripping courageously at the ski mask of one of them, and
what that had gotten Esther everyone had seen.

Rachel remembered seeing stewardesses in crowded planes
who carried their trays of drinks at eye-level, just as this man
carried his machine-pistol. He need not have been so careful,
Rachel thought. All of the thirty-seven passengers were either
terrified or sunk in catatonic sleep. The flight crew might have
been less tractable, but they were out of sight in the first-class
cabin, no doubt with a gun on them every minute. None of the

hostages had the daring to grab for a weapon. If they had tried, of course, they would have failed.

Faintly she could hear yelling from the control cabin—no doubt the chief hijacker, once again shouting into the radio. Whatever they were negotiating for, they were not getting it. It was making them angry. Rachel had no clear idea of what their demands were. In the first minutes after the plane was seized on the takeoff strip, the huge hijacker, the one in the green and yellow mask, had made a little speech. Hawaii, he said, belongs to the Hawaiians. The Americans had stolen it in 1898, and the Chinese and the Portuguese and the Japanese and everybody else had gone on stealing it ever since. It was time for the native Hawaiian people to take back their country, through their strong military action arm, the Maui MauMau, and this was Step One in the war of liberation.

It hadn't sounded bad, really, until they killed Esther.

Still, Rachel reflected, if these terrorists were trying to make a moral case, couldn't that mean that they wanted to be moral people? Was it possible to try to talk to them as one human being to another?

Perhaps it was; and Rachel was astonished to find herself putting the thought into action. She saw herself straighten up and look right into the masked man's black eyes. She heard herself say, "Excuse me?"

The hijacker froze. He was only a few feet from her, looking down out of the wool mask, his eyes opaque. Rachel said shakily, "I only wanted to ask—please, couldn't you put this lady's body outside of the plane?"

The terrorist rotated the machine pistol thoughtfully, staring down at her. Then he said, "Shut up, little haole bitch." His voice was soft and deep, and not at all angry. He stood there for a moment without saying more. If there was anything funny about a man hiding behind a ski mask, part of some organization ludicrously called the "Maui MauMau," Rachel could not smile.

There was a new noise from the front. He turned and loped gracefully away.

Rachel was shaking. Oh, what a stupid thing to do! She suddenly needed very badly to go to the bathroom, but more than she wanted that she wanted to live. She did not dare to call attention to herself again by asking. Certainly she did not dare get up without permission. The male hostages, like the hijackers, had been allowed to relieve themselves out the open cabin door from time to time. For the women (again how unfairly!) it was more of a problem. They had been escorted, one at a time, to the toilets, with the door always left humiliatingly open. The problem got worse every hour as the toilets became really unusable, and there seemed no end to it.

The noise at the front suddenly took on an unmistakable shape. A shot!

It was a hard, flat crack from up front. There was a flurry of activity, and the two stewardesses were thrust out of the first-class section, stumbling back along the aisle to find seats. The older of the two, the one who had been allowed to bring them rations of water and packaged macadamia nuts when there still were any, came back to the row just ahead of Rachel before slumping into a seat. She looked worse than Rachel felt. The woman was hysterical, her perky aloha frock soiled and ripped. She stared back at Rachel with frightened eyes. "Oh, my God," she whispered, "they killed the pilot! They say they're going to take off and dive the whole plane into the nuclear power plant on Oahu!"

She stopped talking to listen as the right-hand turbo engine began to whine and then sing. "Belt up," she whispered, the triumph of training over terror. But she did not get up to patrol the aisle.

All up and down the plane now the hostages' heads were beginning to pop up over the backs of their seats. The engines roared. The plane began to move. Someone was at the controls, co-pilot perhaps, or even a hijacker. The aircraft lumbered along a paved strip, wheeled slowly twice onto a different one, then turned again. The roar of the motors rose in pitch and volume. They bumped and shook, and then they were airborne.

They were on their way, somewhere.

To Rachel at that moment it seemed that anywhere would be better than staying forever at the end of the strip at General Lyman Field, with the commuter jets and the intercontinental DC-10s still taking off on the main runway, and themselves condemned to an eternity of helpless waiting.

But it was not better.

They were barely airborne when the huge man in the green and yellow mask appeared at the head of the aisle. His stance was purposeful and frightening. The machine pistol was in his hand. He stood waiting there while the aircraft climbed—only a few thousand feet; the hijackers were not concerned about the CAB's flight rules—and leveled out on its course. Out Rachel's window she could see the cobalt Pacific and the fleecy clouds that stretched more than two thousand miles to the nearest land. On the left, over Esther's body, were the peaks of Mauna Loa and Mauna Kea.

The hijacker began to move.

Without haste he moved down the aisle. At each row he shot the persons occupying the seats in the head.

After the tenth row he switched to a second machine pistol and continued. He was a tall and strong man, and no one struggled. No one jumped up to grab the gun. It seemed that every hostage was as paralyzed as Rachel herself.

When the hijacker shot the man in the seat two rows forward, Rachel closed her eyes. When he killed the stewardess, she began to pray—not for herself, for Stephen, the very-soon-to-be orphan. When she heard the next shot, she thought it was herself.

But she felt nothing.

The aircraft dipped and turned. She waited. She still felt nothing. She dared to open her eyes, and saw the back of the hijacker, already a dozen rows away, handing himself down the aisle as the aircraft came in for a landing.

The hijackers were not infallible. The masked man had made a simple mistake, and across the aisle Esther's plump face had a terrible new hole in it.

The aircraft gently settled, flaps down, as though it were any inter-island charter bringing its load of tourists to the Kona coast. But it was not a normal landing. The airstrip was too short for the plane. The plane reached the end of the strip, still slowly moving, and kept on going, with quite horrible shudders and lunges, for a few more yards before it finally stopped. Rachel could hear the opening of the emergency door over the wing, and men's voices hoarsely muttering to each other, and then silence.

With silly courage, she dared to raise her head and look out.

The last of the hijackers was still on the wing, doing something with what looked like a beer bottle. The other three were already running across a strip of roughly mowed grass toward a wire-link fence. The hijacker on the wing tossed whatever he was holding back into the aircraft, then swung himself down and followed the others. Rachel could see a four-wheel-drive vehicle waiting outside the fence. As she watched, the last man clambered over the fence and scrambled into it, just as it was beginning to move away.

Half a dozen rows ahead, the object he had thrown was lying in the middle of the aisle. It was a green bottle, with a strip of cloth sticking out of its neck. It leaked fluid onto the carpeting.

The fluid was gasoline.

But the cloth fuse was out. Rachel was alive and alone, in a silence that grew and grew, in the mingled smells of gasoline, and blood, and stopped-up toilets, and Esther.

When the police car from the town of Kamuela raced up, sirens screaming, she was able to thank them calmly for helping her down from her seat on the edge of the wing, where she had been swinging her legs into space and thinking of nothing but the warmth of the sun on her back.

Two hours later, in the police station on Kapioli Street in Hilo, she picked out from their file the picture that looked most nearly like the one hijacker whose mask Esther had torn away. "Oscar Mariguchi," said the police lieutenant who was standing by. "He's one of the Maui MauMau, all right. Are you sure of the identification, Mrs. Chindler?"

"Not altogether sure," she said. "I think so. I could tell better if I could see him in person."

"Of course," the lieutenant agreed, and set about finding her a place to stay pending her return to St. Louis in the morning.

It was two months after that, trimming the Christmas tree with her son, Stephen, that the telephone call came from Hawaii to say that one of the hijackers had, perhaps, been caught.

2

The Hawaiian islands are volcanos, some long dead, some still active. When geologists first began to understand the complex story of the movements and faults of the Earth's crust, it was easy enough to deduce how the islands had formed. It was harder to see why they had formed where they did.

The Pacific Ocean is surrounded by a ring of fire. All around its perimeter are places where the hot soup that is the interior of the Earth forces its way to the surface, and even through it. This upwelling shows itself as ranges of volcanos, regions of hot springs and geysers and areas of strong earthquake activity. The ring is immense. It stretches up along the coasts of the Americas, with volcanos like Parícutin and Mount St. Helens and the great peaks of Alaska, across the Bering Strait to the Siberian cones around Kamchatka, down through Fujiyama and the other mountains of the Japanese archipelago, through southeast Asia. Krakatoa is part of the ring of fire. So are the geyser fields of New Zealand. And what the ring surrounds is a group of tectonic plates—masses of crust that float on the viscous interior of the Earth like puffs of meringue on a pudding—the biggest of which is the immense Pacific Plate itself.

The Pacific Plate is in motion. The whole sea bottom, carrying with it its associated sea mounts and islands, is cruising slowly toward the northwest at a steady speed of centimeters a year. It is where it pulls away from, or rubs against, the other plates that the earthquakes and volcanos occur.

But Hawaii is not at a meeting place between plates; it is actually at the very center of the largest of them.

The answer to the puzzle of why the volcanos formed where they did lay in the understanding of "hot spots"—places far under the surface of the Earth where, for reasons unknown, the temperature of the magma was higher than in the surrounding masses. These hot spots are long-lasting (many millions of years lasting); since heated liquids rise, they produce slow fountains of molten rock that seep sluggishly to the surface. The Hawaiian hot spots (there appear to be two of them, close together) have stayed in the same position for a very long time, as the crust of the Pacific Plate floats past overhead.

Where the upwelling plume of a hot spot penetrates the crust of the sea bottom, a baby volcano is born in the deeps. It grows. Over many millennia it rises to reach the surface of the ocean, and to grow past it; it has then become a volcanic island. All of the islands of the Hawaiian chain were born in that way, as the crust passed over a hot spot. When the plate moved on past the hot spot, the volcanos were shut off from the slow, hot fountains, and they died. Then the sea and the winds and the rains began to eat them away, so that the oldest of them no longer exist except as submerged sea mounts or shallow shoals.

The process has not stopped.

Even while Kilauea and Mauna Loa on the Big Island of Hawaii continue to erupt and grow, they are aging. The moving crust has carried them almost past their upwellings.

South and east of them, a new vent has opened in the sea bottom. Over time, it too has grown, as successive layers of lava build up from its craters. It began on the sea bottom two and a half miles under the surface of the ocean. It is now more than nine thousand feet high, its peak half a mile or so under the waves.

It is still growing.

One day, thousands of years from the present, it will reach the surface, and the Hawaiian Islands will have a new, infant member of the chain. The unborn island has already been given a name: It is called Loihi.

3

Rachel would be met at the airport, the Hilo police lieutenant had told her over the phone, but he hadn't said who would meet her. Once out of the DC-10 she pushed through the glass doors at the bottom of the steps with all the others. She paused in the middle of the transit lounge, glancing around. No one seemed to be looking for her. She settled her overnight bag on the folding luggage cart and walked around the security X-ray machine for passengers on their way to the planes.

When she went through the next set of doors, her first thought was that they'd turned the air-conditioning off. Then she realized she was in the outside air. What she felt was the muggy warmth of the Hawaiian day. The coat she carried over her arm, the pantyhose that had been the absolute minimum undergarment to get her to the airport in St. Louis, everything she wore or carried was suddenly far too much.

And who was meeting her?

It was always possible, she proposed to herself to see how it would feel, that some arrangements would go wrong, some word would get out. Some friend of the hijackers might have discovered she was coming, and then she would be met in a very bad way. She felt around inside herself and discovered that the thought didn't really frighten her. Probably she had been so frightened by such thoughts already that their potential for terror was all used up—

"Mrs. Chindler?"

It was funny. Her name was called twice, from two different

9

directions in two different voices; at first she thought it was some kind of echo. Then she saw that on her left the large old Distinguished Professor Emeritus—Yanami was his name, David Yanami—approached with relaxed speed, carrying a red and white lei and with a welcoming smile on his face. On her right a tiny Oriental-faced girl in a police uniform was also holding a lei, this one all honey-yellow. The policewoman was almost trotting, looking surprised to see Yanami there. "Mrs. Chindler? I'm Nancy Chee. Hello, Dr. Yanami."

The professor nodded, obviously as surprised as she. Rachel accepted both leis and let them sort it out. They did it rather quickly. "Do you need Mrs. Chindler tonight?" Yanami asked.

"Not for anything formal, no. I just wanted to help her get settled in her hotel. Tomorrow morning at ten, Mrs. Chindler, we'd like you to come down to the police station, if that's all right."

"And meanwhile," beamed Professor Yanami, "my grandmother specially wants you to come to our house tonight. Unless you have other plans?"

"The only real plan I have is to take a shower and change into different clothes."

"Fine! Your hotel's only ten minutes away." He reached to lift her bag by its handle, cart and all. He said with real warmth, "I'm so glad you're coming, Mrs. Chindler, because Kushi would never forgive me if I showed up without you—after all, it is New Year's Eve!"

There were New Year's firecrackers going off all along Banyan Drive as she changed her clothes. She didn't dawdle over it, but she didn't race, either. Actually, she decided, she was feeling quite relaxed.

It occurred to her that that was strange. She had wondered, drowsing across the Pacific, if seeing Lyman Field again would terrify her. It hadn't. She hadn't felt a thing, except pleasure at being away from a St. Louis winter for a few days.

She put on her muumuu and pretty sandals, checked her hair, picked up her pocketbook and left. The elevator had a spangly sign across the rear wall that said "Mele Kalikimaka," and when she got out David Yanami was waiting for her next to a tall and very traditional lighted Christmas tree. It seemed incongruous, with the open window showing palms and the blue Pacific stretching away behind it, but David's smile of welcome was real. He looked her up and down carefully. It was not a sexual look, she thought, or not exactly. It was as though she had painted a picture and he was giving it the critical study it had earned. "Very fine," he approved. "You'll be the best-dressed woman on the island for New Year's Eve."

But as they crossed the driveway to his car, impudently parked by a no-parking sign, a string of firecrackers went off behind them. David jumped. "Oh, hell," he said. "I hope you're all right."

Rachel stopped to confront him. "Dr. Yanami," she said, "honest, you don't have to coddle me. I can talk about the hijacking. I won't break. And I won't think every firecracker is a gun going off."

He nodded slowly, then grinned. When this man smiled he did it all the way, the big round face lighting up like a Halloween pumpkin. But a good-looking one. Yanami was as huge as a retired sumo wrestler, head bald, white beard scraggly. He looked around fifty, but had to be much older—he was retired, after all, so sixty-five-plus at least! His eyebrows were white, and so were his lashes, vivid against his khaki skin. And yet, on him, the combination looked good. Like an unpompous Charlie Chan. Like somebody you could trust.

Not counting Stephen, of course, there had not been many men in Rachel's life, since her father died, that she could trust.

On the way up to the town of Volcano he talked about himself. He had lived there, with his grandmother (his grandmother!), for twenty years and more, ever since he had decided he probably was never going to marry. He was Hawaiian-born. His father had been a sugar-cane field hand. He'd had a haole student once, he said, who thought that "cane" was where he'd got his middle name—David Kane Yanami—but actually, of course, it was pronounced *Kah-nay*, and that was his grandmother's Hawaiian part of his heritage. And he was, he said, very glad to show her around, since the problem about being retired was that it was hard to find things worth doing.

Rachel leaned back, content to peer out at Hawaii flowing past the car and listen to David. He was a nice man, she thought. He was making sure she had no time to dwell on the horror that was her purpose in being there. Wasn't it nice that everybody was being so nice about that? And would there ever come a time when somebody would be a little less nice, so that she could face up to that knot of fear and pain that lived just between her breasts, just inside her rib cage, and maybe dissolve it away, or maybe let it explode, no matter how devastating the explosion might be?

Then they were at the house. There was a flower garden behind it, and a scant lawn in front. Neither were very carefully tended. Neither was the house itself—frame, two-storied, with a wide porch both front and back that Rachel had already learned to call a "lanai." It was a comfortable kind of house.

David pushed the door open and shouted, "Kushi?"

In a moment the sliding door at the rear of the entrance hall rattled open, and a huge woman pushed her way in. Rachel had forgotten how immense the woman was. She had long, glossy red hair—it could not possibly be her own!—and at least one thick ring on every finger. She did not bother with shaking hands or even kissing. She reached out and wrapped her arms around Rachel, and it was like being hugged by a loving bear. "You come back, Rach'," she said, and hummed for a moment, resting her cheek on top of Rachel's head. "Aloha, then! Glad you come back. Other guests come pretty soon, now I got you all to self!"

She seemed to want to keep Rachel all to herself, too, or at least to be reluctant to let go of her. Rachel felt swaddled in those huge arms. The woman smelled pleasantly of cooking food and the flowering ginger lei she wore, which made Rachel sneeze. "Now," she said, releasing Rachel at last, "drink before guests come. Sorry only wine. Whiskey no more for me, only wine. Cigars no more, only pipe. Sometimes pot. You like some? No—" She searched for the word she wanted, humming, "No narcs here. David! Get wine wiki-wiki, you!"

When Kushi had carefully poured the wine into long-stemmed goblets and sent her grandson out to look at the pig, she put Rachel to work making a huge salad.

It was astonishing what the old woman remembered. There had been only one short luncheon meeting, and Rachel had not thought she had confided much autobiography in it. But Kushi remembered to ask after Stephen, and even remembered Stephen's name. Not only that, she remembered his age. "You leave eighteen-year-old alone New Year's?" she demanded, scandalized. "*Haole* boy? He get drunk, Rach'!"

"He'll be with friends," said Rachel, amused, and while she peeled and cored some whitish Islands salad vegetable, she listened to Kushi explain about getting drunk. There was nothing wrong with enjoying yourself, she decreed. A good time was a good thing to have. When she was young she had *fine* times—nine kids, too! Even old, when she traveled . . . and she embarked on a long story of a trip to Los Angeles, complete with trips to the Farmer's Market and to X-rated movies; she had come back wearing Mickey Mouse ears, she said, and if she had been ten years younger (what would that have made her? eighty?) she would have come back married again. It was impossible to be uncomfortable with this laughing mountain of a woman, and Rachel hardly even noticed when the doorbell began to ring. She had never met anyone like Kushi Shiroma, once Kushi Yameyoshi, daughter of Albert Kaonokilani's daughter, and no doubt the oldest living person Rachel had ever seen. Shaking pepper and oil onto the salad, Rachel almost forgot that terrorists existed.

The party was not merely a party, it was a luau. It was in the oldest Hawaiian tradition, which meant that there were more guests than Rachel could remember, and almost more than the little house could hold. There was a man who had something to do with solar energy, and another man who had something to do with geothermal energy. There were artsy-craftsy people, for that was the kind of town Volcano was, a sort of Provincetown of the Pacific. Some of them seemed to be related to the academic people from the university. Once or twice it turned out they were the academic people, for the solar-energy man also carved scrimshaw out of synthetic whalebone for the tourists. There was a woman who quilted Hawaiian spreads and got five thousand dollars apiece for them, also from tourists; but basically she was a librarian like Rachel herself, in town from Honolulu to see relatives over the holidays. She was a handsome woman, middle-aged, hair pulled severely back, face so taut that it almost seemed she had had it lifted, and the first thing she did was to take Rachel away for a nice chat about library jobs and prospects. She was very kind. Everyone was. Two painters. Three photographers. A jewelry maker—ten drummers drumming, eleven ladies dancing, and about twelve more people than Rachel really wanted around at that moment. They were all drinking eggnog, which did not seem very Hawaiian, and nibbling at little slivers of fresh pineapple and papaya, which very agreeably were.

Kushi disappeared for a while and returned in her party clothes, red velvet jacket and a plaid skirt. It looked like acres of fabric, and Rachel wondered where she found her size. She had squeezed her feet into gold, high-heeled sandals. She captured Rachel from a woman who taught hula at hotels but also taught ballroom dancing to children and carried her away to meet a great-great-grandson. "My daughter Masuki's granddaughter's boy," she declared. "Name Albert. This his wahine."

Albert was a handsome youth, far slighter than Kushi or David though almost as tall; he had Kushi's perfect teeth and David's engaging smile. "This is Alicia," he said, bringing forward a young woman as pretty as he was handsome. "I understand you're here to catch some terrorists, Mrs. Chindler."

From behind Rachel, David's voice boomed reprovingly, "Albert!" Rachel hadn't even known he was there. His grandmother scowled at him.

"Rachel don't break, David," she scolded. "She know what she here for, right? You take her back to eggnog bowl, cheer up!"

David shrugged helplessly and escorted Rachel across the room. On the way she said, "Kushi's right, you know. I don't mind talking about it."

"So you told me," he grinned, "but I keep forgetting. Oh, here's somebody you ought to meet!"

The somebody was one of the shadowy figures Rachel had already been introduced to, about whom she had retained nothing at all—was he the physicist who carved scrimshaw or

the political scientist who was in the amateur theater group?
He turned out to be neither. His name was Frank Morford,
and, David declared, "Frank has the most interesting job on
the faculty. He makes catastrophes."

"Only computer simulations," said Morford, offering
Rachel a fresh cup. He was a faintly bashful, fresh-faced, not
unattractive man in his late forties. He wore glasses, was identified as single by David and the "catastrophes" turned out to
be computer reconstructions of major geological events. He
had, he said, modeled the growth of the Hawaiian island
chain, island by island, as well as the crunch of tectonic plates
that had uplifted the Rockies and the opening of the Atlantic
Ocean that drove a three-thousand-mile wedge between
Massachusetts and Africa. He paused and took off his glasses
to look at Rachel better. From his pocket he took a neatly
folded Kleenex and began to polish them. "Of course," he
said, "that's all pretty technical, and I don't know how interested you are—"

"I am," said the woman who made the five-thousand-
dollar quilts. Rachel reached for the name and found it: Meg
Barnhart. "Please go on, I like hearing about these wonderful
scientific things."

"Oh, so do I," said Rachel automatically, wondering why
she was beginning to feel giddy. More than giddy; she felt
nervous, ill at ease. Meg Barnhart was a perfectly nice woman,
had even been very helpful about possible library jobs, but the
taut skin of her face looked almost reptilian. Morford seemed
uncomfortable, too. No doubt it was just imagination—and,
of course, fatigue. After all, in St. Louis it was already the
New Year, and she had got up before six o'clock. "I do want
to hear more," she said, "but I promised to help David's
grandmother and I've been forgetting."

The old lady was alone in the back garden, poking a heap of
earth which turned out to contain the pig roasting for the luau.
"You keep me company, Rach'? Mahalo! But you look kind
beat, you know?"

"I'm just tired after the long flight."

Hum. "You want—" Hum. "You want sleep little bit? Got
all kind spare room."

"I'd better not. I want to get my body on Hawaiian time."

"Then you want coffee," Kushi decided, and swept away without waiting for an answer. She returned with a huge mug in each hand. "You sit down right here," she ordered. "Drink coffee, screw off little bit. Nobody come out here because"— hum—"afraid Kushi put them to work, you know? How come you got only one keiki?"

Rachel stopped with the cup at her lips. "What?"

"Keiki." Hum. "Kids, you know? Why only one?"

Rachel hesitated, and then found herself saying, "I was lucky to have the one." And found herself going on to talk about her marriage, and her husband's disinterest in children, and the subtle and complicated schemes she had worked out that had persuaded him at last, half stoned and wholly amorous, to agree that, well, maybe *one* child would not utterly disrupt their lives . . . When David appeared on the lanai she was almost annoyed at the interruption.

He smiled. "Frank told me Kushi kidnaped you for K.P.," he said. "Would you like me to rescue you?"

Kushi declared, "No K.P. No rescue, neither. Rach' and me just having woman talk. Got only one kid, would've had more but husband, you know, not so kind good. Still could have plenty more, prob'ly."

"Kushi!" her outraged grandson cried.

"What's matter, you think I 'barrass Rach'? No, I tell you, David, us woman not 'barrassed so easy. Right, Rach'?"

"Absolutely," Rachel agreed. The funny thing was that it was true. She wasn't embarrassed, although discussing the fact that she had not yet reached menopause with a near stranger was exactly the kind of thing that she would have expected to be embarrassed about.

She took a deep swallow of the cooling coffee, almost relaxed. And then Kushi affectionately scolded, "Good-lookin' woman like you, you marry, you hear? You"—hum—"you try again."

With a sudden flash of anger Rachel snapped, "For what? To get them killed, in this world where everybody's *crazy*?"

She stopped, remorseful. She had not intended to say any of that. She could see that David was upset on her behalf, but as he started to speak his grandmother waved him silent with one huge hand.

"Good, Rach'," Kushi declared. "You too kind calm. Yell some. Cry if you want. You got friends here to yell at."

"I'm really sorry," Rachel began, aghast at herself, but Kushi was shaking her head.

"Keiki always something to worry about, you know? You know that Lono? My daughter Masuki's granddaughter's kid, you met—Albert, his real name? He big worry, Rach'. He the kind Kamehameha Korps, you know. Hate haoles."

David said furiously, "Kush, Rachel is our guest!"

"Rach' is grown-up lady, David," his grandmother told him. "Rach' knows some Hawaiians can't stand the kind haoles, probably"—hum—"the kind some other kind haoles can't stand too, right? See, Lono study history. Lono know what haoles did—done"—hum—"still do, you bet! Haoles come Honolulu harbor with warships and cannons, and first thing you know, Hawaiians don't own Hawaii no more. But, Rach'," she explained, "Lono don't hijack airplanes."

David said anxiously, "Kushi's right about that much. Albert did belong to the Kamehameha Korps in high school—it was just a kid thing to do—and he would certainly vote for Hawaii going independent again if he had a chance. But he wouldn't murder for it."

Rachel said, feeling herself under control again, "I know that, David. He's a perfectly fine young man. I wouldn't mind seeing Stephen grow up like him."

"Because he turn out all right!" cried Kushi triumphantly. "You see? So you worry an' you worry—but keiki they all grow up, turn out fine! Like David here. Only he don' get married."

David laughed out loud, and Rachel found herself laughing too. The sudden shock of anger had evaporated, along with the fatigue. Kushi stood grinning at the two of them, then she snapped her fingers.

"Eat in thirty minutes," she stated. "No, Rach', you got nothing to do here. You go with David. You, David! You show Rach' night-blooming cereus and stuff, okay? Then you both come back wiki-wiki, help serve luau!"

Looking after the huge, disappearing back, David asked
Rachel, "Do you really want to see the cereus?" She started a
polite "of course," but he went right on: "Because you've
been standing next to it for the last half hour. Kushi still hopes
I'll get married, you know, and I'm afraid she's picked you
out as a candidate."

"Don't be afraid, David. She's a wonderful woman."

"Formidable. She's a con-lady. She'll cold read you in two
minutes, like all the old Hawaiians. When she knows what you
want to hear, that's what you'll get." He looked suddenly
serious. "Did they tell you about the man you're supposed to
identify tomorrow?"

She was startled at the quick change, gratified that he had
decided to treat her like a grown-up. "Only that they thought
he might be one of the hijackers."

"I got the word from Frank Morford—he has a policeman
as a neighbor. It's Murray Pereira. They arrested him the
other day on a charge of extortion—a local airline—"

"I think I heard about it. He tried to get fifty thousand
dollars out of them?"

"And they caught him picking it up. That's right," said
David.

Rachel said seriously, "I don't think you ought to tell me
any more about him."

"I won't," David grinned. "I don't know any more,
anyway. Oh, Pereira's picture has been in the paper, but you
won't have seen it on the mainland. Just don't look at any old
newspapers tonight, all right?"

She said, "David, about all I want to look at tonight is my
pillow."

He looked alarmed. "You're really tired, aren't you?
Would you like me to drive you back now?"

"Oh, no—a taxi—"

"No taxi," he said firmly. "Just give me a minute to tell
Kushi, and we're on our way."

"I don't want to take you away from your guests—"

"They'll never know I'm gone. Anyway, I'll be back before
they miss me!"

Or maybe not quite. It was a good forty minutes each way,

plenty of time for David to add to his autobiography. As they turned into the highway, he waved off to the right, toward the park entrance. "That's where I got converted to science," he said.

"Converted from what?" asked Rachel, covering a small yawn. "Didn't you say you used to work in the sugar fields?"

David laughed. "Only until I saved up the fare to Waikiki. I was a beachboy for a year. I lived for surfing and jitterbugging with the tourists. But I couldn't support myself that way forever, so I came back to Puna, my dad's house, over on the other side of the island. Then I came to Hilo, still looking for a job, and Kushi put me up right where we live now, so she could feed me for a while. You don't remember the Depression, you weren't born then. It was bad on the mainland, worse here. But I hit lucky."

Rachel straightened up. She had been drowsing off, which was not only impolite but frustrating. She really wanted to hear what David's life had been. "Lucky how, David?"

"Oh—" He made the turn past General Lyman Field, nearing the Banyan Drive hotel colony. "I hitched up to the crater to see if I could get a job in the hotel. There weren't any jobs there, either, but when I started to hitch back, there was this old man along the road. He was changing a tire on his Model A. He was in the U.S. Geological Survey. He's a famous man around here. He was then, too, but not to me—if he wasn't Cab Calloway or Fred Astaire he wasn't famous, as far as I was concerned. Anyway, I changed the tire for him, and he gave me a quarter and a ride, and we got to talking. And he gave me a job. Five dollars a week, out of his own pocket. I carried his surveying instruments for him. I worked that whole summer with him, and then he got me a part-time job with the Survey and arranged for me to get into the university. That was a good time, Rachel," he smiled, making the U turn into her hotel driveway. "Later on, not so good—but here you are home!"

David parked smack in the no-parking zone in front of the hotel entrance. He left the lights on and the motor running as earnest of his intention to move quickly, but on New Year's Eve no one really seemed to care about such things.

The New Year's Eve noise level had begun to rise as soon as they turned into Banyan Drive, like the machine guns rattling in a war of toy soldiers. "Mele Kalikimaka!" shouted a tourist girl with long blonde hair flying, laughing as she tossed a string of firecrackers into the parking lot below.

"You don't have to come in," said Rachel as he opened the door for her, but he shook his head. She was truly exhausted. She walked that way. He escorted her up to the desk clerk to get her key. When the clerk came from behind the message desk, he was wearing a party hat, and the lobby was filled with drunks and half-drunks, mostly coming from the tourist trap on the top floor. The whole hotel looked like the late stages of a very large party.

David was perfectly willing to escort Rachel to the door of her room, but she excused him at the elevator. "I'll be all right, thanks," she said, and looked hesitant—but finally accepting—when he offered to take her to lunch the next day. He saw her into the car and turned away, rather pleased. She was a nice enough young woman. Pretty enough to be interesting. Old enough to be comfortable . . . but, David decided, very troubled. Of course, she had every reason for that . . .

On the way out he saw the men's room and elected to visit it before the ride back. As he approached the door a woman's voice from behind him said, "Excuse me, please?"

He turned. The woman was middle-aged, and the clothes she wore would have been more suitable to a business office on the mainland than to a Hawaiian New Year's. Her accent was odd. It was almost an Englishwoman's, but with something definitely foreign beneath it. She said, "Did you see the man who just went in? He is my husband. He is wearing a blue and white aloha shirt," she explained as David shook his head. "You cannot miss him, so would you give him this note for me, please? Our daughter is sick and I must take care of her at once." She smiled in a way that cut off conversation, thrust a folded piece of hotel stationery in my hand and hurried away.

It was an imposition, of course. But it did not seem to entail a lot of trouble. David had no trouble finding the man; he was pensively standing in front of a urinal, his eyes closed. David waited until he was through before handing him the note.

"Your wife asked me to give you this," he said. And then, as the man stared at him uncomprehendingly, one hand frozen in the act of zipping up his fly, David added, "It's something about your daughter."

The man's stare did not falter. David tolerated it for a few seconds, then irritably pressed the paper into the man's hand and locked himself inside a stall to urinate. What an unpleasant man! He had looked a little bit foreign, too, in the same way the woman had.

The note itself had been in a foreign language. David hadn't attempted to read it, but as he passed it to the man he caught a glimpse of un-English script. They were not of any alphabet he recognized, curlicued things that might have been Arabic or Persian.

He really wanted another look at the man, but when he came out of his booth, the washroom was empty.

4

A terrorist is not simply a vandal. He (or she) always has a purpose, and the name they give to that purpose is usually "justice." It does not matter if the terrorist's conception of "justice" is wildly at odds with that of the rest of the world. Indeed, it is when the general majority takes no interest in the purposes of the terrorist, or is even opposed to them, that the bombings and burnings and beatings and butchery begin. From the Weather Underground to the Contras, by way of Serbian nationalists, Right-to-Life abortion-clinic bombers, PLO, Black Panthers, IRA, Ku Klux Klan and Irgun Zvai Leumi, there is always a cause to kill or destroy for.

The cause need not be an immediate wrong. Sometimes it can be revenge for something generations old, as when Armenians murder Turkish diplomats today because thousands of Turks murdered thousands of Armenians long ago. None of the original killers are still alive, and most of the revengers were not even born when the massacres occurred. No matter. Blood feuds survive in the blood, and Irish Catholics are still revenging themselves on Oliver Cromwell.

Any surviving Hawaiian of Polynesian extraction need never be without a grievance to revenge. History contains plenty. In the centuries since the first haole ship made port on one of the islands, the balance of trade is clear. The invaders gave the Hawaiians religion, tourists, a written language, syphilis and smallpox. What they took in exchange was the islands themselves. The numbers tell the story. When Captain

Cook first visited Lahaina, there were half a million native Hawaiians. A century later there were hardly a tenth as many. The ethnic rainbow that is the present population of Hawaii contains colors from most of the countries of Europe, from Asia, Africa and the Americas, but the Polynesian tints are fading fast; and of the polity of the original Hawaiians nothing is left at all. The Americans saw to that. Missionaries, traders and adventurers alike, they combined to obliterate the Hawaiian culture and replace it with commerce and Christianity. They overthrew the governance of the kings (which Americans had come to exercise in the King's name anyway) and replaced it with a Hawaiian republic (in which Americans made the laws); they even, in the name of the Hawaiian people, sought annexation by the United States, and the final humiliation came when the American Congress turned the request down.

After decades of limbo the United States grudgingly took on its Pacific islands, but it was decades longer before Hawaii was allowed the ultimate grace of statehood.

Yes. There are grievances aplenty for ethnic Hawaiians to hold, the few of them that survive in the surrounding sea of paks and haoles.

5

Though the note was wadded up tiny in the pocket of his dressing gown, Arkady Bor could feel it. It was trouble. He wanted none of that.

In the two years since he had defected, every day had brought him new proof that he had made the right decision. True, the physical surroundings were not perfect. This drilling ship was no Black Sea resort, and it was a pity they made him spend so much time on it. But the food was good, the occasional shore liberties were fine and every month, in his account in the Maritime Bank of the Pacific, there was another fat deposit in spendable American dollars for his "consultancy" honorarium. So there was no question of allowing anything to endanger this, he told himself, brushing his fine white teeth before the little mirror in his stateroom.

But how was he going to avoid the looming trouble?

There would be a way, he thought while dressing. It was merely necessary to find it. He slicked down his hair, made sure his chin was shaved closely enough, grinned to admire the teeth one more time and opened the flanged stateroom door.

Jameson Burford was standing just outside it, ready to knock. Jameson Burford was shorter even than Bor, but he carried himself with the assurance of a very large man, and spoke with the confidence of a colonel addressing his regiment—he had actually held that rank at one time, though not as the kind of colonel that commands a regiment. "Good morning, Jamie," said Bor with cheer. "Happy New Year. I hope you are not too hung over from our party last night to go to the meeting?"

"That's what I was coming to tell you, Arkady." He pronounced it *Ar-KAY-dee*, but Bor was used to that. "The guys from Sandia are late. The meeting's rescheduled for thirteen hundred this afternoon."

"Ah," said Bor.

"So you've got the morning off. Do you want to go over our presentation?"

"Perhaps—no," said Bor. They had rehearsed it quite adequately already, and Burford nodded to show he accepted the decision. On shore, or in certain specific circumstances anywhere, Burford had the rank to tell Bor what to do, and Bor would be obliged to do it instantly, whatever it was. But in the context of Bor's professional duties on the Vulcan project, Bor was the boss. Bor smiled to take the sting out and practiced a colloquialism in American. "I think I will go up on deck and soak up some rays," he said. He pronounced it "sock up some race," but Burford did not correct him.

"Suit yourself," he said, tipping Bor a soft salute and retreating down the corridor. Bor looked after him with some malice. Very likely Burford did have a hangover, he thought. He surely had had more than the allowed two drinks in the hotel nightclub the night before; otherwise he would have been with Bor in the men's room and things would not have gone as they did. So if Bor decided to take Security into his confidence in this matter of the note, Burford would find himself in trouble. That thought did not displease Bor at all.

Bor paused to decide if he really did want to go up on deck. There were many other choices. He could, for instance, go back in his room and watch the Hawaiian rebroadcast of the morning network news programs. That was an attractive idea. Bor had become a news addict since his defection, OD'ing on the network broadcasts every night, snacking on CBS radionews during the day. The habit had only claimed him late in life, but of course for most of his life in the U.S.S.R. there hadn't been any believable news you could become addicted to. When the debriefing interrogators asked if any one American had helped bring about his decision to defect, he said instantly, "Walter Cronkite."

But he had learned that news, in the Western democracies, was not allowed to happen on Saturdays, Sundays or legal holidays. There was no audience for it at those times, so it would have been wasted. So Bor did what he had told his security blanket he was going to do. He went up on deck.

And that was another way in which his present situation had it all over Leningrad, or even Tbilisi. The climate! You didn't get sun like this anywhere in the Soviet Union!

The deck of the dormitory ship *Hermes*, which he was aboard, was quite stable in the gentle sea, and about a dozen holidayed people were stretched out on air mattresses or deck chairs, drinking coffee. Bor sniffed annoyance: coffee! What foolish rules the U.S. Navy had! But as there was nothing better, he ordered some from a messboy, took it to the rail and stared out at the other vessels in the flotilla, fingering the crumpled note in his pocket.

The first thing he had to decide was whether he still had all his options. If he chose to turn the note over to Security now, how could he explain not having done so at once? There could have been an explanation for a while. He could have said that he didn't dare give it to Jameson Burford because the man was intoxicated. That would have covered him perfectly, at least until they returned to the *Hermes*.

But it did not cover him now.

He swallowed the last of his coffee gloomily, looking out over the sea. It should have been a tranquilizing scene. The *Hermes* was only one of the five major vessels and dozen or so occasional minor ones that clustered around that point in the open sea that lay just over the unborn island under the surface. The biggest was the drillship itself, collateral descendant of the *Gomar Explorer*, colorlessly named the *Sandusky* so that the name suggested nothing of its purpose. There was also the floating hotel he was on, the *Hermes*, as well as an old minesweeper used mostly to store supplies, a small tanker that kept the other vessels fueled—and the missile-carrying frigate, *Alamagordo*, mission never defined but obviously serious. There was no doubt that those missiles would be fired at need. What would be the need? To repel possible Russian or Chinese submarine attack? To—the possibility that made Bor swallow hard—to send the entire flotilla of Project Vulcan to the bottom, if at some mad moment it became necessary to establish "deniability"?

Such fancies did not improve Bor's mood.

Even the sun was hiding now. Bor looked gloomily out over the sea. Clouds hung all around, and vertical streaks of darker gray dangled under some of them to show where rain was falling. To the north, the peaks of Mauna Loa and Mauna Kea were swallowed in cloud.

Bor watched a tug pull a pair of barges through the plume of mud that stained the sea around the drillship. One barge carried pipe lengths for the drill string. Container pods concealed whatever the other held from outsider, or satellite, eyes.

Even on New Year's Day work went on. Drilling stopped briefly, now and then, while they hoisted a new hundred-foot section of pipe to the top of the Christmas tree on the *Hermes*. It was an ugly ship, in profile something like a tanker with an oil derrick riding on its midsection, and when it was in operation, which was nearly always, it sounded like a boiler factory. Soon enough the noise would stop. The drilling now was only a sort of checking out of already dismissed possibilities and a tidying up of unimportant loose ends. The drills had already stabbed Loihi, the infant volcano that reached up toward them from the sea bottom below, in enough places. The biggest wound was ready to receive its implant. Then Loihi would be what Arkady Bor had designed it to be, the final answer to all vexing questions of world rule.

Even in the middle of the Pacific Ocean one could not escape those problems. Behind Bor, one of the riggers had abandoned coffee cup, deck chair and Japanese transistor radio for a quick trip to the men's room. The radio was blaring, and now it had given up rockabilly music for a moment of news reports. The news was no more to Bor's taste than the caterwauling music. The news was the same old Arab accusations of Israeli violations of airspace, of protests against deployment of the same old high-tech weaponry, of the same tedious fighting in the same tedious places. In Latin America. And in Africa. And in Southeast Asia, and—oh, well, why not say in the world and be done with it?

Bor scowled at the sun as it began to reappear. Such things were, after all, not his problem to deal with.

His problem was closer at hand—in fact, in his pocket.

He leaned into the sunny wind and thought about the note the fat Jap had handed him. Was it possible that the Jap was KGB? Probably not; he was too American. The KGB recruited from all nationalities, and there were plenty of Japanese who were sympathetic to the Soviet cause. But the KGB didn't need to recruit idealistic sympathizers. Idealists might do something idealistic at an inappropriate time, and it was much safer simply to buy a traitor on the open market, for there were always plenty for sale.

As Bor himself had been for sale.

He fingered the note in his pocket. He didn't have to take it out to read it. He had its contents by heart, in that graceful Georgian script that, all by itself, had convinced him it was authentic. How many Americans could write Georgian? How many Russians, for that matter? No, it was real, and it had said:

> *Your daughter, Serafina Borboradzhvilana, has been tried and convicted of espionage and anti-Soviet activities. A preliminary court has sentenced her to internal exile. Sentencing on the more serious charges has not yet occurred. If you wish to help her, call 555-5917 at once.*

There was no signature, of course. He had not called the number—also of course, for he had not dared.

Bor tossed the empty paper cup into the Pacific and watched it bob in the long swell. He tried to imagine his seventeen-year-old daughter in a Gulag camp—if that was where she was; if the note had not been a fiction to trap him with.

If she were even alive.

He had tried to call her, once, from his room in the Mayflower Hotel in Washington, during the first weeks after he defected. That had been a blunder. Of course he had not got through, and when the Americans heard about it they were furious. So he had not heard her voice in more than two years, two months—since the last time he had been in Tbilisi. And naturally he had not dared speak openly to her then. He took her for a ride in the chrome-yellow cable car, swaying in the wind on the way up to the amusement park on the cliff. Wonderfully, they had been alone in the car. There was little chance the car was miked, yet, even so, he spoke in only pretended confidence. "Fina, if anything should happen to me you must be strong. Do not hesitate to denounce me!"

She had put her knuckles to her mouth. Even a fifteen-year-old knew what "anything" was. "Father! Are you in trouble?"

"I am not now in trouble," he said in partial truth, "but there are some unpleasant things going on. Others wish my downfall. If only your mother were still alive . . ." But that had been a mistake, and Serafina's eyes had showed it. She remembered well that he had not ever wished his wife were still alive. What he had wished was that Serafina had taken after her, with that clear, fair Lithuanian coloring—the blue eyes, the golden hair, all the things that had made Bor want to marry the woman in the first place, without stopping to think that beneath that pretty exterior there lived a shrew. She had made him hate all women, Bor reflected bitterly. And thus, to be sure, led directly to the difficulties in which he found himself!

Slipping across Grosvenor Square to the American Embassy, on the pretext of that meeting in London, that had been his way out of those difficulties . . .

But there were difficulties still, it seemed. The KGB had lost him for a while. But, somehow, now he had been found.

Such thoughts were useless. If he could not solve the problem of the note, at least he could make use of the time. Bor went below again, to the tiny office under the water level where he was allowed to do his private work, and attacked his desk.

Bor's desk was not actually a desk. It was a computer monitor, and the clutter on it was not stacks of papers but displays of abstracts awaiting his attention in his "mail bag." Most were of no interest to him. A few were tangentially so—for example, *Low-Neutron-Emitting Nuclear Configurations*, a highly classified paper resulting from researches somewhere among the Defense Department's study teams. But he no longer had to worry about keeping the numbers of neutrons low in his devices, because the least important aspect of them was how much tritium, and therefore how much loss of human life, they caused. *4.8 Richter Event in Western Siberia*—he groaned, and tagged it for request for copies. They were still at it! But where in Western Siberia was the "event"? For what purpose? Almost certainly it was an underground nuclear explosion, but was it one of the waste-disposal projects he had pioneered? A seismic study looking for mineral deposits? What? It was frustrating not to know. Since Bor had left the U.S.S.R. in rather a great hurry, there had been at least twenty Richter 4 or larger disturbances that registered on the seismographs of the West. Two of them had been actual earthquakes—not big enough to do much damage, not interesting enough to be worth much study.

The others had been Bor's specialty at work.

The difference between an underground nuclear explosion and a tectonic event was easy enough to detect. The seismograph trace showed the distinctive frequency patterns. Earthquakes, which resulted from the shifting of bodies of rock far under the surface of the Earth, took measurable seconds to happen. The seismograph displayed a measurable blurred tracing. A nuclear blast took less than the wink of an eye.

Bor knew. He had been perhaps first among all in planning them and supervising their detonation. It had been Arkady Borboradzhvili who supervised the placement of the hydrogen device that blasted out the thousand-meter cavern in the Urals that now held the Soviet Union's most dangerous radioactive wastes. It had been Bor who had provided the explosions that let Soviet petro-geologists identify the big, deep, new salt domes near the Caspian sea that would pump oil into Soviet aircraft and armor in some future war—if there was another war. It was Bor who had blown out the great underground bubbles around Astrakhan that were now filling with natural gas condensates, settling out so that the gas could be piped off the top and the liquids out from the bottom. That had been a particular triumph! There had been talk about the Order of the Red Banner—not often given to a person who "needed a clock." (If you needed a clock, you were nobody, because the only somebodies were those who told time from hearing the bells in Moscow's Spassky Tower.)

It was too bad that, just then, that foolish militia cadet had become frightened and told all sorts of things to his commandant. There was no prosecution, to be sure—a cadet's word was not to be taken against a senior scientist's. But there was also no Order of the Red Banner.

He rubbed his eyes fretfully—damn these cheap Navy CRTs, they bothered one's vision so! Also the noise that sometimes one forgot became quite annoying when one heard it again. The drilling went on regardless of holidays, and so there was the constant, repetitive, scratchy, rattly, boom of the drill string, and the smell of drilling fluid and exhaust from the engines on the drillship when the wind was foul. Bor allowed himself to hate where he was and what he was doing for a moment—one needed such moments occasionally. And it was so unfair that he should have been made to come here! If only he had not been born a Georgian! Or, better—since no Georgian ever truly wished to be anything but a Georgian—if only he had been a Georgian a couple of decades earlier! There was a time when it was worthwhile to be Georgian, because the great Vozhd himself was. But then Stalin died. Then that imbecile Khrushchev read his secret report. Then they hit bottom, all Stalinists, all Georgians. Then that same son of an imbecile bitch, Khrushchev, put Bor out of business with the anti-surface-explosions embargo, so that the thing he trained for—digging canals and leveling mountains through the peaceful uses of nuclear energy—became outlawed. It had been a scramble to find the loophole that allowed underground explosions to continue, and then—

Then that moment's drunken intimacy with the militia cadet—and then here!

Bor broke out into a cold sweat. For it had not been quite like that. It had not been direct from Astrakhan's triumph to defecting, but what had been in between he did not like to think about, even here.

And even "here" was in jeopardy, because of that accursed note!

He switched off his computer, leaned back and stared at the

gray bulkhead behind it. Think, Arkady! Make a plan!

Was it too late for him still to go to Security and say, "This was handed to me last night and I have not been able to make up my mind—" Oh, no! No such admission was permissible at all!

Very well, second alternative. Suppose he called the number he was given. Suppose he received instructions to meet some person at some secret rendezvous, what would happen then?

He prepared an orderly list in his mind of possible outcomes:

1. Would they kidnap him and force him back to the Soviet Union? Likely not; he was of more value here.

2. Would they punish him? Perhaps simplify the whole situation by shooting him through the head? Not likely. If all they wanted was to kill him, they could easily have done that in the hotel. A bomb could be passed as well as a note.

3. Would they try to "turn" him back to the Soviets? Make a deal? Say, his daughter's life and security for, perhaps information? Bor frowned. That was not very likely, he thought, because if they had been able to locate him, they already had quite a lot of information. Then what? Sabotage? Oh, God! Would they make him sabotage Project Vulcan and then leave him to the vengeance of the Americans?

If only he had acted at once . . .

And then he snapped his fingers. It was not too late after all! Run fast! Arrive breathless at Security! Say, "Oh, my God, listen! I just found this in my tuxedo jacket! Now I remember, someone handed it to me last night, but we had been drinking—" It would work! They would be annoyed, oh, yes! But the worst of the anger would fall on Jameson Burford, not himself. Too bad, of course. Yet in this world one had to look out for oneself. Arkady Bor could not take the responsibility of protecting an incompetent security man—

Or—he thought, as he began to run in conspicuous panic down the passage, clutching the note—of protecting a daughter who was, after all, old enough to look after herself.

6

To sink a hole through rock is not, in principle, a complicated matter. All you need is some sharp-edged tool, harder than the rock, to twist and scour away at the rock inch by inch with brute force and persistence. On land you build a derrick and hang pipes and bit from it; attach engines to lift and turn the pipe chain; then thud and twist, thud and twist as the hole deepens. In shallow water you build a tower with legs resting on the bottom, and the process is the same.

In deep water the process is harder. The tower must stay where it belongs, above the hole at the bottom of the sea. The drillship *Sandusky* solved that problem with dynamic positioning—with small screws, commanded by computer, that thrust it this way and that in response to every urging of wind, current and wave. It steamed constantly, twenty-four hours of every day, but it never moved from its position.

To keep that drill turning and digging required a large crew. There were three complete drilling teams of eleven men each, for round-the-clock operation. There was a barge engineer and his assistant; nine rig technicians; four welders; a Navy diver; three cranemen; the *Sandusky*'s own six-man security detachment; four electricians; a motor team of six motormen plus two supervisors; and ten roustabouts for dumb labor. Those were just the people who served the drill. The *Sandusky* had its own crew of forty more, captain, mates, cooks and stewards, gunners, radiomen, engineers and oilers—only forty, in this confining duty, because the *Sandusky* was not, after all, going anywhere.

Then there were the satellite ships that supported the *Sandusky*, with their crews; plus the scientists and naval officers and specialists who directed it; plus the helicopter pilots and their mechanics, and the boat crews that plied between Vulcan and the Hawaiian port, and the cryptographic clerks and the computer technicians and the signals personnel—and, of course, the security force that soaked into every phase of every operation . . .

Altogether it was a community of some size. More than 250 persons lived and worked out on the open ocean, all of them there for no other purpose than to direct that wasp's sting that penetrated Liohi's rocky crust . . .

And they were only the preparatory crew. There were twenty more persons on their way, bringing with them a complex object the size of a kitchen stove to tuck into the hole the *Sandusky* had opened for them. The wasp's sting had broken the surface of the submerged infant volcano. Now it was time to plant the egg.

7

It was past seven-thirty in Hawaii, therefore nearly noon in St. Louis. Therefore there was a chance that Stephen would be awake, even on New Year's Day. While Rachel's tub was running, she dialed home. Wonder of wonders, Stephen answered on the second ring. He didn't even sound sleepy. "It must not have been a good party," she guessed.

"Ma? Oh, naw, it was fine, really *fine*." And she knew that was all she would get out of him. No names-dates-places. Certainly nothing about how much he had had to drink—or smoke. Positively nothing about whether he had "scored" with one of the girls who sometimes showed up in her living room. To keep her from asking he went right on: "And how was yours? Did you see that guy yet? Are you all right?"

"In order," said Rachel, feeling very fond of her son, "my party was quiet but nice, I'm going to try to identify the man this morning and I'm fine, really *fine*." She frowned at a muffled, not identifiable sound from Stephen's end of the line and added, "If I'm through, I might try to catch a flight back tomorrow—"

The muffled sound turned out to be Stephen chewing something. He swallowed and said, "Oh, Ma! The he—heck you will! Soak up some of that sun. How many free trips to Hawaii are you going to get in your life?"

"What are you eating, Stephen?"

"Eggs Benedict, and don't change the subject. Stay! Take a week at least—the library doesn't open till the eleventh, right? I promise I won't burn the house down."

"Well—" But she had left the tub running. "We'll see."

"No, we won't. Do it! And Happy New Year," he boomed, in that way he had of suddenly sounding like his father.

Like the best side of his father, Rachel reflected in the bath. Without that treacherous, unpredictable meanness, especially without the lying. As far as she knew, Stephen had never lied to her. He had told her to get out of his face, oh,.yes, a lot. But she had conceded that right to him long ago.

In any case, there were questions she didn't need to ask because she could deduce the answers from clues. Clues like eggs Benedict. Stephen had learned how to make them, but didn't much like to eat them. The girl, Sandy Corrado, who had helped him drive his mother to the airport, on the other hand, did; so if Stephen was eating eggs Benedict on New Year's morning it probably meant that the year was starting out fine, really *fine*, for him.

Rachel had never been in a police car before. She was interested to see, craning her neck to look back over her shoulder, that there were no handles on the insides of the back doors, and a heavy steel mesh separated the back from the driver's seat. She was glad she was riding up front. Chee was her driver, friendly and unthreatening. She said, "Mrs. Chindler—"

"Please call me Rachel."

"—do you know how a showup works? They'll have five or six men lined up—"

"I've watched a lot of Kojak, Nancy," Rachel smiled. The girl looked awfully young to be a police sergeant, and awfully small.

"Of course," said the policewoman, returning the smile. "Well, since you didn't actually see the man's face, I suppose they'll do this one a little different. I really don't know."

Rachel gazed at her speculatively. "Do they know which of the hijackers this man is? I mean, did he do the actual"— she swallowed, surprising herself—"killing?"

The smile slipped away. "I really can't discuss that with you before the showup, please. It's the rules of evidence, you know. I don't know what a judge might make of anything I said." She changed the subject briskly, nodding toward the greenery around them. "That's Queen Liliuokalani Park. I guess you've seen it? It's beautiful. And up ahead"— she waved—"that was all tsunami damage. What they call a tidal wave? That park used to be the whole business section. My father's office was here, and he took me down the day after the tsunami and it was all just *gone*." She threw a quick, considering look at her passenger as she made the turn toward Kapiolani. "I could give you a tour this afternoon if you'd like it," she offered.

"Oh, that's sweet of you, Nancy. Actually I think Professor Yanami is taking me to lunch, and we hadn't planned much beyond that."

Nancy Chee turned into the lot marked *Official Cars Only*, and advised, "Get him to take you for a flight around the island—he's in the same aviation club as my father, so I know he can get a plane. Maybe he can find some gray whales to see." And she slid out and waited for her passenger to join her to go into the police station.

Rachel found herself swallowing quite a lot. She was not as calm as she had thought she was; in fact, she had to go to the bathroom pretty badly. Sergeant Chee was patient and unsurprised.

Even so, they had to wait, in a little windowless office. Rachel declined the offer of a cup of coffee, and listened inattentively while the sergeant chattered pleasantly about the Waipio Valley and the Pu-uhona O Honaunau, where the Hawaiian kings had set up a sanctuary, and the inlet where Captain Cook had been killed along the Kona coast. She was glad when the door opened and Captain Wasserling came in. Although the sergeant was a pretty mixture of Chinese and Portuguese and the captain was missionary white, they wore identical expressions of official compassion as they courteously led Rachel to another room. He sat her down before a curtained wall, explained that behind the curtain was a one-way mirror so that she could see through, but those on the other side could not, and asked her to tell him when she was ready.

Rachel was not ready. She did not think she ever would be ready. It was, she decided, terribly unfair of them to ask her to do this. How could she be sure? Even Kojak admitted eye-

witness identification couldn't be trusted. Anyway, Orientals
were scarce in St. Louis. One might look like another to
her—how could she tell? What you saw when you saw an
Oriental in Missouri was that basic quality of Orientalness; the
ability to recognize that fine detail that distinguished one from
another would come only a lot later. And in that one
lightning-flash instant, with all her mind full of the horror of
what was going on, there hadn't been any later . . . "I'm
ready," she said, untruthfully, and the captain pulled the curtain back.

On the other side of the window, the five men in ski masks
looked toward the sound of the curtain rings sliding.

She knew at once, even in the masks, that not one of them
was the man whose mask Esther had died to pull away. They
were all too big. Nevertheless she studied them carefully, and
jumped when—there must have been some signal, but she
hadn't heard it—unexpectedly the first one in line spoke:

"Don't anybody move. We're taking this airplane over," he
said.

That one said it like a stenographer reading back dictation.
The second man said it like an actor trying to memorize a part.
The third said it offhandedly, as though in a hurry to get to his
waiting lunch. The fourth—

The fourth had a voice that was deep, and gravely amused,
and not at all worried.

"Mrs. Chindler?" said the captain.

She realized she had been silent for a long time. She shook
herself but stayed silent, glancing helplessly at the captain.
"We'll try without the masks," he said, and made the im-
perceptible signal again.

The men began to take off the masks.

They didn't need to. That huge head was not easily forgotten, nor the black eyes. She had no difficulty imagining
him—remembering him!—moving gracefully down the aircraft aisle, with the Uzi held shoulder-high and ready.

Without the mask, the head was even huger. Rachel could
not make herself believe in the opacity of the one-way glass,
for the black eyes looked right at her.

She said, "I'm afraid none of them is the man who shot
Esther."

The captain frowned at Sergeant Chee, then turned back to Rachel. Politely he said, "You can't identify any of them at all?"

"How can I be sure?" Rachel asked reasonably. "One ski mask looks exactly like another, you know."

"You're sure?" asked Sergeant Chee.

"I'm sure I'm not sure," smiled Rachel. After all, how could she be? Even if she made an I.D., what would happen if they came to trial? Then the defense lawyers might pull some of those sneaky Perry Mason tricks—mix her up—maybe even substitute some other Oriental with wide-set eyes and fat lips. How could she tell the difference? And, she reflected indignantly, what would the penalties be for perjury, if some lawyer tricked her into a contradiction? She said firmly, "I'm sorry."

"The thing is," the captain said, "I thought when you were looking at one of them you did seem to sort of get uptight."

He was regarding her with the sort of detached puzzlement one might give to a jigsaw piece that didn't fit anywhere into the pattern. She shrugged. The captain added, "The big one with black eyes, I mean. His name is Murray Pereira, but they call him 'Kanaloa.' He's an Army veteran. Dishonorable discharge. The D.O.D. didn't give us very complete information, but he seems to have worked with very sophisticated explosives. Even nuclear."

"How worrisome," said Rachel politely. "I'm really sorry to have put you to this trouble for nothing, captain, but may I go now?"

When David Yanami met her in her hotel lobby he was surprised, and pleased, at her air of cheerful calm. It wasn't just the expression on her face. She had evidently found time to visit the dress shops on the lower levels, and now she was wearing a peach-and-white aloha shirt with her white slacks. "Very pretty," he complimented her, meaning more than the new shirt. "I guess everything went all right this morning?"

"Oh, all wrong, I'm afraid. I bombed completely," she said ruefully, and added, "I'm really hungry."

David was too polite to speak his surprise, but he felt a lot of it. What was happening with this young woman? It was one thing to be relaxed the night before her ordeal—that was a tribute to her strength of character. To be so cheerful after failing to make an identification was something else. David could not decide what; and the more she told him the more puzzling it became. "It *could* have been the one the captain thought I flinched at," she said, spooning curried chicken out of a papaya half. "But I wouldn't swear to it. Supposing it had been a policeman?"

"I'm sure they would have told you if it were a policeman."

"Well, but suppose it was just someone they'd picked up for, oh, jaywalking? And I got him in trouble? The more I looked, the more I couldn't be positive—say, this is lovely!" she added, holding up a bite of the chicken and fruit.

"I'm glad you like it." That wasn't too understandable to him, either. In David's view, papaya was splendid and curried chicken also sometimes splendid; but putting them together made about as much sense as serving corned-beef hash on watermelon slices. Tourists ate that sort of thing. Nobody else did. "Actually," he said, "I think from what you say that that one must have been the real terrorist."

"Oh, really?" Spooning the papaya out now took most of her attention. "They said his name was something Pereira."

"That's the one. They call him 'Kanaloa'—that's one of the old Hawaiian gods. You could say Kanaloa was the god of Hell."

"A sensible name for a terrorist," Rachel smiled, but her smile was strained. "He extorted money from an airline?"

David was surprised. "I see I've underrated your sources of information, Rachel. Yes, SunAir—he said the Kamehameha Korps would declare it kapu."

"Taboo?"

"It's the same word—'kapu' is the Hawaiian version. And to prove they meant it, they put a smoke bomb in the baggage on one of the 737s. So the president of the airline dropped fifty thousand dollars where he was supposed to, and the police had a helicopter watching the spot. They caught Kanaloa."

Rachel said thoughtfully, "I suppose they'll convict him of that, so he'll go to jail."

"For extortion. Not for murder."

She sat back and gave him a considering look; but all she said was, "Do you suppose I could have some iced tea?"

He flagged the waitress, turned to say something to Rachel, caught himself, then said determinedly, "I don't understand you. How can you be so forgiving?"

She frowned into her glass as she stirred her tea. "I don't know if there's anything to forgive," she said at last.

"Murder?"

"Of course I can't forgive murder!" she said sharply. "But—but I can feel a little compassion, maybe. David? You know what I do for a living? I'm a librarian. When something puzzles me, the first thing I do is look for a book to look it up in. Maybe that's why I didn't do so well at being married, because the right book wasn't written. Or I couldn't find it . . . Anyway, I wanted to know what Hawaiians could be so *angry* about."

David nodded, comprehending. "So you read some Hawaiian history."

"I read months of it," she corrected. "Michener to start. Then King Kalakaua, and the story of Queen Liliuokalani, and all the history of the monarchy and the republic. There were half a million Hawaiians when Captain Cook landed here. A couple of generations later, less than fifty thousand!"

"Dear Rachel," said David somberly, "as a fifty-three sixty-fourths semi-pure Hawaiian, I *know*. But that's all old history. It doesn't matter any more—except," he added, "to lunatics like Kanaloa . . . And even some non-lunatics, like Kushi, and my nephew, Lono."

"Lono?"

"That's his Hawaiian name. You met him at the party last night. He was in the Kamehameha Korps too, in high school. On the basketball team, as a matter of fact; 'Kamehameha Korps' was what they put on their T-shirts, the whole team. He took the name 'Lono' out of Hawaiian mythology—Lono is what you might call the god of the underworld. The shark god. He's something like Lucifer, a fallen angel. I don't think the symbolism meant much to my nephew when he was fifteen, except that it was romantic." He picked up his empty cup, noticed it was empty and put it down again. "They still do that, though. Kanaloa is also a god's name."

"I see," said Rachel. And then, brightly, "Sergeant Chee says you fly a plane."

He grinned, welcoming the change of subject. "So does my grandmother," he said, "although I try to talk her out of it these days. As much as anybody can talk Kushi out of anything. You're a lot safer with me. Would you like to try it?"

"Sergeant Chee said we might be able to see whales."

"Not too close—there's a twenty-thousand-dollar fine for disturbing them—but, yes, there's a good chance of that. And I've got field glasses in the car."

She was smiling and shaking her head in wonder, as carefree a tourist as ever wore a lei. "Gosh!" she said. "Whales! Let's go!"

When they stepped out of the general aviation building the wind caught Rachel unawares, hair flying, skirt whipped up her thighs, almost making her back up a step. David did not seem to notice the wind for himself; evidently wind was an old story in Hawaii. He did obviously, however, notice how the skirt pressed against her legs, intimate as any lover. David was far too old to be considered in any such romantic way, thought Rachel, but she was nevertheless pleased to catch him staring.

Pleased, too, to be sitting with him as the little plane lifted off the runway and circled out over the Pacific. Unfortunately there weren't any whales that day, at least not nearer than the roads off Lahaina. Apologetically David declined to go that far. "Another time," he said, leaning toward her so she could hear over the whine of the Comanche's engine. "I'll give you the guided tour, anyway." And he flew her back between the two great volcano peaks, down along the Kona coast, over the black-sand beaches and the condominiums. There were no whales over the southern tip of the island, either, but David pointed the nose of the aircraft out to sea, throttled back so they could talk more easily, and said, "Would you like to see Vulcan?"

"What's Vulcan, David?"

"Ah," he said, peering out across the empty ocean before them, "that's the question, isn't it? It's a Navy operation, and they're not talking. The best rumor I heard is that there are manganese nodules on the sea bottom, and they're trying to mine them.''

"Why would they keep that a secret?" asked Rachel.

"Why does the government do anything? It could be something entirely different. Another rumor is that they're trying to develop geothermal power. There's a baby volcano under the water out there somewhere.''

"Or they could be planning to start world war three," said Rachel dreamily.

David glanced at her. "Or," he agreed, "they could be planning to start world war three. But that would be a funny place to do it, wouldn't it? Even if it made sense to want to do that.''

Rachel was silent for a moment, staring out across the cobalt sea. When she spoke it was rapidly and grammatically, as though she were dictating into a machine. "After the hijacking," she said, "I was scared, and mad, and—helpless. I felt absolutely—well—raped. I've never been raped, but it must feel like that. I wanted out, David. I wanted to run away and hide. I thought of leaving the United States, only I couldn't think of where to go. Israel was a possibility. I've never been religious, but I'm the daughter of a woman who had a Jewish mother, so by definition I'm Jewish—even though my parents were Ethical Culture and I brought my son up Dutch Reformed, because that was what my husband was. But I couldn't go to Israel. The PLO and the Syrians spoiled that for me—not to mention the Israelis themselves. So where, then? Sunny Italy, where they kneecap tourists? Latin America, where they shoot nuns? There wasn't anywhere. If it wasn't the PLO, it was the IRA, or the Puerto Rican Nationalists, or the Cubans, or the Free Serbians, and if there's a place in the world where there isn't somebody with a grievance who wants to kill and maim other people for revenge, I don't know where it is." She shook herself and smiled. "So that's why I'm not so sure that if somebody were going to start world war three, I'd lift a finger to stop them," she said sunnily, "and what's that up ahead?"

He cleared his throat. "It's Vulcan," he said. He changed course slightly to pass well west of it, glancing at her out of the corner of his eye.

For a little while neither of them spoke, as what had looked

like a lump on the horizon changed to look like a ship, then a
cluster of ships, then an artificial archipelago in the middle of
the blue sea. This woman, David was telling himself, this
woman is a lot more shaken up than she lets herself show on
the outside. I wish I could help her. She doesn't need to be
shown the sights. She needs somebody to care about her, and
let her cry, and hold on to her. And that somebody isn't going
to be anybody who was nearly thirty years old when she was
born; so I wish I'd brought Frank Morford along this afternoon.

But he hadn't. Out loud, all he said was, "According to
the NOTAM we have to stay at least ten miles away. You can
probably get a good look through the glasses."

Rachel was already focusing them. "There are a lot of
ships," she reported.

"A whole lot," he agreed. "The big one in the middle is a
drillship, I think—at least, that big mast-looking thing is what
I think of as a drilling tower. Might be some kind of pump for
manganese nodules, though, I suppose. That next biggest one
is supposed to be a sort of floating hotel, and I don't know
what the others are. See the two helicopters on the drillship?
They ferry back and forth to Hilo every day. Mostly it's for
people coming in and out of the airport. They have a lot of
mysterious visitors."

Rachel took it all in, studying the little flotilla. The sun was
high enough to make a bright spot on the sea, burnished cop-
per in the middle of all that cobalt. The Vulcan complex was in
the middle of that great, coppery, egg-shaped patch, black
ships against the glow. "I'll circle around," he called, "and
we'll get a better look from the south—oh-oh."

Company was coming. From the deck of the drillship, a
dragonfly was bobbing up to meet them. At the same moment,
an angry voice rattled David's radio: "Comanche Nancy
Three-six-six-eight-Poppa, you have entered prohibited
airspace!"

He gaped at Rachel, then addressed his radio microphone:
"This is the Comanche. We are at least fifteen miles away!"
No answer. He shook his head. "What's the matter with the
man?" he demanded. Rachel had no answer; but the
helicopter was climbing steadily. It would intercept their

course, like a shotgun group leading a duck in flight. The copter pilot would be directly in their path in a matter of moments. David grumbled, hesitated, then altered course to pass still farther east.

Helicopters are clumsy things compared to fixed-wing planes. This one was a big Navy Sikorsky Sea Rescue jobber, with power to burn. David's Comanche did not have the same reserves. The chopper held its course until it reached their altitude, and then suddenly lurched directly toward them.

Rachel gasped. David swore violently. "That asshole!" he yelled, turning away in a dive. The Comanche was not meant for aerobatics, and he had never treated it so violently before. Nor had he ever been exposed to such reckless handling of another aircraft. In this empty sky there was no excuse!

For a moment he had the crazy fear that the chopper pilot was going to chase after them—catch them, ram them, shoot them down—

The fantasy evaporated, as he peered over his shoulder. The helicopter was already small in the distance, sinking back down toward its landing pad on the drillship.

"I will most certainly report him!" he told Rachel furiously, but she only shrugged.

"He's crazy, I guess," she remarked. "I think it's catching."

Neither said much as they headed back toward General Lyman Field. David saw a big DC-10 sliding in from over the ocean and stooged around for a while before asking for landing clearance, waiting his turn and then waiting a little extra to let the jumbo's turbulent wake subside.

When they were down, and rolling toward the general aviation terminal, David saw a police car with its flashers going. His first quick thought was that it was a pity it was there, since it would remind Rachel of that other day at that field with police cars flashing away. As he parked and leaned across her to open the wing door, he felt her shudder and heard a faint gasp. She scrambled out on the wing and stepped carefully to the ground, staring toward the terminal.

The police car, oddly, was barreling toward them. It pulled up directly in their path, and a Federal Aviation Administration man got out. David said, irritated and puzzled, "What's the matter?" His anger was on Rachel's behalf, but then it became his own as the FAA man said:

"Dr. Yanami, I've had a reckless flying complaint against you. You're charged with endangering another aircraft."

"That's preposterous!" David exploded, and it was, but it was nothing he could laugh off. If the helicopter pilot pressed the charge, there would have to be a hearing. The bad part of that was that, no doubt, they were out of routine radar observation range of the Hilo tower when it happened, so there would be no air-traffic evidence to back up his claims.

Fortunately, Rachel could be a witness for him. But when he was at last through, for the moment, with the police car and the FAA, his witness was stiff with fear. "I'm sorry, Rachel," he said, concerned for her. "These things happen. I'm sure it will get cleared up."

She looked at him as though she had not been listening. "He's gone now," she said.

"Who, the helicopter pilot?" he guessed, puzzled.

She shook her head. Her eyes were bright with fear. "The terrorist. The one who killed Esther. I saw him in the parking lot when I got out of the plane, but when I looked again he was gone."

8

The Soviet orbiting satellite Kosmos 993 was a RORSAT—a "Radar Ocean Reconnaissance Satellite." It had been launched from the Tyuratam Spacedrome, between heavy snows, on an F-1-m booster; now it was sliding over the Pacific Ocean, up from Fiji, radar-mapping a strip of sea surface four hundred kilometers wide as it came.

Kosmos 993 was a subtle and complicated mechanism. The heart of it was its Topaz nuclear furnace, where enriched uranium-235 heated a shell of molybdenum metal to some fifteen hundred degrees Celsius. The furnace did not need to make steam to pass through turbines. It had a better way. At that temperature the molybdenum boiled off electrons. They passed through a thin film of gaseous cesium to another, outer shell; this one was made of niobium. As long as the niobium was kept cooler than the molybdenum within (which was done by liquid sodium and potassium flows), the niobium would collect the electrons: thus an electric current was passed. The current was nearly ten kilowatts, plenty to run the RORSAT's controls and instrumentation.

The Topaz furnace was the heart of the RORSAT. The radar it carried was its reason for existence. Nothing on the surface of the ocean larger than twenty-five meters could escape its detection. It was not interested in dolphins or small boats. Still, among the things it was very interested in were submarines, and it was true that a partly submerged submarine, even a big nuclear one, might be invisible to its rather coarse radar resolution.

However, Kosmos 993 had another trick in its repertory. It could measure sea swells. It could determine their patterns, and it would recognize when those patterns were disturbed by some rapidly moving object under the surface—even hundreds of meters under the surface. If such an object moved swiftly and steadily in a fairly straight line at a considerable depth, the RORSAT would not need to see it with its radar to know that there was a submarine down there.

On the second day of January, Kosmos 993 passed over the Hawaiian islands, as it did every day. Its course took it almost directly over Mauna Loa on the Big Island. Project Vulcan was at the fringe of its radar range. Nevertheless, its radars registered a significant upwelling of wave motion near the clustered ships of the project. As it was designed to do, it reported this observation.

This led to another event.

The RORSATs hunted in pairs. Kosmos 992, its mate, was twenty-two minutes behind it in the same orbit, and it was Kosmos 992 that the RORSAT notified of its interesting observation.

The second RORSAT, Kosmos 992, then took two significant actions.

First, it activated its ion microthrusters to bring it closer to Vulcan on its pass. Second, it caused the beryllium reflector around the reactor core of the Topaz to rotate slightly. The shutters of neutron-absorbing boron retreated; those of neutron-reflecting beryllium enlarged. The result of this was that the reactor heated up slightly. More electrons flowed through the cesium gas. More electrical power went into the radars.

The image the second RORSAT produced of Vulcan and the seas around it was admirably clear. The RORSAT's internal cameras took a picture of the scene, and got ready to deliver its messages to its masters.

Although the RORSATs were capable of transmitting taped pictures by radio, for clearest images the physical photographic film was best. For this purpose they were in an inconvenient orbit—or, rather, the objects they were looking at were in an inconvenient place, due to the constraints of terrestrial geography and orbital ballistics. On a Mercator projection of the Earth their orbits looked like sine waves, floating above and below the equator, reaching up into the Soviet land mass only along its southern edges. Strategically this was ideal—what need did the U.S.S.R. have for looking down on its own territory? Tactically it meant retrieval was limited to only a few possible moments in each ninety-minute orbit.

So as the RORSAT came up over the Aegean Sea it opened a hatch in its side; and at almost its northernmost point it ejected its little gift for its owners. The packet fell through the airspace of the Crimea, easily surviving the buffeting of reentry, until it reached an altitude of twenty miles. Then it popped two parachutes, a tiny braking chute no bigger than a bath towel, then a larger one from which it swung for the balance of its fall. Soviet radars, which had eagerly been seeking it, locked onto its blip at once. The capsule dropped into a snowy birch and pine forest on a mountainside and Russian helicopters, zeroing in on its radio beacon, retrieved it from a snowdrift in less than an hour.

Six hours later the film it contained had been delivered to a low, gray building in Moscow, developed and projected on a screen for an audience of four serious men.

They could easily see David's little plane, frozen in time as it turned away, and the helicopter that soared up to challenge it. These were only mild curiosities. What interested them most was the submarine track heading toward the flotilla. They muttered to each other as they touched each feature in turn with a light-pointer or a stubby finger, the submarine track, the drillship, the barges, the boats.

Then they sat back and looked at each other. "Is it perhaps OTEC?" one asked. He pronounced it "Aw-tech."

The second shook his head. "Geothermal power," he said. "Or perhaps oil drilling, or mining for manganese nodules."

The one in the uniform of the Internal Army said scornfully, "And supplied by a submarine?"

"We do not know that the submarine is supplying anything," the second man objected. "It is perhaps a routine patrol."

"Or," said the Internal Army officer heavily, "it is perhaps—something more serious."

"We need more information," suggested the first man.

"We will have more information," the officer said grimly. "Now let us see the next slide."

9

Arkady Bor's principal social relaxation aboard the floating dormitory ship *Hermes* was Scrabble. He said it was because he wanted to improve his English. To some extent it was, but it was also the best available way of getting another person into his stateroom. After that anything might happen.

It was true nothing ever had. The few interesting female members of the crew either didn't care for Scrabble, or didn't care for Arkady Bor. He was reduced to playing with one radioman, either of two sonar operators or a deckhand. All male. All, actually, rather good looking, and looking better all the time to Bor. "Please," said Bor kindly, "it is not so difficult to spell a word. Make your move, please?"

The deckhand put the tip of a finger between his lips and did not answer. His name was Marvin Poke. He was nineteen years old and black, and he wore musk oil somewhere, perhaps in his hair. Bor sighed and looked away. To have all this free-floating libido was a terrible thing. Why did not the Americans recognize that provisions must be made? Even for someone whom the American women did not find attractive? A woman in his stateroom, for whatever natural purpose, would cause no trouble—a few jokes, yes, but the sort of jokes one could respond to with only a smile or a leer. A young man, especially an attractive one who daubed himself with sensual perfumes—now that could cause trouble of a kind Bor did not want to have again.

To be stuck on this ship, that was the truly terrible thing.

You might as well be in an aul, one of those Georgian hilltop
hamlets where the average man lived for a hundred years. Or
maybe it just seemed like a hundred years? Each day here on
Vulcan, even, seemed like a hundred years, when you were not
allowed to leave it simply because some filthy KGB person had
passed you a note. Anyone could be passed a note! It was not
cultured to punish someone who had done nothing worse than
to accept a piece of paper from a stranger! And the result had
been that he was confined to this ship pending investigation—while even this Marvin got his regular pass to go ashore.
Where, with those tapering fingers and smooth cheeks and
long-lashed eyes, he would no doubt cut a great figure among
the tourists. "Do you go often to Waikiki?" Bor demanded
suddenly.

Marvin kept his eyes on the tiles. "What?"

"I bet that in Waikiki you get plenty of pussy, do you not?"

Marvin took a last slow reconnoiter of his pieces, then
raised his eyes and took his finger out of his mouth. "I don't
go to Waikiki anymore. You could get killed, flying there."

"Ah, the airline troubles," nodded Bor. It had come over
the news. Those strange people who called themselves the
Maui MauMau had shot a chief pilot as he came out of his
home, and the same people had thrown a Molotov cocktail
over the chain-link fence at a parked DC-9. Neither attempt
had done much harm. All the gasoline in the Molotov cocktail
had done was to scorch some suitcases on a baggage truck,
and the pilot had gone home from the hospital with no more
than a patch on his shoulder. But the MauMau had declared
the airline kapu. No one wanted to fly on a plane that might
be a bomb target. The airline's owners were leaking blood
with every flight, as their load factor dropped to sixty percent,
forty percent, still going down.

Marvin had not finished answering Bor's question.
"There's plenty of stuff on the Big Island anyway," he continued. "You go over to the black-sand beaches and there's
always tourist ladies. Only it's hard to find a place to take
them. Around Kilauea's better. There's plenty of them there,
and they've usually got cars you can get into. Or you can go
down in the ravines where it's all nice and warm and nobody
can see what you're doing because it's all like jungle, you

know? Or up by the Kona hotels is best. Except they're usually in tour groups and some of the chicks don't want the others to see them fooling with a sailor, like. But you go up the east shore, up toward the canyon, where there's a lot of little towns. Sometimes you'll find some local girls that can really give you a good time. Or hippies. The hippies are good. They've got grass, usually. Maui's the real place for dope, you know, but there's plenty on the Big Island. That little island in the bay at Hilo, there's usually a couple of guys selling there. There's chicks, too, only some of them've got herpes or something—"

"Make your move," said Bor nervously. He got up for a gloomy look out the porthole. There was nothing to see there but the motor launch carrying somebody from the helicopter pad to the dormitory ship. Bor's main concern in getting up was that he seemed to be getting an erection. At certain times he would not have objected to Marvin's observing that. In fact, that was sometimes the first step to a rewarding encounter. But that particular kind of encounter had been what had cost him the Order of the Red Banner—and very nearly more than that! Bor shivered when he thought how narrowly he had escaped the Moscow Neuropsychiatric Institute and five-grain injections of haloperidol four times a day—as though that had anything to do with one's expressions of love!

The Americans did not do that sort of thing, quite, but Bor did not want to find out just what they did do. This boy was not worth it. "Well?" he asked over his shoulder.

"I'm done," said Marvin. "Let's see. M-A-I-Z-E, maize, that's triple-letter score there for the Z, double word score for the whole thing, plus it changes that 'the' to a 'them' so I get that too—"

The erection had disappeared. Gloomily Bor sat down to enter the seaman's score. And to enter the one after that, and the one after that; and in ten minutes, at a nickel a point, he had lost thirteen dollars. He was not sorry when the public-address system out in the passageway rattled, whistled and blared:

Dr. Arkady Bor. Dr. Arkady Bor. Report to Room 314, Deck C. I say again, Room 314, Deck C. That is all.

He was not sorry, no, but annoyed. The dormitory ship had

once been a cruise liner. There were still telephones in every
stateroom. Why not just pick up the phone, instead of this
public-address misch-masch? And why give the pettifogging
room number instead of saying, what every human being on
the ship knew Room 314, Deck C to be, namely, the security
office?

"We'll play some more later," he said.

"You want to settle up first?" Marvin inquired.

"Oh, God! I can't keep them waiting. Later, I said!"

They kept him waiting, though. "They" were the lieutenant
commander who had ordered him restricted in the first place,
along with a stranger, a pale young civilian in a turtleneck
sweater twice too heavy for Hawaii. Bor was not given the
young man's name. For a moment, sitting in the yeoman's
tiny office and waiting to be invited to join them after their
private talk, Bor had a hope they were planning to tell him his
privileges were restored. No such luck. The civilian said as
soon as Bor was in the room, "You are Arkady Borboradzhvili?"

"Of course," said Bor. He observed that the lieutenant
commander was keeping his mouth shut and his eye on a tape
recorder. The spools were spinning. How many thousands of
kilometers of tape did these people consume in a year? Bor sat
himself down without waiting to be invited, moved his chair
closer to the machine and repeated, "Of course. I am Dr.
Arkady Borboradzhvili, technical consultant to Project
Vulcan, and this is the third of January at approximately 2:15
P.M. Hawaiian time."

The man in the turtleneck looked at him without expression.
He said, "Two days ago you received a written message.
Describe the circumstances."

Bor sighed. "I have done this," he grumbled, "but, if you
wish—I had gone to have a pee in the toilet off the hotel
lobby. While I was urinating a very large man, whose identity
was unknown to me, handed me a piece of paper. I glanced at
it, but I had been drinking. I did not take it in. Later I found it
in my pocket, realized what it was and at once delivered it to
Lieutenant Commander Youngblood, here."

Youngblood glanced up at the sound of his name, but immediately returned to watching the tapes. The civilian asked, "Had you ever seen the man who gave you the message before?"

"No. Well, perhaps yes, in the lobby of the hotel. I cannot be sure. He is a big old man, Oriental. I think I passed him on my way to the men's room."

"Did you see anyone else you recognized, other than the persons in your party from Project Vulcon?"

"No."

The man in the turtleneck was silent for a moment, studying his notes. He let the tape go on recording nothing, and Bor frowned at the waste. Then the man said, "The identity of the man who passed you the note has been established. He is Professor David Kane Yanami. He has been interviewed, and states that he knows nothing of the provenance of the note. He states that it was given to him by a woman who stated that it was for her husband, describing you as her husband. This woman is described as about forty-five, approximately five feet four, dark hair, dark complected, rather heavy build. Can you identify her?"

Bor spread his hands. "Every woman in the Soviet Union looks just like that."

"I see," said the civilian. Further shuffling of notes while the tape spun. "Professor Yanami," he went on, "has been identified as the pilot of an aircraft which entered prohibited airspace over Project Vulcan yesterday. He was warned off. Further investigations of this matter are underway. Do you still claim that you do not know him?"

"Me? Of course not! What I do have to do with some rural college professor? I grant," Bor said reasonably, "that it is an interesting fact that the same person who passed me the note from the KGB is also showing an unusual interest in the project. One would suspect some connection. However, I know nothing of this."

"No one has mentioned KGB," the man in the turtleneck pointed out. "How do you know where the message came from?"

"Oh, for God's sake!" cried Bor. "Who else? I must demand that you ask more sensible questions. Am I at fault because your security has become so lax that Soviet agents can approach me at will? What will you say if next time they come not with a letter but a pistol?" He looked around with indignation, not all of which was pretense. "Well?" he demanded. "Am I to look forward to months of this harassment and suspicion?"

The man in the turtleneck didn't open his mouth but after a moment his mouth opened slightly. He might have been saying no. The other man said placatingly, "Certainly not for months, Dr. Bor. A week or two, perhaps."

"Then what?" asked Bor. The man in the turtleneck gazed at him. He might have shrugged. Such boneheads! Worse than KGB . . . almost! Bor said with dignity, "Then, if you have no further unnecessary questions for me, I must go to my two o'clock meeting. My fourteen hundred, that is," he added, annoyed at himself for spoiling the effect.

There was no answer, but at least when he turned to leave neither of them moved to stop him.

It was always better, he told himself as he made his way to the conference room, to take the offensive with such persons. If he had done so in Tbilisi, who knew, he might still be an honored scientist in his homeland, and these exasperations would never have occurred. If he had dared . . .

But if he had dared too much perhaps it would have been something worse than the psikushka he would have been sent to. Might even be something worse here, he reflected, his mood dampening, for these Americans were not without their own unpleasant resources. Such distracting worries! How unfair the world was, when all one really wished was to be effective in the practice of one's scientific skills!

All the same, he seemed to have got away with it. He felt himself expanding as he walked; he grew taller, his chest broadened, his step was more firm. He marched into the room where the geological team waited to go over the latest photographs and computer simulations with him and nodded crisply to the gathering. "Gentlemen," he said, and, to the black WAVE lieutenant who would run the screen, "and lady, of course. You may proceed when you like."

He seated himself, of course, in the center chair of the first row, mildly annoyed to see that they were not quite ready. The civilian consultant, Dr. Frank Morford, was still fiddling with his floppy disks while Lieutenant Mannerley, the black woman, conferred with him in low tones. Nothing could be said, of course, while Morford was in the room. Bor sat upright with his hands on his knees, the model of an important person whose patience is being pressed a little too hard.

At last they were ready. The civilian was banished to a nonsensitive part of the ship, the lieutenant played a tune on her keyboard, and the screen on the wall of the room displayed, successively, a plate of unintelligible data, a pulsing dot of color as the machine digested its inputs and, finally, the image they were there to study: the simulation of the undersea volcano, Loihi, that lay half a mile below them.

The simulation showed the lava flows and magma pockets of the volcano in color. It looked, as much as anything, like a large, transparent cowflop. The cow had not been well. There were pockets and clots of dark blood-red inside the heap. As Lt. Mannerley rotated the image, the illusion of three-D showed clearly where the magma reservoirs swelled, and where new flows stretched toward the surface. There, where the skin of Loihi was thinnest, the lieutenant stopped the rotation. Three bright blue scars pocked Loihi's surface. She increased the magnification and said, "The three sites under consideration are marked in blue."

"Yes, yes," said Bor testily, glancing around at the geological team. Everyone knew that. Site A was at the base of the mountain, and half a kilometer of dead rock lay between it and the nearest pocket. Site B, halfway up the slope, was no more than a hundred meters from the nearest reservoir. Site C, a quarter of the way around the mountain from B, was a compromise. The stretch to the nearest magma was two hundred meters and a bit, but there was faulting all around it.

"The device is ready for emplacement in Site C," said the head of the drilling team. The lieutenant, present only to speak when spoken to, listened with her head on one side. Bor nodded.

"I have voted to approve, yes, although geology is not my field."

"It's the best emplacement by the criteria you gave," said the drillmaster, covering his ass. "Also, you are the one who must tell us if your charges will alter the geology. Can you guarantee there is no risk of premature explosion? Or of stirring up volcanic activity through the emplacement itself?''

"Of premature explosion positively none," said Bor with contempt. Then, returning the serve, "Of stirring up volcanic activity, how can I say? That is again a risk for geology to assess. I have never said there is no risk at all.''

"If I may be excused," said a new voice from the doorway, a rich and honeyed voice. Bor jumped, and turned in his seat to see General Brandywine smiling winningly on the group.

"Yes, general?" said Bor. "You were about to say?"

The general was usually somewhere about the flotilla, almost never seen. Just what he was a general of Bor had never been told, but what he knew was that when the general spoke everyone else in the command listened attentively. Bor did the same. "Ah," said the general, "I simply had a question. What if we plant the device at Site C and then a new crater forms there? Would that not destroy the device? Or worse?''

Bor looked sternly at the drillmaster, who of course looked away. Naturally. They all wanted Arkady Bor to take all the responsibility. Very well, then. "I do not think that will happen, general," he said, making his voice sound as assured as the general's own. "No, I will put it more strongly. We have submitted these data to specialists in rheology, tectonics, seismology, every discipline that in any way relates to this subject. There is good consensus that Site C is an adequate choice. Of course, we will continuously monitor the site. Of course, if the situation should change in a worsening way we possess the capability to retrieve the device and relocate it. Of course, also, for the device to be effective there is a critical distance from the magma pocket which we cannot exceed, so in any case there will be some unavoidable minimum of risk.''

"To be sure, Arkady," smiled General Brandywine. "I am only asking if you feel sufficient study has been given to all aspects.''

"What I am sure of, general, is that the device is ready for planting and, as you know, the fuse testing is ready to be carried out. I do not wish to be responsible for any delay at this time.''

"Yes, of course." The general smiled around the room,

especially at the woman lieutenant. "Nice to see you again," he acknowledged, and looked around the room to include the members of the geology team. To Bor he said, "If this session is complete, perhaps you'd walk up on deck with me for a moment's sunshine."

"To be sure, general," said Bor promptly. It was not an attractive prospect. If the general wanted to speak to him privately, what he would have to say would not likely be enjoyable. The whole meeting, short as it was, had left a bad taste in his mouth. How desperate these Americans were to protect themselves! Asking him for assurances that were not his to give! As though, if some worst-case accident occurred, it would matter in the least who was to blame. Who would be left to point a finger?

At the top of the stairs—*ladder*, he corrected himself angrily—he panted, "You wish to speak to me privately, general?"

"Of course, Arkady," smiled the general. "You've given our friends from the department a bit of a hard time, haven't you?"

"So they have complained? Well, general! They ask foolish questions, to which I cannot possibly have answers."

"Of course not," the general agreed amiably, and Bor's heart lightened.

"So will you overrule them, then? If you please? There is no real reason for me to be on this ship at all, you know. What I do could be done just as efficiently, and a lot more comfortably, in an office in Honolulu, even better in San Francisco or New York." And that was true. The shape of the undersea mountain, the measurements of its density, the hardness and chemical composition of its rock, the faulting and stressing the test drills revealed—all these things amounted only to numbers. Numbers could be processed anywhere.

"There is the fuse test," the general twinkled, reminding him.

"Yes, of course! Certainly. But after that—"

"Ah, after that," said the general regretfully. "I don't think you see the whole picture, Arkady. I know you would like to be in Waikiki—who could blame you for that? But there's terrorist activity on the islands these days."

"Yes, yes! The news broadcasts have mentioned it."

"And we can't be sure that there isn't some Commie activity behind that, you know. You're pretty precious to us. We really can't risk you."

Arkady Bor's heart sank. Gamely he tried to score a smaller point. "Of course, the fuse test must be done. I presume you will permit me to visit the Big Island to monitor the transmission, at least?"

"Transmission, reception," smiled the general. "Does it matter which end you're at?"

"General! I must protest! I cannot perform my work if I am confined to this stupid ship!"

"Of course you can, Arkady," soothed the general.

"Impossible! The fuse coding is the most important test we can make!" And that was true, he thought but did not say, because it was almost the only part of Vulcan that could be tested at all. For the rest of the project, the first test would be the last, and also the only.

The general looked tolerantly amused. "You can't be in two places at once, can you? So your assistant will cover the transmitter, and you the receiver, instead of the other way around. What's wrong with that?" he asked genially; but when Bor opened his mouth to reply the general answered for him. "Nothing's wrong with that," he said definitely. The tone was still friendly. The eyes were not.

Bor's eyes flickered away, then, sadly, resignedly, dropped. "So I am not to leave this ship ever," he said.

The general was all amiability again. "Who said that, Bor? Far from it! There is a meeting at Sandia, and you are going to be there to explain the project!"

"Sandia?" cried Bor. "What is this about Sandia?"

"A meeting," the general nodded. "It is time to announce the Vulcan project to our masters, Bor, and who would be better than you to explain it?"

"I was not told!"

"You're being told now," the general smiled. "I'm surprised. I thought you would enjoy it! After all, there's plenty to do in Albuquerque. You haven't tasted real Mexican food until you eat the guacamole and chocolate chicken at La Duena. You'll have a fine time, I promise. And then, when you come back, you can check the emplacement of the device, and then there's the fuse test—the time will pass very fast for you, Bor."

"Of course, General Brandywine," said Bor formally. Hopelessly. "Now, if you will excuse me, I have some work to attend to in my office."

It was true that he had work to do, since he always had work to do in his office, but Bor's mood was not constructive. How quickly things had turned bad for him!

And how bad had they turned? To be sent off like a messenger boy was insulting, but was there anything behind the insult? He sat down before his screen and punched up his Mailbag program. Yes, there was, as always, a great deal of it, and even some real mail from the afternoon courier delivery. None of it would be of any importance, of course.

Something the general had said stuck in Bor's mind. A small incongruity. Was it something about the emplacement of the device? He gazed listlessly at the screen with its action memos (of which he got only information copies; action was not allowed to Bor), the strings of data for computer simulation (by the civilian consultant, Morford, or if too sensitive for a civilian perhaps by the black woman—certainly not by him), the titles and abstracts that his search programs had found him in the journals. Yes, he thought gloomily, he would have a fine time in Albuquerque—with at least two security agents never out of sight, this time surely not even when he went to relieve his bladder! Oh, he would be permitted some follies, no doubt. If he were to pick up some hotel-lobby hooker, the security agents would grin and joke leeringly—and, of course, then listen with stethoscopes through the door of the adjoining room, to make sure he revealed no classified information while achieving the surgical release of his accumulated sexual tensions. But even that tolerance would be quite limited. If, for instance, Bor were to encounter some handsome young man in a bar—then, no! There would be no forgiveness there. No grins. No jokes.

Bor sighed. Ignoring the crawl of electronic data on the screen he began to open his letter mail. A bank statement —some satisfaction in that, anyway. A bill from American

Express—no satisfaction at all, because it was for so little that it pointed out to him how little opportunity he had to spend money on enjoyment. A Christmas card—

A Christmas card! Who in the world would be sending him a Christmas card, especially one postmarked in Hilo on the first of January? There was no signature. The card itself was one of those foolish American comic things, with a Santa Claus face that popped up menacingly when he opened it, and a silly doggerel verse about Christmas carols ending all quarrels—not even a decent rhyme, he thought contemptuously.

Then he suddenly felt a chill.

Carefully he unfolded the card, searching the blank inside sheet. There was nothing. He thought for a moment, then retrieved the crumpled envelope from his wastebasket. He smoothed it carefully, slipped a ballpoint pen under the gummed edges and flattened it out; and, yes, there was something written on the inside, tiny curlicue letters, almost invisible in the fold of the paper.

It was in Georgian, and it said:

"You made a foolish mistake. Don't make another."

10

In 1913 H. G. Wells wrote a book, *The World Set Free*, in which he talked about the possibility of atomic bombs. Twenty years later Leo Szilard, remembering the story and thinking about the recent discoveries in nuclear physics, decided that such a bomb could really be built. Twenty years after that Szilard and others in the Manhattan Project had finished the design and begun the manufacture of the first atomic weapons . . . and on August 6, 1945, the American B-29 bomber *Enola Gay* took the fruit of their inspirations and labors and dropped it on the Japanese city of Hiroshima. The time from fiction to fact was forty-two years.

Why did it take so long?

It would make more sense to ask how it could be done so quickly, for between the inspiration of a science-fiction writer and the deployment of the weapon itself were immense problems of both engineering and theoretical science.

The scientific facts behind the A-bomb were immensely difficult to discover, but fairly easy to understand once found. They rest on Einstein's great revelation that matter and energy are only different forms of the same essential thing.

If you add up all the individual weights of each proton and neutron in the nucleus of an atom of uranium (it doesn't matter which isotope of uranium you choose), and then balance this aggregate weight against an intact nucleus, you will find a surprising thing. The whole weighs less than the sum of its parts. Some mass has "disappeared." When the nuclear particles came together, they lost some of the mass they possessed in isolation.

This mass did not disappear; Einstein's conservation law says accurately that this would be impossible. What the mass did was to become energy—the "binding energy" that holds the nucleus together, in spite of the fact that its protons repel each other so violently that otherwise they would cause the nucleus to fly apart.

The nucleus of an element lighter than uranium—say, of iron—has more binding energy per nuclear particle than uranium does. That is why the uranium atom is fairly easy to split, iron impossible. Being more tightly held, each nucleon in the lighter elements has less energy of movement—kinetic energy; so that when a uranium atom "fissions" (or splits into two or more lighter atoms), each nuclear particle has lost some energy. The amount it has lost is about one million electron volts (written as 1 MeV) per nucleon. For an element as heavy as uranium, that comes to about 240 MeV per atom.

This is not much at all. The smallest firecracker releases a hundred million billion times as much energy as that. But there are a great many atoms in even a tiny lump of uranium—say, one the same mass as a firecracker. If these atoms were all to fission at once they would release the energy of twenty billion firecrackers.

That is what happens in an atomic bomb.

Not all elements—not even all atoms of the element uranium—will fission readily, or even at all. But some forms of some elements fission more easily than others. Uranium-235 and plutonium-239, in fact, will fission all by themselves, if only you put enough of them together in one place and thus achieve what is called "critical mass."

The two basic engineering problems of the A-bomb were, first, to laboriously produce large quantities of uranium-235 and plutonium-239; and, second, to devise a mechanism which would hold smallish (subcritical) lumps of them far enough apart, so that they would do no harm, until such time as the bomb was to go off, and then bring the separate lumps together into one critical-mass–sized piece instantly.

For accomplishing this there are many engineering designs. One can put a smallish lump of plutonium in the barrel of a "gun" and then fire it into a larger lump (that was the Nagasaki bomb). Or one can surround a group of small lumps with a shell of chemical explosive, so that when the chemical is detonated all of the lumps are forced into each other (in one configuration or another, the basic design of most A-bombs).

That is quite simple, really. What made it difficult was to so design it that the bomb would never go off by accident, and never fail to go off by intent . . . and to fit all the necessary fusing and safety precautions into something that could be dropped from an airplane.

But all that was achieved by the summer of 1945. Then the scientists and technicians and soldiers of the Manhattan Project had the satisfaction of bringing about the biggest damned man-made explosion the world had ever seen, the equivalent of forty thousand tons of TNT going off at once over the naked city of Hiroshima.

That was a small bomb by modern standards—why, it delivered no more explosive force than a thirty-aircraft B-24 bomb group could have delivered on a target if they had flown a mission every day for eight or ten months. However, that energy wasn't delivered over a period of months, but in a fraction of a second. It demolished buildings, blew away bridges, boiled the eyeballs out of the heads of people looking at it and killed others by the tens of thousands.

That was one bomb.

Now there are fifty thousand or more nuclear bombs in the world, and almost all of them are bigger than that one. Some are a thousand times more powerful; because now we have the H-bomb.

11

Although her body was in the islands, Rachel's biological clock was still on Central Standard Time. Six-thirty, said the digital alarm by the bed. The internal one was sure that it was pushing eleven—disgracefully late to be abed—and would not let her go back to sleep.

That was a pity. She had slept soundly, dreamlessly—and safely. While she was tucked under the light blanket she was safe. Or had that illusion; and any illusion was worth having, when reality was so nasty. The nastiest part had been seeing that man, that Oscar Mariguchi or whatever his name was, at the airport. Or *thinking* she had seen him, because when David told the policeman about it, no one had been able to find the man.

Perhaps it was just her imagination?

The policeman evidently thought so—well, her credibility with the police was a lot less than it had been, since she failed to make the identification they were hoping for of the other terrorist.

She pushed the blanket off and got out of bed. Since the hotel was paying for all, she called down for coffee in her room, then dressed quickly and set out to explore a little. David would think that was very reckless of her, she thought abstractly, because he had not believed she was imagining things. But David Yanami was taking more charge of her life than she really enjoyed.

Twenty minutes later she was sitting on a paintless park

bench, with the names of a hundred pairs of lovers carved into
it, on a little island in Hilo Bay. Behind her was the little
bridge she had crossed, and behind that her hotel, with a line
of others beyond it, warm in the rising sun. The sun was hot
on her back. It was a pretty place, with the flattened bulge of
Mauna Loa and the craggier, taller Mauna Kea across a narrow stretch of the bay before her. She looked at them appreciatively, but what she was seeing was the face of Oscar
Mariguchi. She saw it three times. She saw it in that frozen
moment on the airplane, when Esther had ripped the green ski
mask away and she had seen the startled, almost boyishly
frightened face of the terrorist, just before he had fired the
shot into Esther. She saw it again as it had appeared in the
police book of known criminals. The same face, definitely.
And she saw it in that fugitive glimpse at the airport.

Still the same face?

She stretched lazily and put that question, along with
everything else about Oscar Mariguchi, firmly, completely,
out of her mind.

There was a more important question to ask.

Why hadn't she identified the other terrorist in the lineup?
True, she could not be certain in a technical sense, since she
had never seen his face before. But that deep, contemptuous
voice, that huge head—there could not be many like that in
Hawaii! She could at least have told the lieutenant what she
thought, and let them make a case of it if they could.

Why hadn't she?

Was it because she was sorry for him? Ridiculous! The man
was a murderer many times over, it was only by the flimsiest
of chances that he hadn't killed her too. Was it because she
was afraid of retribution from one of his accomplices, still
uncaught? Of course. It had to be. That was, Rachel told herself, the only explanation for her behavior that made sense at
all. It accounted for everything. Almost everything. Everything but why she had come here in the first place and exposed
herself to risk (but you could explain that, too, because she
hadn't really thought it out back in St. Louis, because a free
trip to Hawaii had looked a lot better than jumping puddles of
slush in Missouri). So everything was accounted for—or
everything except the fact that she was sitting here, all by

herself, a prime target for whatever the terrorists might want
to do to her and no help in sight.

Rachel folded her hands in her lap and leaned back against
the uncomfortable planks. The other question—all this being
so—was, why wasn't she frightened?

Frightened she was not. The dominant emotion on the surface of her mind was in fact a faint regret that she had not
worn her shorts and halter top on this stroll, so that she could
be working on a tan. She sat there with her mind slowly pursu-
ing its self-interrogation, not very interested in what it might
discover, and she went on sitting there while traffic began to
grow on the bayfront drive and the sun rose higher behind her
until she heard a step. Even then she didn't turn. She waited
until she was sure the steps were moving away. Then she got
up and glanced casually at the man in the wetsuit and flippers,
walking away from her toward the other end of the island. It
was interesting that he had not been a terrorist, her mind
registered; and as long as she was standing anyway, she turned
toward the bridge and her hotel.

She had barely reached the first banyan tree on the drive
when a car accelerated madly, made a screeching U-turn
around the center divider, and roared to a stop beside her.

It occurred to Rachel to be surprised that a blast from a
sawed-off shotgun did not take her head off. Instead, the person in the car was the policewoman, Nancy Chee. "Mrs.
Chindler!" she cried. "Where have you been? Really, you
mustn't leave the hotel alone. Dr. Yanami came to pick you up
and you weren't there and he called me at once. Get in,
please!"

Rachel was mildly surprised again to see that the girl was
really upset. "I just wanted to be by myself for a while."

"But that's terribly dangerous, Mrs. Chindler," the
policewoman scolded. "You shouldn't go out alone! I'm not
sure you should stay in the hotel alone, either, for that matter.
We have an extra room. If you'd be willing to—"

"That's very kind," Rachel said, as Nancy Chee turned
around the divider on Banyan Drive. "Really, I'm better off
in my hotel room."

"But you'd be much—"

"No," Rachel said definitely. The policewoman looked at

her, then slid the car into its parking space. Before they got out she said:

"We haven't been able to find Oscar Mariguchi."

"Maybe I just imagined it, Nancy."

"I don't think so. We're pretty sure he was seen on the Kona side yesterday morning. He could have got here easily enough to be at the airport when you and Dr. Yanami landed. But we haven't found anyone at Lyman who recognized his picture."

"He knows I saw him—if it really was him, I mean—and so he's probably a thousand miles away by now anyway," said Rachel comfortingly.

"Not on this little island," the policewoman said. She led the way into the hotel lobby, eyes on every person in sight, peering into every alcove.

Rachel realized she had given the sergeant a fright. That being so, she was less surprised to see when David Yanami hurried up to them that he was panting and sweating, having just come back from a tour of the hotel grounds to make sure that her corpse was not floating in the swimming pool or hidden behind a hedge of dirty-boy anthurium. "I'm really sorry to have made trouble for you," she said to both of them. "Would you like some breakfast?"

They exchanged looks, then both declined. "I should get back to the precinct," Chee said. "Would you like to come with me, Mrs. Chindler? I'm afraid it's not very luxurious, but—"

"I really don't like police stations much," Rachel smiled.

"Then you'll come with me," David said firmly. To the sergeant: "I'll see that she's with somebody all the time."

"If you're sure—" Chee said uncertainly.

"I'm sure," Rachel said. "I'd much rather do that. Is that your car out there in the no-parking zone, David?"

It was. "They're making a real federal case out of that thing yesterday," he grumbled as he helped her into it. "So I've got to file a report. I thought I might take you up to spend the morning with Kushi, but she wants us there for dinner tonight and maybe that's more time than you want to spend with her. So Frank Morford has been wanting to show you around his projects—"

"The one I met at your house?"

"That's right, Rachel. He's a very nice man, just divorced—"

Rachel shrugged. "All right." She gazed idly out of the window. What a nuisance to have someone you barely knew trying to matchmake with someone you didn't know at all! She was able to work up quite a feeling of indignation about it, which wholly submerged any of the worries stirring under the surface of her mind about terrorists or possible death or why she had failed to make the ID for Sergeant Chee.

The reason Frank Morford switched from stars to computers had nothing to do with his hopes for advancement in his career. It didn't even reflect his interests. He still liked stars. The solar and sidereal universe delighted him more than silicon chips did, but it was vastly remote. You could look at it. You couldn't touch it. Especially you couldn't shape, change or improve it, and Frank Morford was a hands-on kind of man.

He was fond of his old teacher, David Yanami—probably fonder of him than of any other person alive, since he had no family left. Once there had been a wife of whom he had been very fond indeed! But she left. Fondness would not stretch as far as Fargo, North Dakota. North for God's sake *Dakota*. It was bad enough that she had left him for a man older than he, poorer than he, even, dammit, duller than he—but in order to do it she had left the island paradise of the Pacific for North *Dakota*. How much more shattering could a rejection get?

She had not, however, quite deprived him of his interest in women.

That was a whole other problem. Fond as he was of David, Morford had had a few sharp words with him about this new malahini woman, Rachel Chindler. The worst thing—no, the second worst thing—no, the *third* worst thing about being ditched, after you'd got past those really nasty ones like the hurt to the vanity and the emptiness of the bed, the third worst thing was the way you became quarry. You knew that you were a large, bright blip on the radars of unattached women who didn't want to stay that way, and that your best friends cooperated to flush you toward their blinds. This Rachel

Chindler might be all very well. If he had run into her on his own, he would no doubt have considered interestedly the prospect of, at least, taking her to bed once or twice. But not with David and Kushi looking on, certainly in the spirit, however physically absent they might be in the bedroom.

Besides, she had been rude to him at David's party.

So when David woke him up that morning to ask if he would entertain the woman for a couple of hours while David talked his way out of some reckless-flying violation, Morford couldn't say no, but was aggrieved to be forced to say yes. He was still surly as he bicycled up the hill to the campus, but once on the grounds he cheered up. He loved his school. It was, in spite of everything, an attractive prospect to have someone to brag to about it.

For a school that had started as a land-grant college, principally concerned with instructing plantation people on what they had to put back into the soil so that they could keep on pulling sugar cane out of it, Hilo State had come a long way. The volcanos were right out the window, so it was natural to teach earth sciences. The ocean was there: marine biology, hydrology and all the associated disciplines came easily. Mauna Kea loomed just down the road, a 12,000-foot platform to put telescopes on. Canada, France and England, lacking good mountains of their own, borrowed its space to build their instruments. Therefore adding a major astronomy faculty to the university was cheap and easy. There were other advantages. It wasn't the mere presence of the mountains, the sea and the scopes. It was the kind of people who came to work with them that turned out most valuable of all. To its great surprise, Hilo State came out of the cocoon to spread its wings as a first-class scientific school. Well, maybe not *first* class. It was still quite small. But it was definitely a place to mention right after Stanford and Cambridge and M.I.T. The computer department flowed naturally from the others, because how else could you digest their data?

It wasn't quite all roses. Frank Morford's office was at the very edge of the campus because there had been a plan for the university to start its own Silicon Gulch or Route 128, with a better view than California and a better climate than Boston. That hadn't worked out—yet, anyway—so Morford had a long walk from the parking lot to his building. He met David and the Chindler malihini coming in the front door as he was coming through from the back. "I'll be back as soon as I can, Frank. Noon at the latest," David Yanami promised. *Noon!* That meant three hours! What did you do with a strange woman for three *hours*?

Well, first things first. "Let's see if they've got the coffee on yet," he said to Rachel Chindler, as David hurried out the door.

Actually, it wasn't painful at all. Rachel Chindler was of a sensible age. She had had a husband, as Morford had had a wife, and they'd both been rotten—a palpable bond. She was willing to talk about anything Morford had on his mind, and they spent two cups of coffee discussing—no, Morford explaining, Rachel listening to—the myriad tourist attractions of the Big Island. It wasn't until he realized that not only had she no doubt heard this whole spiel before but in fact he had said the same things at the New Year's Eve party that he broke off. They had pushed as far into each other's domestic miseries as either felt it right to go at that point. The next thing interesting to them both would have been the terrorists but, he thought, it would surely be a painful subject for her. So he thought; and did not test his conclusion by asking Rachel how she felt about it.

Instead, he took a different kind of a chance. "Mrs. Chindler," he said, smiling diffidently, "would you like to see how the world came to an end?"

She looked as he had expected her to look, startled. "I mean the Cretaceous extinction," he explained. "That was the time, maybe seventy million years ago, when all the dinosaurs became extinct. I've done a computer simulation of the event for, ah, for a government agency. Would you like to see it?"

She was either truly interested or pleasingly polite. "Oh, may I?"

"No problem at all," he told her, stretching the truth slightly. Well, more than slightly. There was a problem. The simulation was classified Top Secret by the government-agency people who had ordered it, for use in their Project Vulcan. Frank Morford was not one to be intimidated by some bureaucrat's classification stamp, though, and, anyway, how would anyone know if he showed the tape to this unalarming visitor? He said, "The theory is that a big asteroid hit the Earth around then, say 70,000,000 B.C. Its impact threw up so much dust that it darkened the sky for several years. Without light, everything died. There's a refinement to the theory which says that the place where the asteroid hit is now the island of Iceland."

"Were there dinosaurs on Iceland?"

He said impatiently, "No, of course not, it's too young. Iceland was built up out of undersea volcanos, just like Hawaii. That's the point. The speculation is that there was a volcano where the asteroid hit, and so the impact not only threw up debris from its kinetic impact, it released a huge explosion from the volcano itself. Remember Mount Saint Helens? The big blast there was when a landslide weakened the side of the mountain, and all that compressed material inside exploded out. Well. The Iceland idea is that you got both kinds of explosions at once, do you see?"

"I think so," said Rachel, watching Morford work at the computer.

"Anyway," he said, bent over his keyboard, "I have a consultancy with this, ah, government program, and they asked me to simulate the theoretical Iceland episode, only rewritten to assume that the point of impact was right here in Hawaii."

"Why would they do that?" He glanced up to shake his head humorously: Why did any government agency do anything, the gesture said. "Could that really happen? I mean, one of these volcanos go off that way?"

Morford hesitated. He wanted to give her a convincing answer to that question—to tell her how silly was the notion that a shield volcano could be made to blow up by anything at all—but, after all, he *was* taking liberties with classified material. The Vulcan people had a lot of power behind them. He compromised by giving her a grin and an "I hope not." He looked around the room. "I'm going to display it for you on the big screen so you can see the detail, Mrs. Chindler, only you'll be able to see it better if we get the room a little darker. Could you pull those blinds down for me?"

Obediently Rachel rose, fumbling with the cords until she

had blotted out the bay on one side, Mauna Loa on the other.
"It's what you call a maximum-risk scenario," he was saying.
"I've taken the assumed volume and velocities of the Iceland
situation, same proportions of heavy solids, dust and gases,
only I've put it here with the local wind and upper-air patterns—ready? All right, here we go."

The "big screen" was not all that big; actually it looked like
the twenty-four-inch television in Rachel Chindler's living
room, only what it showed was not Johnny Carson. It showed
a map of the world on the Mercator projection, except that it
was centered over the Pacific. The Hawaiian islands were dots
of red in the middle of the sea. Off to the right were the shapes
of North and South America, to the left the huge Eurasian
land mass with Australia and New Zealand hanging at the
lower corner of the peninsulas and island chains of Indochina.
A diamond-bright dot of white appeared on the right of the
screen, heading for Hawaii. "That's the asteroid," said Morford. "After it hits, we see the detritus cloud in yellow."

"I see," said Rachel politely. What made this program most
different from any she watched in her living room was that it
was silent. Without sound the bright asteroid dot crossed the
continent and the sea. Without sound the red dot of Hawaii
erupted into a brilliant golden flash. "We've just been
pulverized," Morford explained. Still without sound, a bil-
lowing splash of gold obliterated the islands and grew.

The golden cloud spread. At first, the low-level winds
spread it harmlessly into the broad Pacific. Then the upper-
level currents began to tug it remorselessly toward the North
American mainland. Portland and Seattle were clouded over,
then the mountain states. Butte and Omaha and Kansas City
came under the pall, and Chicago and Detroit, and it spread
around as it moved. Los Angeles and Phoenix and Albuquerque looked up to unexpected overcasts. Where it went it did
not depart. Its first tendrils reached the East Coast, blanketing
Boston and New York and Richmond. Then it leaped off the
map and reappeared on the other side to shroud Ireland and
England and Scandinavia and France. It did not go away.

At the bottom of the map, just above Antarctica's Amund-
sen Bay, a digital time hack measured the passage of hours
and days. In nine days the eastward-moving upper-air clouds

reached and blended with the ones that had been milling about the Pacific, and Tahiti and Bora Bora were drenched in unseasonable rain. The rain stopped. The clouds remained.

The clouds remained, consolidating their conquest of the Earth's sky, and spilled over the equator to the southerly lands. The time hack read off two weeks, ten weeks, fifty weeks, one hundred weeks, two hundred weeks—

At that point, at the end of the fourth year of the simulated event, they began to weaken. Patches of clear sky appeared again, as the particles slowly clustered together and fell out of the air.

But by that time every sun-loving plant would be dead.

"You can open the venetian blinds now," said Frank Morford.

"That was very interesting," Rachel said, complying. As she turned around she saw Morford glancing at his watch. "Mr. Morford? I know you're busy, and really I can fend for myself. Why don't I go out in the waiting room and just sit for a while until David comes to pick me up?"

Morford hesitated. "Actually," he admitted, "I've got to make a conference call about a grant pretty soon."

"Well, then."

"But I'd really feel better if you stayed here, if you don't mind. There are magazines." He waved at the bookshelves. "A lot of them are pretty technical, but there's *Scientific American* and *Omni* and a couple of others—"

"I'll be fine," Rachel assured him.

What a remarkably obedient woman she was, Morford thought as he dialed the three people at the University of Hawaii with whom he had to discuss the allocation of an N.A.S. grant. How many grown women would let themselves be ordered around as placidly as she? She had taken the top magazine off the pile and was compliantly turning the pages one by one—*Nature*, it was, and a fat lot of good she would get out of reading that.

Then he got involved in the question of whether Hilo State or U.H. was to be considered the prime grantee and hardly noticed when a secretary appeared at the door and spoke to Rachel Chindler. The woman came over to him. He looked up abstractedly. "David's waiting for me in the parking lot," she said. "Thanks for letting me keep you company." He waved politely, but his mind was on the three hundred and fifty thousand dollars of the grant. And stayed there until an hour later when David Yanami appeared and denied, first irritably and then in panic, that he had ever called to say he would meet Rachel in the parking lot.

12

What makes an H-bomb explode is what makes the Sun shine. It is the fusion of two atoms of the lightest element, hydrogen, into one atom of the second lightest, helium. This is a "thermonuclear" reaction and, as the prefix "thermo" shows, it happens only under the application of great heat.

There must also be great pressure. These conditions are easily met at the core of a star like the Sun, where the immense weight of the star itself squeezes its core to the critical point—and, at the same time, tamps the explosion process, so that, from our comfortable 93 million mile distance, the Sun appears only like a bright light, with no hint of the violence that rages inside.

Such conditions do not naturally exist anywhere on (or even inside) the Earth. To make an H-bomb work, they must be created artificially. There is only one practicable way to do that: You must first detonate an ordinary plutonium or uranium-235 atom bomb, and use the resulting furious heat and pressure to set off the reluctant (but vastly more powerful) fusion reaction.

That is the basic "secret" of the H-bomb. The rest is engineering.

The engineering, to be sure, is enormously complex.

For one thing, the hydrogen in a hydrogen bomb cannot be exactly the familiar element shown in Mendeleyev's periodic table. There it possesses the simplest possible structure for any atom—one proton in its nucleus, one electron in orbit; that's the element that makes the water that we drink, and is overwhelmingly the most common substance in the universe. Ordinary hydrogen can be made to fuse, but only in the core of a star. For military purposes its reaction is too difficult to initiate, and too slow.

However, most elements exist in isotopic forms—that is to say, in forms that contain the same number of electrons and protons as the simple form, but with one or more neutrons added in the core. Chemically the isotopes are the same. Physically they are heavier than the simple form, because of the added neutrons. Hydrogen has two significant isotopes. With one neutron added, it is called deuterium; with two, tritium.

Either deuterium or tritium will fuse more readily than simple hydrogen. They are, in fact, the fuel that makes the H-bomb explode.

They are not easy to work with, however. Both are gases, which presents problems in storing them and in compressing them to the point of fusion. Tritium, moreover, is poisonously radioactive.

To these problems there is an elegant solution. The metallic element lithium fissions readily when bombarded by neutrons (as it is in the presence of an exploding A-bomb), and when it splits it produces all the tritium one needs. Moreover, lithium combines chemically with hydrogen very well, to produce the compound lithium hydride—or (to select the most effective isotopes of those two elements) lithium-6 deuteride. In its handiest form, lithium-6 deuteride is a heavy grayish sand; it is easily storable—and, when it undergoes fusion, violently explosive.

That is the first problem solved. There are others.

The overpressure in the vicinity of an A-bomb explosion is certainly adequate to compress the lithium deuteride; the radiation from it is plenty to ignite the fusion reaction. Troublesomely, the two effects come in the wrong order. *First* you need to compress the fuel; *then* you must ignite it with heat and radiation. But the radiation travels faster than the shock wave. Left to itself, the reaction would begin too soon, expanding the fusion elements before the blast could have time to compress them.

Solution: Place a heavy metal buffer between the A-bomb trigger and the H-bomb fuel, so that the fuel is shielded from radiation long enough to be compressed. (While you're at it, make the shield of uranium—in fact, make as much of the structural parts of the device as you can of uranium. Ordinarily nonexplosive [and thus comparatively cheap] uranium-238 will do, since under these conditions it too will fission and add its energy to the blast. This isn't negligible; perhaps half the energy of an H-bomb comes from the fission of the uranium and plutonium it contains.)

Next problem: If the shock wave itself strikes the lithium deuteride directly it is more likely simply to blow it away than to compress it in place. There must be a way to convert that outward-thrusting explosive energy into inward-forcing pressure.

Solution: Fill the otherwise empty spaces around the lithium deuteride with some substance—properly doped polystyrene will do—which the A-bomb explosion will instantly convert into plasma, hot and violently squeezing the H-bomb fuel.

Then, to make sure that the lithium deuteride fuses promptly, stick into the heart of it (as you might steady a beach umbrella by thrusting its shaft into a can of sand) a spike of fissile uranium-235 or plutonium, so that the secondary explosion of the spike will ignite the lithium deuteride at once.

Your bomb is complete.

Many refinements are possible. If you want to cut down the radioactive fallout to make a (relatively) "clean" bomb, you take out as much of the uranium as possible and replace it with another heavy metal that does not fission readily—say, tungsten. If you want to make the fallout even nastier, replace it with cobalt. If you want to be able to adjust the size of the explosion to the target—what is called the "dial-a-blast" feature—arrange to pump in as much more deuterium and tritium as you like while arming the bomb. You can build an H-bomb as large as you like simply by adding more ingredients. One hundred megatons has already been achieved. There is no known upward limit to the size of an H-bomb, except, perhaps, Chandrasekhar's limit to the maximum size of a star.

An H-bomb need not be very large. A cylinder no bigger than a household garbage can will hold one that will blow up with the force of twenty or so million tons of TNT, enough to annihilate most cities—

And easily enough to open the side of an undersea volcano.

13

Past the orchid farm, past the macadamia-nut plantation, out of the traffic and up the slopes of Mauna Loa the boy drove the Honda pickup truck, skillfully and easily, with his mind obviously not on his driving. The truck was a wreck. From where Rachel sat she could see the right-hand fender was missing, and half the gadgets on the dashboard were gone, only holes remaining. It was a farm truck, the kind the cane operators used on their private dirt tracks and never put on the road. "Don't you worry about the police?" Rachel asked, making conversation as she would have with one of the college students waiting for a book to do his term paper—the jocular reproof of an older person. The boy didn't turn his head, but it was a moment before he answered.

"It isn't the police we're worrying about, Mrs. Chindler."

"I mean about motor vehicle inspection," she explained. "Don't you have it here in Hawaii?"

This time he grinned. "They don't patrol much here, Mrs. Chindler." He had an unusual sort of grin. He was a handsome boy, a lot more haole than Hawaiian or Oriental, but with the golden skin and black, bright eyes of the beachboys. But when he smiled he looked like a wolf. "We're turning off here," he announced, glancing in the rearview mirror. No other car was in sight. They entered a driveway, not one used very often, it appeared, because there were fronds of uncrushed dead vegetation blown across the asphalt. They pulled into a parking turn-around in front of a boarded-up home, and the boy cut the ignition. "I didn't exactly tell you the truth, Mrs. Chindler," he said. "Uncle David told me to pick you up, but the part about taking you to stay with Kushi wasn't right. That would be the first place they would look for you."

Rachel nodded placidly. She glanced around at their surroundings. The first thing you noticed was the quiet, no sound at all except for a faint scraping of branches and leaves in the perpetual wind. The house looked as though it had been through a fire, and the plantings around it had not been tended for months. Dirty-boy anthuriums had grown tall, and coconut palms had dropped greenish-yellow pods onto the driveway. "I thought that part wasn't right," she agreed, "because David told me we were going to his house tonight, not today. I don't even think Kushi's at home."

The boy looked startled. "And you still got into the car with me?" he demanded. "Really, Mrs. Chindler, you have to be more careful! What if I'd been one of the hijackers? I could have been Kanaloa himself!"

"Is that his name? The one that was in the lineup? The one that's in jail now?"

"The one that got out on bail this morning," the boy corrected savagely. He looked at his watch, then recollected himself. "I didn't mean to yell at you," he apologized, charming—consciously charming. "Well. How are you liking Hawaii so far?"

Rachel plucked a green stem from the foliage. "It's beautiful."

"I don't mean the scenery, I mean us crazy Hawaiians. Somebody like my great-great-and-so-forth-grandmother must be quite an experience for you."

Rachel twisted the bit of greenery through her fingers. It smelled tropical. "I like Kushi very much," she declared, watching him thoughtfully.

"Of course you do," he grinned. "Everybody does. She's practically a tourist attraction, with her stories about old Hawaii and the gods and heroes."

If the boy was determined to play conversational games,

Rachel was willing to go along. "I don't think she's told me any of those."

"She hasn't? Not even about me?" The boy smiled confidingly. "They call me Lono, Mrs. Chindler. It's a kind of nickname; he was one of the supreme gods, along with Kane and Ku. He was the one that really did things, you know? And when I was young they thought I was really going somewhere —I guess I've been a disappointment to them lately."

"Oh, surely not," said Rachel politely.

He shrugged. "Kushi's favorite of the gods is Pele, of course. I guess Kushi was a feminist way before her time, even for gods. Pele was female."

Rachel set her face in the appropriate expression of polite interest; encouraged, Lono went on: "You have to remember, Mrs. Chindler, that legends are the closest things we Hawaiians have to history. We didn't have a written language until the missionaries came. Our historians were all poets— like Homer. Singers sang the meles—that's the traditional, historical songs—and other singers listened, and then they went away and sang them somewhere else. As far as they remembered. With whatever creative additions they thought up by themselves. There are twenty-five different stories about how Pele, the volcano goddess, came to Hawaii, and at least a hundred more about her sisters and her lovers and her enemies —all mutually contradictory."

"But all interesting," Rachel murmured. Although the boy was talking directly to her, his eyes were everywhere but on her face—watching the road, glancing up at the sky, peering around the weedy garden.

Lono chuckled, still not looking at her. "We had a haole astronomer here once," he said. "French fellow. With the big telescope on Mauna Kea. Kushi told him all about astronomy, Hawaiian-style—all about the creation of the Earth, and the stars, and the planets—none of this Big Bang stuff, believe me! Do you know why the sky is black at night? Because once it fell down, and got pushed back up with a muddy stick. And the stars come from, excuse me, Mrs. Chindler, from splashes from when the sky god was masturbating." He was looking right at her now. "And once the shark god made love to a pig, and so the famous humahumanukanukaapuaa was born.''

"Very interested in sex, they were," Rachel commented.

"They were. And so's Kushi, at least theoretically now—I *think* it's theoretical.''

Rachel said carefully, "Was Kanaloa the name of a god, too?"

Lono's face hardened. "Who?"

"Kanaloa. The terrorist in the lineup. The one you say just got out on bail. Did he have a god's name, too?"

The boy said sullenly, "It's not exactly a god's name. It's the name of a couple of old princes of Hawaii. They were very brave."

Rachel nodded. "That seems fitting. I suppose it takes a lot of courage to be a terrorist." She leaned back, drowsy in the sun. "Actually," she said, "that's what Kushi and I talked about, more than about the old gods. About the Maui MauMau and the Kamehameha Korps and those others."

The eyes that had been humorous and friendly just a moment before were now hooded. "As a matter of fact," Rachel added, "I think Kushi has some sympathies with some of them—at least, as you say, theoretically."

The boy looked thoughtfully at his watch. After a moment, he said, "In a theoretical way, I'd say every Hawaiian does. To some extent," he added carefully.

Rachel said, "How about yourself, Lono?"

"Me?" She nodded. Lono pursed his lips. "In a theoretical way," he said, pronouncing each word as though it were part of an invocation, "I'm not sure that I'd even call them terrorists. Terrorism is a matter of dates, isn't it? Wasn't your George Washington a kind of terrorist? And Menachem Begin—he definitely was one. Even had a price on his head. And then he became a world statesman, even won the Nobel Peace Prize. No, Mrs. Chindler," he said earnestly, " 'terrorist' is only the dirty word for what every soldier and statesman does as a matter of course. No offense, but if Kanaloa had shot that plane down in war, instead of hijacking it on the ground, they'd have given him a medal for it."

"I see," said Rachel. "He did do it, then?"

The boy sat straight. "They *say* he did. Maybe he did." He stopped in mid-breath and stared at her. Then the beautiful smile took over again. "But that's all theory, too, Mrs. Chindler. Look at the time! I wonder when Uncle David will get here."

Rachel Chindler leaned back and half closed her eyes. She put her hand on the sill of the open window to enjoy the warmth of the sun before she spoke.

"I don't think David's coming here," she said.

Lono swiveled his head to look at her, the dark eyes half shut. "Tell me why you say that?" he asked, his hand negligently going to his pocket.

"Well," said Rachel obediently, "partly because you've been lying to me. Your uncle wouldn't have sent you to pick me up, because you're a member of that Kamehameha Korps. So you're not waiting for David. Who is it, Lono?"

He stared at her silently for a moment. Tiring of his gaze, Rachel shifted and looked out the window. It really was a pretty spot to build a house; too bad it had burned. It was a suburban-America, white-painted, clapboard house with green shutters. It was the kind of house you saw in children's books, where Mummy made gingerbread and Daddy came home from work with a loosened tie, a smiling face and always something in his pocket for the children.

"Why did you get in the car with me?" Lono repeated, his face so close to the back of her head that she could feel his breath.

"You told me to, Lono. Who's coming?"

Pause. "A friend," he said. Another pause. "He's bringing a different car because they might be looking for this one by now." Another pause. "Aren't you going to ask me what we're going to do with you?"

The pause this time was lengthy. Rachel was watching the way the ti blossoms moved in the wind.

"I've got nothing against you, Mrs. Chindler," said Lono. "This is a political matter. Just do what we tell you to, and—"

He didn't finish the sentence.

Rachel nodded to herself without speaking. He didn't finish the sentence because the only way to end it would have been "—and we won't hurt you," and, although the boy was a terrorist, he wasn't a liar.

•   •   •

But the sun reached its zenith and began to climb down toward the mountain. The boy dragged Rachel with him to the back of the house and an old, but workable hand pump because they were getting very thirsty. Rachel had to beg permission to retire behind the anthuriums to relieve herself because her bladder was full . . . and still no one came.

"I don't think he's coming, Lono," she said when the shadows were as long as the trees were tall. "I think something must have gone wrong."

"You shut up," he ordered, and added, "Please." It was obvious that he had reached the same conclusion himself. Lono had not taken the failure of his plans well—whatever his plans were; Rachel did not allow herself to speculate on them. He was nervous. Every time the sound of a car motor changed on the road, every time a plane appeared heading for Lyman Field he tensed. "I ought to tie you up," he said, "but you've got no place to go. If you try to run I'll catch you, you know that. If you yell, there's nobody to hear."

"I know."

He nodded and ordered her over nearer the house. There was a garage, locked, no car inside, filled with what looked through the window like fire-damaged furniture. Lono made her sit down in plain sight while he forced the lock on the door and began shifting furniture, stacking it against a wall, finally making a space just big enough to run the battered pickup into. Then he closed the door and gave the sky a glance, as if to tell any possible police helicopter that now there was nothing for them to spot.

"It isn't the Kamehameha Korps," he said suddenly.

"What?" Rachel had lost the thread.

"The Kamehameha Korps, they're just loonies," he said savagely. "Half of them fink to the cops on the other half. They never really do anything but scare tourists."

"Then you're with the, the other ones—"

"The Maui MauMau, right. We're serious." He stared at her belligerently, as though waiting for her to deny it. "You haoles have to get out of Hawaii."

Rachel said, as though she were making conversation at the library's Christmas party on a subject that really didn't much matter to her either way, "But if the United States got out, wouldn't the Russians just move in?''

"Americans and Russians! That's all you hear! As if the whole world had to belong to one or the other!''

"Well, wouldn't they?'' she persisted.

"We can kill Russians as easily as we can kill Americans,'' Lono said grimly. "Haoles are all the same.''

Rachel sat down on a lump of that aa lava, apparently carted to the house's front lawn for decoration, and continued the discussion politely. "I know that you have a grievance,'' she said. "I've read about how the Europeans came to Hawaii, gave all the women syphilis and smallpox, stole the land, all that—it's not unlike the history of the American Indians, you know, Lono. I know about the American naval vessels that made the Hawaiian royal house abdicate because the United States was going to accept them as a colony or a possession or something—and then Congress wouldn't do it. I know about the sugar companies and the land grabs.''

"How do you know so much?'' he demanded.

"I'm a librarian,'' she explained. A librarian who had been hijacked and nearly killed over these issues, and had made a clean sweep of everything on her shelves that bore on the subject. "But, Lono, that was all long ago. Are there any pure Hawaiians left, really? If you could make amends, who would you make them to?''

"I'm left!''

"Your real name is Albert,'' she pointed out, "and, excuse me, but aren't you pretty much a mixture?''

But for that he had a pat answer. It started with a sneer. "Haoles! Just because the original Hawaiian blood is mixed you want to pretend it doesn't exist, so you can forget the whole thing. Like the Tasmanians!''

She was startled. "I don't know anything about the Tasmanians.''

"If you did know, you'd probably say they were extinct—that's what the textbooks say. But there are thousands of Tasmanian aboriginals still left. They're part haole, because the Europeans raped their women, but they're still there, they live like the abos, they think of themselves as abos—only the Australian government pretends they never heard of them! I'd say about ten more years and the

Americans will pretend there aren't any more Hawaiians, either! You people from the mainland don't know the difference."

All Rachel could think of to say was "I'm sorry, Lono," but her conversational training made her add, "All the same, I really don't see how getting the American government out would make things any better for you."

"You don't have to see," said Lono fiercely. "What's important is that we see, and we have the means to drive you out!"

Rachel nodded seriously. "You mean terrorism," she said. "You mean shooting and killing."

"If necessary!"

"Just like every other terrorist in the world. They're shooting everybody, Lono, even the Pope!"

He was angry now. "You don't understand," he told her severely. "We're not just terrorists. We're not the May 19th Coalition or the Weather Underground; we're not revolutionaries at all. We're just Hawaiians and we want our country back! Now," he finished, jumping up, "we are going to get out of here."

"Your friend isn't coming then?" asked Rachel—not argumentatively, just out of interest.

"That's none of your business. Come on! I've made a new plan, and we're going to carry it out."

"But where are we going?"

He said crushingly, "You'll find out when we get there."

They didn't seem to get there. Rachel Chindler was not sure that Lono had a real "there" in mind. Obviously something had gone wrong with his plans, obviously he was improvising. It was interesting to observe him and to try to figure out what was going through his mind, but it was also hard work. The burned-out house was on the fringe of the volcanos park; even Rachel knew when they had passed out of private land and onto the park sector, because there stopped being any houses. They took hikers' trails sometimes and sometimes no trails at all. Lono seemed to know where he was going. He didn't seem happy about it. He was tense and erratic in his movements; he made Rachel stop every few minutes while he listened for sounds. He led her to a declivity and sat her down. "We wait here for a while," he said. "Don't talk."

She nodded and leaned against a tree trunk. Like most of the sheltered ravines that had been undisturbed for any length of time, this was tropical jungle. There were dead logs scattered about the forest floor. Shoots grew out of them to make the trees of tomorrow—rapidly, in the steamy, jungly air. It was still broad daylight, but the sun was out of sight; only the tops of the trees still shone where sunlight struck them.

Next to her Lono was listening intently and breathing hard. The boy was frightened, Rachel realized. Not frightened in the way that would make him want to stop what he was doing; frightened of failure, unsure of what should come next. Whatever had gone wrong with his plans, whatever his plans actually were, he had not foreseen the need of a fallback strategy and now he was making it up as he went along.

Distant sound of a car. Rachel had barely realized she heard it when Lono's hand caught her and dragged her down to the damp, uneven ground. "Park rangers," he whispered in her ear. "Be very quiet." And the arm that remained about her neck was in a good position to choke off any attempt she might make to scream for help. She considered the prospects philosophically. By the time she had estimated that no attempt would work, the car, moving slowly, was well past; but of course she wouldn't have done that anyway. "They're making a last check for tourists," Lono muttered. When he put his mouth close to her his breath was foul—a pity, in such a good-looking young man. Easily and naturally, she turned her head toward his and kissed him.

Rachel had not known she was going to do that, and certainly Lono had not expected it. But once it was done it seemed inevitable. He drew his head away instinctively, instantly—not very far—then returned the kiss. His hand slipped under her T-shirt, and hers under his buckskin. The ridges of muscles along his spine were hot and hard, and when her exploring hand reached inside his denims, his penis was hotter and harder still. Still kissing they began to undress each other and themselves.

For all of Rachel's life she had been a moviegoer, had watched a new generation of film stars each year making love au naturel, in among the hibiscus and the coconut frond, from Dorothy Lamour to Brooke Shields—and, oh, wow, what a difference between the fantasy and the fact! The lush jungle growth had spikes and stickers in it. The ground was jagged where it was not damp, and in all places unyielding. Those pretty ferns had sawtooth edges. The sheltering trees had roots that lay, iron-hard and bruising, along the surface of the ground. Under Rachel. She would be bruised from hips to shoulders; and the young man needed to have his teeth fixed. Some Hawaiian, she thought; didn't they all have perfect teeth?

Men were probably not as faithful as women at keeping their teeth brushed and their breath dainty; Rachel had had unsavory tongues inside her mouth before. This boy was something special. But it was all cultural anyway, wasn't it? A smell was only a smell. The importance you put on it was in your own head, put there probably by six million toothpaste ads and ten million commercials for breath fresheners. She made up her mind to accept it, just as she accepted the thick, hot invader of her vagina.

And she had stopped the Pill after her last trip to Hawaii.

Since the end of her marriage—actually, since quite a long time before the end of her marriage—Rachel had found sexual intercourse sometimes mildly pleasant, sometimes boring, never very important one way or another. In spite of all the circumstances this was no different. She thrust against Lono's thrusts, reached out with her hands to cup his buttocks to pull him toward her with every lunge; she gasped—but it was more the mechanical squeezing of air from her lungs than excitement; she stabbed her tongue into his mouth and accepted his—until she needed air too much, and turned her head away. When the thudding had gone on long enough to convince her it was not going to get any better for her, she slipped her fingertips down through the crevice of flesh between buttocks and thigh and plunged a finger into his anus to make him come. It worked. He cried out, with a strangled sound, and she felt the hot drenching inside her.

He rolled off her, looking at her, with his breath coming hard.

She returned his gaze absently, thinking of other things.

Would David be worrying about her now? What would Stephen think if he had a baby brother, with a father no older than he? Was it raining outside the lava tube? You could not tell until you felt it, since the fall of raindrops and the clicking of the palm fronds made the same sounds.

Lono said suddenly, "You recognized Kanaloa in that lineup, didn't you?"

She didn't answer, only watched the boy's face. It was almost dark inside the tube now, but she could still see him clearly.

His breathing was still not under control. He panted hard for a few moments, then said, "You should have stayed in St. Louis." Rachel shrugged, and he added, "This doesn't mean that I won't kill you if I have to."

"I know," said Rachel. "Can I go outside for a minute? I have to pee."

14

The device implanted in the drowned slope of Loihi was a fission-fusion-fission bomb with a calculated yield of sixteen megatons. It was a big one, though much bigger had been built. It had to be big, because it was meant to scoop out of the side of the undersea mountain a bite of six cubic kilometers.

When the device had done its work, those six cubic kilometers of solid rock would no longer be solid, nor would they any longer occupy so small a volume. They would be a plasma, a sort of gas of charged particles, very hot and in the process of violently expanding. Not only would the rock be so, but the sea water nearby as well.

This event would produce two consequences.

First, the side of the undersea volcano would be removed, as a breakfaster might chip a segment of shell off his soft-boiled egg, and the yolky, runny mass of magma inside would be exposed. Second, the surrounding ocean would disappear. Sea water from the site of the device up to the surface would be, at least, vaporized; the magma would therefore no longer be constrained by its pressure.

So Loihi would erupt.

The eruption of a shield volcano, like those which make up the Hawaiian Islands, is comparatively gentle and restrained, as long as the volcanos are left to themselves. Loihi would not have been left to itself. With the cage that contained the magma removed, the eruption would be of that specially explosive and violent kind called "pyroclastic," which is to say that a great part of the tectonic energy would be expended in hurling itself, along with associated dust, rock and sea water, into the air.

The prompt effects on the Big Island of Hawaii would be considerable, though the usual symptoms of a volcanic eruption would be almost the least of them. Loihi was too far from the Big Island for hurtling red-hot boulders to be a threat. There would certainly be some fall of volcanic dust, made nastier than usual because fission products from the bomb would be present; but with any luck at all the prevailing winds would carry most of the immediate fallout over the Pacific Ocean. The lava that would follow the first explosion could not flow uphill, so none of that would reach Hawaii. The associated earthquakes would make interesting patterns on the U.S. Coast and Geodetic Survey seismometers, but no Hawaiian would give them a second thought. Even the tsunamis, the gathered swells of water that would rush up onto the land, would spend themselves on the southern shore of the Big Island. A few villages would suffer, perhaps a condominium development or two would be wiped away, but most of that shore was bare recent lava flows from Kilauea anyway. In any case, the configuration of the sea bottom did not encourage large tsunamis. There is no continental shelf around the Hawaiian Islands. There is on the exposed southern shore no good-sized bay, like the one that funneled the disastrous wave of the 1960s that walloped Hilo. And the rest of the island chain would hardly notice waves at all.

It was not prompt effects, then, that would seriously harm the Hawaiian island chain. The worst effects would come more slowly, and Hawaii would by no means suffer the most.

The erupting plasma, that plume of incandescent rock and sea water and mud, would cool into a cloud. It would not just be a normally large cloud, like the kind that, for instance, overlays the Indian subcontinent during the monsoon season. It would be a *big* cloud. It would not be made of simple water vapor, like the fleecy lamb's-wool cumulus or towering L-5 thunder-bangers. The cloud that Project Vulcan deployed would be full of particulate matter. Of dust. Starting from the point of explosion at Loihi, it would spread to girdle the northern hemisphere of the Earth—not in Ariel's forty minutes, but in forty days or so.

And it would stay there.

The length of time a dust cloud stays in the air does not depend on where it comes from—volcano, or dust storm, or cometary impact. Nor does it depend on the amount of dust involved. Its dwell time is determined by the size of the particles and their other characteristics, and even more by the altitude they reach. If they remain in the lower reaches of the atmosphere they will be washed out by rainfall fairly quickly; if they go higher than the regions of raindrop formation, they will stay a long time.

In the case of Project Vulcan, that dwell time was enough to span at least two growing seasons in the northern hemisphere.

So for more than a year, from the Tropic of Cancer north, the sun's rays would have to penetrate a veil of dust to reach the surface. Much sunlight would be reflected away, or soaked up in heating the dust particles themselves. Surface temperatures would fall. Growing seasons would be shortened. And, because of the curvature of the Earth, the farther north any point on the surface was, the worse the effect would be.

That was what Project Vulcan was all about.

15

Under the right circumstances, thought Arkady Bor, this wild goose chase to New Mexico could have been almost pleasant. Even though he was being kept waiting like a peasant. Indeed, almost because he was forced to wait. The "public relations" person who had been assigned to sheepdog Bor around the Sandia base was young, good-looking, friendly—was even sexy, for there was that widening of the pupils that indicated sexual interest that Bor relied on. He would have been definitely interested, except that she had one fault. She was a she. One could achieve a certain physical release with a female, to be sure. But the probabilities were large that she would leap out of bed, assuming one could get her there, and go at once to telephone some Security person about everything Bor had whispered in passion, the sexual interest as feigned as her improbable breasts. Why take that chance?

So he returned her warmth with frost. Frost was appropriate. He was shivering as he allowed himself to be shown around the photovoltaic farms and the queerly shaped windmills that this open part of Sandia specialized in. Although he did not enjoy any of it, he was docile—up to a point. He let himself be taken through the long tunnel under the acres of movable mirrors to the Solar Thermal Power Tower, but he drew the line at climbing the tower itself. When she offered him the huge elevator, big enough to carry a tank, he shook his head and declared, "It is too cold for this sightseeing, and it is a great waste of my time."

The woman was professionally soothing. "Would you like some coffee, Dr. Bor?" she offered.

Coffee! The great American wonder drug which cured all ills and solved all problems! It could do nothing for Arkady Bor, the intellectual giant harassed on every side by pygmies. Suspected of heaven knew what by the security dunces. Threatened by the KGB. Worst of all, sent out of the way like a troublesome child while the device which was his own creation—well, nearly his own creation—was being emplaced. He snapped, "How much longer must I wait for Gener—"

"Hush," said the woman, glancing around. This was the open, peace-and-plenty half of Sandia, where anyone might wander around uncleared and listening; it was not a place to mention names. The invitingly wide pupils began to contract. "It will be at least another hour, sir." No names even to himself, Bor observed. He pulled the London Fog coat around him, that had seemed just right for inclement weather from the perspective of Hawaii but was hopelessly inadequate against New Mexico in January.

"Some coffee, then," he complained. "Some warm place, at least!" For this whole solar-energy project Bor had amused contempt, anyway. How silly the Americans were! To devote all this time and effort to the soft-headed, idealistic attempt to capture usable energy from the sun—oh, technologically somewhat interesting, he conceded, with that American trickiness of gadgetry that still persisted in spite of everything—but if one wanted energy, why, then there was limitless energy in the atom! Risks? One learned to accept risks—when one was in charge of large ventures one did, and was not deterred by vague fears of the uneducated masses. Although Bor's expertise lay in the explosive uses of nuclear energy, not power generation, he had seen enough of the Soviet nuclear plants to know that they were cheaper, better adapted to industrial use, above all quicker to pay back in the chronically capital-short noncapitalist Union of Soviet Socialist Republics. Of course, there were certain penalties. There were penalties to any use of nuclear energy—witness the devastated area between the Black Sea and the Urals, where an annoyingly large quantity of radionuclides had dispersed themselves around the sacred soil of the motherland—

He caught himself up short. How strange, that the clichés of one's childhood should recur in one's adult mind.

If he was amused by the solar-power research in the open part of Sandia, he was not amused by—but still contemptuous of—the nuclear warfare museum where in desperation the PR woman parked him to wander at will. Here were copies—no, the real thing—here were actual nuclear weapons, emptied of their fissionable contents to be sure, but nevertheless the very devices that were once ready to blast a Japanese city, or a Russian. This was the second "Fat Boy," whose duplicate had killed a hundred thousand Japanese in Nagasaki one August morning in 1945; here the Hiroshima weapon, here an early ICBM, here an air-to-air missile. It was a vast secondhand store of weaponry. All obsolete, of course.

But not nearly as obsolete as Arkady Bor himself was about to make them all!

General Macklin was West Point courteous. The three stars on his shoulder blade did not absolve him of the need to say "sir" to civilians, even émigré Soviet citizens. Though he did not smoke himself, he obligingly lit the cigarette of the young woman who was there to take notes. Though he took his coffee black, he was expert with the silver tongs to heap four lumps of sugar in Bor's cup, and careful to pour so thin a stream of cream that Bor could stop him at the ideal second. "We're very informal here, sir," he said benevolently—to Bor, but in a voice pitched loud enough to cover the three senators, the four congressmen, the Deputy Assistant Secretary of Defense and the six others in the room. "This isn't going to be a meeting, exactly, just a discussion among the people who need to know what's going on."

"Thank you, general," said Bor. He hadn't needed to be told that. It was implicit in the casual way the men—and the one woman—were seated around the room, all with coffee or tea or soft drinks. It wasn't even a meeting room. It was more like someone's living room—some rich one's living room, of course. From where Arkady Bor sat, on a gray leather loveseat, with an end table for his coffee cup comfortable to his right hand, this top-secret part of Sandia looked no more menacing than the wide-open solar research facility. Of course, this was an illusion. This room did not represent the reality of Sandia's secret functions. Somewhere not far away were places Arkady Bor would never enter, where new configurations were being studied and new plans devised. Even his own Project Vulcan might not make some of these devices entirely obsolete, although it was very unlikely that he would have any chance, ever, to see that for himself.

The door opened, admitting a white-haired colonel—ruddy face, athletic step, yes, but with that hair one would think him rather overage in grade. He was also very apologetic. "Sorry, General Macklin," he said hurriedly. "My plane was late."

The general was gracious. "No harm done, Colonel Petterman. It just gave us all a chance to get a little better acquainted." Gave some of us that chance, thought Bor morosely, as General Macklin introduced the meteorologist from Weather Wing around; others of us just had to stay out in the cold. But then he perked up as the general took his place under the screen at one end of the room and said, "Might as well begin, I think? First we'll hear from the man who has contributed more than anyone else to this project, Dr. Arkady Bor."

Dejection melted away. Bor stood up rapidly. "With pleasure, general," he said happily, beaming around the room. "I take it all you gentlemen know the general purpose of what Project Vulcan is designed to do, yes? So I will confine myself only to the technical aspects of which I am in charge. Lights, please? And the first slide?" The captain at the slide projector was all thumbs as he tried to get it into focus, but Bor only clucked forgivingly. Who could be disagreeable when he has just heard these very important people told how significant his work was? When at last the picture cleared and the computer-enhanced model of Loihi was steady on the screen, he began. "This is an underwater volcano," he said. "I have designed a nuclear device which is being implanted in its slope just there, where you see the orange circle, as I point out." He held the little flashlight with its arrow firmly on the circle, and was pleased to see that his hand was not shaking. "When the device is detonated—perhaps I should say *if* it is detonated—a large section of the crust of this mountain, Loihi, will be removed. What will happen after that is the point of the project, but I will leave it to experts to describe; my part is only with the device and its fusing.

"I should add, however, that the quantities and pressures involved are well established. As some of you know, I have conducted large underground nuclear projects in the Caucasus, the Urals and elsewhere. Other varieties of nuclear devices were employed, because it was necessary to minimize subsequent radiation problems, and the yield was much smaller. Nevertheless, this is a tested technology and there is no doubt the device will perform as I have described.

"The fusing is a slightly different question. With the previous projects of this sort it was quite simple: you connected your detonator to a cable and a switch of some sort; when you depressed the switch—of course from a safe distance—the device was activated, just as I light this flashlight with this button." He demonstrated and called for the next slide: representation of the undersea mountain with its H-bomb, and the waves suggested far overhead. "The only suitable method is by radio. Unfortunately the deep sea is opaque to conventional radio signals; we may use very long wave signals, and such antennae will subsequently be installed in a ground station. But such activity will be all too clearly visible to Soviet reconnaissance satellites. So we have adopted a temporary triggering procedure. Next slide." Sketch of the Vulcan flotilla floating over Loihi on one side, the Big Island and the slopes of Mauna Loa and Mauna Kea on the other. "A buoy with a radio receiver, attached to the device by an anchor cable, will be permanently in position. As you see"— he swept the red arrow from Mauna Kea to the flotilla—"there is a direct line of sight from the top of this mountain to the site of the buoy. As a first measure, the signal to detonate the device, should that be necessary, will be sent from the mountaintop. Other options are possible—I mention only signals from an aircraft, or even from a satellite—but that is what we have determined to be most suitable at present. Are there any questions?"

The elderly senator in the deepest of the armchairs raised his hand—not far; he might only have been planning to scratch his cheekbone instead of seeking attention. But Bor responded quickly. "Sir?"

"How do you know this fuse is going to work?"

"It has been very thoroughly tested," Bor assured him, "in the laboratory. On my return I will of course give it a complete test—without connecting it to the nuclear device, to be sure." He twinkled.

No one twinkled back. Another elderly man in civilian clothes called, "When do you put the bomb inside that volcano?"

"It is being done even as we meet here," Bor assured him.

"Without you?" the senator interrupted. "If you're so all-fired important, how come you aren't there for this part?"

Opportunity to vent his grievance! "As to that, I certainly intend to pro—" To protest being sent away, he had been about to say, but General Macklin's eye was on him. "Intend, that is," he amended, "to perform complete tests to make sure it is properly emplaced. After all," he went on, salvaging what he could, "that is only a mechanical process, best handled by those who are skilled at operating cranes and other machinery involved." He glanced around the room for further questions. There weren't any. Silently he took his seat, hardly hearing the words of the next speaker, a civilian consultant whose specialty was tectonics, as he reassured the gathering that the Hawaiian Islands would not suffer significant direct damage.

"Thank the lord old Sparks isn't here," grinned the senator, "because he'd have all our hides for messing up his islands!" There was general laughter, not shared by Bor, who didn't even know who old Senator Sparks Matanuga was.

The final speaker was the Air Force meteorologist, Colonel Petterman, who had not only slides but a can of motion-picture film.

"The effect of all this," he said, "will be the generation of a very large cloud. It will start from the point of explosion and proceed as shown in this simulation—if you please, captain?" The officer at the projector had threaded the film into the other machine. He began to run what Bor recognized at once as a copy of Frank Morford's computer simulation, and the assembled dignitaries watched the golden cloud erupt in the Pacific and overspread the northern hemisphere. "For security reasons," said the meteorologist, "this simulation was designed to illustrate what may have been an actual event in the Earth's history. At that time, sixty-five million years ago, it is believed that an explosion caused by a very large meteoroid striking an active volcano projected something of the order of billions of tons of dust and chemical aerosols into the atmosphere, causing the sunlight to be kept from reaching the surface of the Earth. This resulted in reducing the average temperature of the Earth by as much as thirty degrees Fahrenheit, as well as interrupting photosynthesis so that plants could not grow. As a consequence, all large animals died out over the five years while the dust remained in the air.

"Our venture is much smaller, by a factor of one hundred. It will not cool the Earth that much—by no more than three degrees, according to calculations. Its principal effect will be on agriculture—specifically, on major grain crops grown at northern latitudes. The United States will suffer considerable losses on all farmland from about the forty-two degree parallel north—that is to say, north of about Omaha and Des Moines. The farther north, the more severe the effect, of course.

"However, the amount of dust is carefully calculated. It will reduce the yields of wheat, in particular, by about twenty percent over a period of two years, but of course the United States normally produces large surpluses in any case. There will be no such surpluses for those years. However, with a certain amount of belt-tightening, supplies should be adequate. The worst effect will be that it may be necessary to divert grain from animal feed to human diets, thus shortening the food chain. No American will lack for bread, but steaks may be scarcer.

"The Soviet Union, however, is a different matter.

"If you look at the map, you will see that much of their best grain acreage lies well north of forty-two degrees. Their short growing season, the average temperatures and all the other climatic factors are already semi-marginal. In a normal year they need to import considerable tonnages of cereals. In the two years while the dust cloud remains effective, they will suffer what is calculated to be an average seventy percent reduction in yields. They will not be able to meet this by diverting grain from animal feed. They will not be able to import anything like adequate quantities from abroad, for the surpluses will not exist.

"The result will be famine on a very large scale.

"The social, economic and political consequences of this are outside of my area of expertise, so I will not comment on that—beyond saying that the effects on the Soviet state will be comparable to the effects of World War II.

"Are there any questions?"

There was only one. "Ah, just one thing," said a portly man in the first row. "Won't Canada be affected as badly as the Soviets?"

"Actually, senator, rather worse, yes, sir. Again, this is not my province, but as I understand it the rather relatively small Canadian population has been considered in the total calculations for North America."

"Meaning we'll feed them out of our own stocks? Reason I ask, my constituents grow the best wheat in the world. I don't know how happy they'll be shipping it out of the country when our own people are in need."

The director stood up. "As I understand it, senator," he cut in, "conversations will be held with Canada at the appropriate time, but this is a matter outside our sphere. If there are no further questions, the bar is open in the next room."

Because the committee had heard all it wanted to hear from him, Bor was excused the rest of the three days. His heart sang. When he got to the Transport Office he found—oh, surprise!—a sympathetic and willing clerk, who agreed at once that it would be no faster, really, to change planes in Los Angeles than it would to take the direct flight to Honolulu and overnight before catching the inter-island to Hilo. The clerk did not ask why Bor preferred the Honolulu routing. She didn't have to. The gleam in his eye was enough. And so by eleven o'clock that night, Hawaiian time, Bor was checked into the Ilikai Hotel. By eleven thirty, he was out cruising the bars on Kalakaua Avenue, the closest thing Waikiki had to Times Square.

All that was left along the strip was the regulars. Half the tourists had gone, with the end of the holiday season on New Year's Day; the other half seemed to have flown to the night clubs and luaus of the big waterfront hotels. Ten days earlier Kalakaua Avenue had been jammed all night long with Christmas vacationers. Now the bars were almost empty, but what was left was what Arkady Bor was looking for.

In the secret life of Arkady Bor, Waikiki was the only place where he dared be himself. On the Vulcan complex there were always Security people nearby; when he went ashore they attached themselves to him like Siamese twins. They were always in sight when he was eating, drinking or sightseeing, always in the next bed when he was sleeping. It had taken a stormy session to get the man out of the room when he was entertaining one of the Kona coast's lovely whores, and then he was uncomfortably certain that somewhere near the bed a microphone was still keeping tabs on him. And that was a female whore. That deeper, less public need that Bor from time to time felt strongly could never be satisfied while Security was nearby—and only in Waikiki had he ever been able to get away from it.

Before midnight, at a dissipating luau down the beach, Bor had made contact with a very pretty young boy who was quite willing to come up to his room. That was one of the nice things about the Ilikai. It was neither better nor worse than any of a dozen other hotels along the strip, but its elevators were nowhere near the registration desk. No desk clerk had a chance to observe what sort of company the hotel's guests took up to their rooms. Not that any Waikiki hotel ever endangered its volume of business by inquiring too closely into such matters; but Bor was not worried only about desk clerks.

It did not occur to him at that time that he should have been worried about more than Security, too.

It was not until the pretty boy from the luau had gone and Bor was just ready to go smiling to sleep that the phone by his bed rang.

It had to be a wrong number, thought Bor angrily as he reached out of his drowsiness for the phone. It was not. It was for him, all right, and the person who spoke to him spoke in Georgian.

So at a quarter of two in the morning, when his body was still savoring its recent release and wished to be asleep, Arkady

Bor checked out of the Ilikai Hotel, demanded a taxi and sat glumly through the long ride through Honolulu and around the bay. His orders were to check into a chain motel near the airport and wait for further instructions, and whether he was wise to be following them he began to doubt. Should he not simply have called the Vulcan security officer? The answer was easy. Yes. He should have. But Vulcan was hundreds of miles away, and the woman on the other end of the phone line could have been right outside his door. It was not his daughter's life that was in danger now. It was his own.

He paid off the driver with a mingy tip and marched belligerently up to the registration counter of the motel. "I want a room for this night only. I have no reservation," he blustered, half hoping there would be no room; but in this hotel in this place there were plenty of rooms. He signed the register with the name he had been told to use, William P. Johnson, and although he did not in the least look or talk like a "Johnson" and had no credit card for imprint in that name, the sleepy woman at the counter asked only to be paid in advance, in cash.

In the room he sat on the edge of the bed, glowering around. Tacky place! The lobby had been almost pretentious, but this room was almost like a jail cell, a minimal box with white walls. The bathroom had a liquid-soap dispenser, like a public toilet—a long way from the suite at the Ilikai! But here he would be entertaining no pretty young men, so what did it matter?

It was three before his phone rang, and the instructions that came over it were simple. Go out the side entrance. Walk ten meters to the corner. Buy a cup of coffee, sit down, wait.

And that was nearly another hour. Bor understood the reasons. Whoever it was who was pulling his strings was being very careful at each step to see that he was not followed, that he had not indeed made that telephone call to Security, that Naval Intelligence storm troopers were not lurking about to pounce as soon as contact was made. He wished it were the case. Now that it was too late, he decided he should have called for help. It was very improbable that it could have arrived in time anyway, although there had been moments, in the cab, when he thought he was being followed. He inspected the other patrons of Sam's All-Nite. Were some of them KGB? CIA? FBI? And how could you tell, when they were not so obliging as to wear name badges? He took his place in line behind two huge youths, muttering to each other in what was either a language unfamiliar to him or that jivey Islands version of English that was almost equally undecipherable to someone who had learned his English in the Poly at Tbilisi. Sam's All-Nite Drive-Inn was not much more than a corner parking lot, with a fast-food structure in one corner, a few wooden tables and benches in another, and a menu that soured his mood even more. His pleasures had left him a touch peckish. He would have welcomed a slice of fresh papaya, or perhaps some of those American scrambled eggs with home fries that sounded so awful but were actually quite edible at three o'clock in the morning. Not here. Tacos. Burgers. "Specials of the House" turned out to be fried-chicken platters and jumbo shakes. He took a chance on a curried beef combination. He lost. When he sat down to open the foam-plastic container it was a greasy stew with two scoops of cold rice.

The coffee was as bad, acid and thick. He drank it anyway, to ward off drowsiness. Half an hour later, when the few others sitting around had gone and been replaced by still others, and there was still no sign of further instructions or a meeting, he dumped the empty container and the untouched curry in a trash can and went up for another cup.

It was worse than the first. What had he done wrong to wind up in this place?

Really, though, what alternatives had he had? His whole life had been taken out of his hands almost from birth. He was barely two when his uncle, the division commander, was shot in the Tukhachevsky purges, ten when his cousin, the paratroop captain, was shot for going over to the Vlasov armies that fought on the German side. In between all he remembered was war. As a seven-year-old he received partisan training. Partisan training! For a boy who still sometimes wet the bed! Ordered in the event of a German victory in Georgia to take to the mountains around Tbilisi, snipe, raid, spy, kill! To Bor who was more than fifty years old it seemed a horrid fantasy, but at the time it was only horrid. There was no fantasy in the map that showed Soviet Georgia pinned between two seas, one already a German lake, with the Turkey his grandfather had died fighting to the south and to the north the Nazis already enveloping Stalingrad.

But Bor had distinguished himself as an infant guerrilla, in training, and fortunately the Nazis had never got that far. So his relatives were overlooked. He was given a chance at the preferred schools, the ones that led to careers. Not military careers; little Arkady had known better than that, with the example of his relatives before him. And when as a gawky teenager he had been paraded before the All-Wise Himself, he and twenty others to receive decorations for their steadfast political activism and their splended scholastic accomplishments, it was Arkady Bor who got Stalin's personal pat on the head. Because he was a fellow Georgian? Because he was very small for his age, and Stalin preferred people shorter than he was? No matter. The head that the very hand of the Marshal had touched was sacred to his teachers and fellow students, and Bor had had no trouble graduating first in his class.

Of course, there were tricky times ahead—after that damnable Khrushchev's "secret" speech denouncing Stalinism, and especially, much later, when the lab assistant had threatened to tell of what it was he and Bor did those nights when everyone else was gone . . . Bor was sweating in the trench coat that that morning had been too light, and woke to the realization he had been allowing himself to drowse.

The Toyota that had been parked near the curb had been there for a long time. He stood up, peering toward it.

The door opened, on the driver's side. The woman that got out was vaguely familiar to Bor; he had seen her somewhere before, perhaps? Tall, dark, with a beaked nose—of course! She should have been wearing a red evening dress! It was the one the Security officer had described to him. "Well, Arkady Semyavitch," she said, smiling, in fluent Georgian, "you have had quite a time for yourself, have you not?"

He sank back onto the bench.

For all of his adult life he had wondered how it felt to hear the midnight knock on the door, or feel the hand on the shoulder as you left work. He had wondered how it was that the father of his school chum, the manager of the factory where he had worked as a youth, the hundred others who had been taken by the KGB—neighbors, parents of friends, acquaintances from school or work—how each one of them had gone so unresistingly along to what they surely knew was hopeless destruction. Now he knew. He could not lift a finger. He saw that the woman wore a shoulder bag and carried an umbrella, neatly furled, held like a weapon, pointed at him. He knew what those umbrellas might be. But it was not the fear of being shot on the spot that held him frozen. It was almost like anesthesia. None of the muscles of his body wished to move. A psychedelic van screeched up and slammed to a stop in a no-parking area of the lot; two huge beachboys got out, cracking jokes with the girl at the counter. Bor stared after them wistfully: how marvelous it must be to have nothing on your mind but to get laid now and then, and perhaps steal money for dope!

"Talk to me, zek," the woman ordered.

"I was never a zek!" he protested.

"No, you were not as elevated as that," she agreed. "You were in difficulties because of your disgusting sexual practices, is that not so, Arkady Semyavitch? And are you not again?" She shook her head, and then jerked it to signal that Bor should rise. She marched him over to the counter, ordered a soft drink for herself and a cup of coffee for Bor. "Now," she said, "let us sit down and talk, my friend."

"I am not your friend!"

"Ah, but you will be, Arkady Semyavitch. The logic of the situation demands it." She took a sip from the paper cup, grimaced, fished out half the crushed ice and threw it on the asphalt. "Of course," she said, "those pederast friends of yours have no loyalty. They telephoned us as soon as they saw you. Perhaps they telephoned others as well, who knows?"

"They would not!" he protested, but his stomach had another opinion. The stale, steeped coffee was like lead in it.

"For such as you," she said seriously, "there are no friends anywhere. Not even the Americans enjoy such filth as you, Bor. Your records of hospitalization are still available. They can fall into CIA hands very easily."

"That would be a meaningless act!" he protested.

"Of course it would not! And of course that would be very

bad for you. So I have a solution for you. You will help your motherland, as you are required to do. Do you think that because you have traveled a few thousand kilometers you are no longer responsible to the state?"

"But if I spy for you they will shoot me!"

She shrugged and sipped her 7-Up. "And if your wretched life comes to an end, is that not a blessing? But this will not happen. The state has compassion for such as you. You will not be required to endanger yourself. They will not shoot you. You will merely supply me with reports and information." She reached over and patted his hand. "How nervous you are, Arkady Semyavitch. Perhaps you would like an injection of haloperidol, to relieve your tensions?"

"No! What do you want of me?" he croaked.

"I? I want nothing. It is your country that wants something of you, Arkady Semyavitch. And that only a little." She glanced at her watch. "In just a few moments we will go to a place where we can talk easily and will not be disturbed. We will talk, you and I and some others who are interested in this Vulcan. Nothing more. Only a talk among friends, and then we will take you back to the airport so that you may catch your flight to Hilo and no one the wiser, eh?" She paused and looked at him with amusement, or was it contempt? "I see you do not ask how your daughter is," she commented.

He shrugged and avoided her eyes. It had been a very long day, with exhausting things in it, and he was physically exhausted. How badly things had turned out, to bring him here in this filthy hole, with those hooligan beachboys shouting and joking with the counter girl and his life in danger!

"Ah," said the woman, nodding, "a man like you cannot be concerned with a single life, of course. I understand. Not when he has on his mind such vast things as the destruction of the fatherland of the working class, perhaps the entire world? What shame, Bor!"

He was stung by her silly failure to understand. "No, no! Exactly the opposite! Don't you see, what we do can save the world? Nuclear war is obsolete. The nuclear winter would kill everyone, if only a few hundred missiles go off—"

"Whereas you have found a better way! So that you need

only one bomb, and you can kill everyone. My compliments, Bor!"

"No! Not one soul will be killed by Vulcan. It is *crops* that will be destroyed. *Harvests* will be ruined. Not even cities, not even factories or missile bases."

Her look was pure contempt now, perhaps with some fear. "And when the crops fail, will the Soviet people not starve?"

"Only if they insist on it! There are huge granaries in America, Australia, Latin America—plenty to feed the world for a year. Of course, there must be certain adjustments. No more squandering of grain to feed animals so that the animals can be eaten; that is too wasteful. For a year or two everyone will eat bread instead of steaks, but is that so awful?"

"Oh? And how will our Soviet people get this grain? Will we simply say to the Americans, 'Oh, yes, now you have made your point; we see you are in earnest, so feed us, please?'"

Bor mumbled, "Well, of course, there must be something in exchange."

"What? Speak up, Bor. What in exchange?"

He shrugged again, more morose than ever. The woman simply refused to comprehend. How much easier it was to explain these things to a Pentagon team or a congressional committee! To people who did not have guns pointed at you! In a well-lighted, air-conditioned, leather-chaired briefing room, instead of this dreary greasy spoon. "Diplomatic agreements," he said. "Agreements for disarmament. Treaties to be signed. Perhaps changes in troop dispositions in certain places—"

"Places like Afghanistan and Poland and Czechoslovakia, perhaps? And the disarmament all one-sided, so that the Americans keep their cruise missiles and their MX? Oh, Bor! You mean the Soviet Union must surrender!"

"And why not?" he flared. "Why not surrender to *freedom?*"

She laughed, one metallic cough of a laugh. "The freedom you prize, of course," she said cruelly, "such as the freedom to perform your grotesque sexual acts on the mouths and behinds of other men—or is it that you prefer the woman's part, Bor? That they do such things to you? You disgust me,

Bor! Get in the car now!'' She gestured with the reefed umbrella, then prodded him with the tip.

Submissively Bor rose. He was defeated on all fronts.

And yet—

And yet, he schemed, something might be retrieved from all of this. Suppose he did what was wanted of him. If he were clever and cautious the Americans need never know, and he would insist on caution. Perhaps he could insist on even more, he thought, walking unseeing past the psychedelic van on his way to the woman's Toyota. Money? Why not? Certainly to keep him happy the secret funds of the KGB could afford a few thousand dollars every month, to go into a bank account in perhaps Switzerland—and, oh, yes, certain unbreakable guarantees about the well-being of his daughter—

He was astonished to hear a muffled cry from the woman behind him.

He turned, appalled at what he saw. The beachboys at the counter had broken off their chatting with the girl and were drifting toward them. The door of the van had opened and a large man had come out; he had struck the KGB woman savagely across the back of the head with what looked like a baseball bat. And then everything happened in a flash. The huge man grabbed the woman by the shoulders and pulled her into the van; the pair from the counter took one of Bor's arms each and dragged him after her. In the wink of an eye he was inside, and the door closed behind them.

Inside the van were a couple of mattresses and a wooden bench fixed along one side. The two men preempted the bench, the unconscious woman thrown on one of the mats. The third man scrambled up to the driver's seat and started the van. Bor was left to kneel awkwardly on the other mattress, tumbled about as the van accelerated out of the parking lot of Sam's All-Nite Drive-Inn.

As the van screeched around corners and up a ramp Bor tried to brace himself, staring around. The van was windowless on the sides, but it was not wholly dark. There was enough light from the street lights that filtered back from the driver's compartment for Bor to see the two men in with him. They were big, bronze-skinned, more Oriental than not. One still held the baseball bat; the other was curiously examining the KGB woman's lethal umbrella. They seemed to be paying no attention to Bor.

Out of the frying pan into the fire. Bor realized sickly that the person who had phoned the KGB about him had also phoned someone else, and these men could be nothing but the terrorists who had been in all the newspapers.

He did his best. When he caught his breath he called, "Are you the, what is it, the Maui MauMau?"

The man with the baseball bat laughed. "Kamehameha Korps, haole pig," he corrected.

Bor dismissed the difference with a wave. "In any case, you must listen. This woman is a KGB agent! I must thank you for saving me from her."

"Shut up," the man said softly.

"But really! I promise that you will be well rewarded for this, only you must take us at once to a telephone so that I may call a Security officer!"

The man didn't speak again. He only grinned and raised the bat, playfully threatening. Bor sighed and closed his eyes. What was going to happen would happen, and he had no control over anything anymore.

It was odd, though, that the man had smiled. Bor did not understand that smile until, half an hour later, the van slowed down and stopped. There was a muttering exchange between the driver and someone outside.

The KGB woman, snoring stertorously, had rolled over onto Bor's lap. He untangled himself frantically, leaning forward to see what he could, as far as the man with the baseball bat would allow him to move. He could see very little, and that for a moment; but what he saw was astonishing.

The man the driver was talking to was in a sort of guard booth, studying a paper the driver had handed him; and he wore the white helmet of an Army MP.

16

The ring of fire that surrounds the Pacific Ocean basin is fueled by the terrible heat and stresses inside the Earth. There are other rings of fire. They are not natural, but man-made. The fire is nuclear. And they do not surround oceans, but nations.

The purpose of nuclear arms, as of any weapon, is to force someone else to do what you want him to. This is the doctrine of *force majeure*. It works well—regardless of whether what you want is moral or fair, and certainly regardless of what the other party wants—unless he, too, is armed. Then about all you can do is kill each other.

The existence of the United States, for example, is very inconvenient for the Soviet Union. If the U.S.S.R. were the only nuclear superpower in the world, it would have no difficulty in imposing its will on any other nation, or on all of them at once. A single ballistic nuclear missile, dropped on a single city, would show it was in earnest. If there were any resistance after that, why, there were ten thousand or so additional nuclear missiles on hand to repeat the lesson. The supply of nuclear weapons for each of the superpowers is larger than the world's supply of cities. Would China show signs of disobedience? Take Beijing out; the rest will fall into line soon enough. Did Poland try to writhe free of its chains? Warsaw, then, could be obliterated. A non-nuclear United States might be somewhat more of a problem, but with Washington, New York, Chicago and Los Angeles seared and dying, any objections the survivors might have would no longer matter.

The balance of mutually assured destruction spoiled all such wistful calculations—on both sides—and the missiles targeted for the cities of the West were as impotent, for fear of retaliation, as those targeted for Moscow, Havana and Hanoi.

Non-nuclear wars could still be fought. They were: in Africa and Latin America, in Vietnam and Afghanistan, almost anywhere except on the territories of the superpowers. But between the giants, the power of the nuclear weapons overrode all other considerations. Navies were obsolete against each other; a single missile cruiser like the U.S.S. *Columbus* alone wielded enough power to have reversed the outcome of any naval battle in history. Armies, however powerful, were enchained; what was the point of winning battles with an army if that army's country were destroyed behind it?

For forty years the two superpowers schemed and strove to outbuild and out-threaten each other. The rings of fire each drew around the other tightened. Nuclear Pershing IIs on one side of a border confronted nuclear SS-20s on the other. Submarines of one power circled the coasts of the other, with nuclear missiles always ready, in warm seas and cool ones— even under the Arctic ice, where Soviet *Typhoon* submarines and American subs of the *Los Angeles* class equally could puncture the surface ice to launch their warheads. At certain times, in certain ways, one nation had more weapons than the other; whereupon the other redoubled its efforts and itself gained some partial and momentary advantage. Nothing changed. The balance of terror was robust against minor fluctuations. It was as if an American tunnel rat had met a Vietcong defender in the underground mazes of Vietnam: it made very little difference if one had six hand grenades and the other only four. Neither would survive.

So the attainment of a really significant advantage always eluded both superpowers, for each always possessed the power to annihilate the other . . . provided it were willing to be annihilated in return.

Terrorist bands capture individuals and hold them hostage, enforcing their will on them by threat of death. Superpowers do not bother with individuals. They hold entire nations hostage.

17

David had slept very poorly—had got up half a dozen times in the night to call Police Headquarters to ask if there were any news of Rachel Chindler and got the same answer every time. It was growing light when at last he drifted off, and his alarm went off at seven. So when the door chimed a few minutes later he was still in a robe, a cup with a spoonful of instant coffee at the bottom in his hand.

It was the young police sergeant, Nancy Chee. "Have you found her?"

Chee shook her head regretfully. "There's something that might bear on her kidnaping, though. You know a young woman named Alicia Patterson?"

Humming sound from the doorway and Kushi entered, majestic in a muumuu the size of a hot-air balloon. "Of course know her. Grandkid's girlfriend. Give me cup, David." She poured from the kettle she carried while she listened to the police sergeant.

"Alicia Patterson was arrested yesterday for trying to steal a car."

David said in surprise, "I'm sorry to hear that. Are you sure of the case?"

"Oh, yes, Dr. Yanami. She hot-wired a Toyota in the Hertz lot at the airport. She did a good job jumping the ignition key, but she must have been nervous. Anyway, she rammed a Post Office truck on the exit road and tried to run in the Toyota. A police car saw the whole thing." She hesitated. "The thing is," she said, "she and your nephew, Albert, are in the file as Hawaiian nationalists."

"There's no law against that," said David instinctively, and then shrugged. "Reflex. Sorry. Are you suggesting that Lono was involved in the kidnaping?"

"That's what I came here to ask you, Dr. Yanami. Patterson says she only wanted a joy ride, but that doesn't seem very logical. There's nothing in her personality to suggest she'd do such a thing."

"No," David acknowledged. "Nice girl. Serious."

"And there's a missing vehicle from up near Waimea. A farm truck. Matches the description of a truck that was in the university parking lot."

David was puzzled. "Do you think Alicia stole both cars?"

"No—she could have, I suppose, but we don't think she was the one who kidnaped Mrs. Chindler. She was arrested right around that time, and Mrs. Chindler certainly was not with her. A better guess is that the kidnaper took Mrs. Chindler away in the truck, then abandoned it somewhere to change to another car. Patterson was supposed to provide the other car, but she got arrested. Of course, we've had an all-points out for the truck ever since we got the description of it in the parking lot, but so far no sign. It seems likely that there's either a third party, who did provide a car, or that Mrs. Chindler and her kidnaper, or kidnapers, are still in the truck somewhere. If so, they can't go far in it."

"And either way," said David slowly, "you think my nephew is part of the kidnaping. Of the hijacking, too, I suppose."

"We're checking everything out," Chee apologized. "One thing is sure. Whoever kidnaped Mrs. Chindler knew where she was going to be. Who knew that?"

"Well—I did, of course. Frank, and his secretary. You knew—" He frowned. "Oh, and I told the duty officer at Lyman, I think. No, I know I did, and his secretary, too. I wanted them to speed things up so I could go back to Frank's office and pick Rachel up."

The sergeant sighed. "And any of them could have told anyone else. Well, at least you didn't put an ad in the paper."

"I had no reason to think any of them would tell," David said huffily.

"Of course not. Anyone else?"

"No, I don't think so," said David, considering. "I didn't really see anybody else."

"Saw me, David," said his grandmother, tamping tobacco into her pipe. David looked at her in alarm. The sergeant said quickly: "But did you mention it to anyone?"

"Did," said Kushi heavily. "Lono called up. Talked long time, very friendly—long time since had nice talk with Lono. Told him where wahine went."

While Nancy Chee was on the telephone to Police Headquarters, David sat staring at his grandmother. She removed the pipe from her mouth, returning his gaze. "You David"—hum—"you right. I made bad mistake."

"You didn't tell me anything!"

Kushi said, "What is to tell? So last night I try to call Lono, no answer. All right, he out with girl maybe. This morning I call again, still no answer. I going to tell you right away. Then lady cop come."

"You should have said he knew about it."

"You right, David," she said gravely, "but he great-grandkid."

David stared at his grandmother. Lono? The bright little kid who only yesterday had been delighted with Eisenhower half-dollars and Susan B. Anthony coins? For the boy to take a philosophical position against the European destruction of the islands was one thing—not a bad thing, either, because David shared the resentment. The *philosophical* resentment. But to join the terrorists? Maybe to have been one of the gang of hijacking thugs who had methodically murdered twenty-some people?

"I don't want to believe it," he said.

His grandmother hummed sympathetically for a moment. "Too much huhu," she agreed. Then, "You, David! What about kid?" She turned to the door, where Nancy Chee's light step had just announced her return. "What say, Nancy sergeant? You think so too?"

The policewoman paused to untangle Kushi's communication. "About the kid? Oh, you mean Mrs. Chindler's son?"

"Rachel kid"—hum—"right. Name Stephen. He come here."

Nancy Chee looked at David, who looked noncommittally
back. "Well, I don't know," she said. "I don't know if there
are any funds for such a thing, or if the captain would approve."

"You fix easy," said Kushi agreeably. "Easy for you. You
get kid here, stay this house till find ma."

"I really don't know—" Chee began, but Kushi shook her
huge head.

"Do know, Nancy sergeant," she observed. "Know kid all
by himself"—hum—"not know bad news about ma. When he
hear on telly, how much huhu? No! Call kid, tell him. Then
bring kid along here. You fix!"

The policewoman thought it over for a moment, then
regretfully nodded, sighed and went back to the telephone.
David went to the window and stared out. It had been raining,
on and off. He wondered if Rachel and his nephew had been
out in it, absently rubbing his chin. Irrelevantly he said over
his shoulder, "I'm thinking of shaving my beard."

Kushi chuckled. "Good idea! Shave make you"—hum—
"look young." He turned to see what his grandmother was
grinning at; but, actually, he didn't need to guess. There was
a causality there: shaving off the white beard, looking
younger—young enough so that a forty-three-year-old woman
might not think of her father when she looked at him. "Is all
right, David," scolded his grandmother, surprisingly gentle.
"No reason you shouldn't like that Rachel. Meet kid, too."

"Her son?"

"You bet, David, you meet her son, you find out how you
get along. Then you shave off beard, see what happen."

"Kushi, she's in desperate trouble!"

His grandmother nodded. "Can do nothing about that
now, David," she proclaimed. She hummed for a moment,
then said, "You go out with Nancy sergeant, look for Lono,
okay?"

David hesitated. "If he's really one of the terrorists—"

"Then maybe is bad, yes, David. Even shooting bad. So
you go, maybe you talk to him."

But before David could answer Nancy Chee was back in the
room. "They'll try to get Stephen Chindler flown here," she
said, "but there's something else that came up while I was on
the phone. Dr. Yanami, they want us to go to the park.

They've found something there that they want you to identify for them.''

The lava tube was a major tourist attraction because of its shape and its history. When lava flowed down the hill it was a slow-moving stream, like chocolate syrup trickling down the side of a can. As it cooled, the outsides of the stream hardened. Molten rock continued to flow inside the pipe it had created. Then the mountain stopped its flow of lava, the liquid in the tube drained out and the hollow pipe remained. At first it was on the surface of the mountain, of course, but then later lava flows covered it; then erosion opened up one end of it to be discovered by human beings.

What it looked like, more than anything else, was a short section of tunnel going from nowhere to nowhere. The Park Service had trucked clay and gravel into the tube to make a level floor, but the shape of the old lava pipe remained. It was lighted. It was even spacious, yards in diameter, running four or five hundred feet underground. Though David had seen it dozens of times, escorting children or off-island visitors, he shuddered with a vision of what it would be with the lights out, if they were marooned under all that weight of overhead earth. At the end of the tube a busload of tourists, held back by crime-scene posters and a couple of uniformed police, gaggled and chattered. The police admitted David and the sergeant. Halfway down the tube, right in the middle, was a knot of policemen, uniformed and otherwise; and as they approached one of them held out a red plaited-straw woman's sandal. "Can you identify that?" he asked.

Sergeant Chee looked first at the man who was holding the sandal out—without recognition—then at her own Captain Fielding. It wasn't until Fielding nodded that she said, "I think so, sir. Rachel Chindler was wearing shoes like that yesterday morning."

David searched his memory. "I think so," he said doubtfully. "I'm not very good at noticing women's clothes."

Captain Fielding said, "I think that establishes it. One of the park rangers found the shoe. He was going to throw it away—it's not unusual to find shoes in here on a morning, not to mention the occasional brassiere—but Mrs. Chindler's return United Air Lines ticket was inside it. The ticket could have been stolen, but nobody would have stolen one shoe—so she was here. Put the car on the air," he ordered, and a patrolman nodded and headed for the exit to the tube. "I think they stayed here last night to get out of the rain. Then, before dawn, they stole a car at the Volcano House. If they drive the car again we'll get them."

David frowned uncomprehendingly. "Why do you keep saying 'they'?"

Captain Fielding hesitated, then said, "We're not exactly sure what part Mrs. Chindler plays in this. I grant that she might have got into a strange car in the parking lot without argument, especially if the driver really was your nephew, whom she had met socially. I even grant that he might have held a gun on her and made her stay with him for a long period of time—but not forever. It's now nearly twenty-four hours since she was kidnaped. The car was stolen not more than twenty feet from the hotel. She could have yelled for help. She didn't. At some time in the last twenty-four hours, in the dark, up here in the park, she might easily have had chances to run, with a pretty good chance of getting away. She didn't. And then there's the matter of Kanaloa. I think she recognized him, Dr. Yanami. But she denied it."

"That's insane," David flared, but as the police captain opened his mouth to reply the man in civilian clothes said: "Hold on a minute. Before you go any farther, Fielding, we've got some questions to ask Dr. Yanami."

"So do I, Murchison," said the captain.

"Oh, you can. But we go first. Not here. I want him to come down to our office—"

"No way. You can question him, here."

"No." Murchison pursed his lips, then said, with an obvious effort at amiability, "Up in my car, so I can tape the answers."

"Then you'll let us have him?"

Murchison shrugged. "Depends, you know that. If there are no charges, yes."

Charges! In all of David Kane Yanami's sixty-some years he had never before confronted the possibility of charges being laid against him. You didn't use words like that for traffic tickets. And traffic violations were not investigated by the

FBI. When David studied the laminated-plastic card and saw, next to the color photograph of Mr. Muchison, the words *Federal Bureau of Investigation*, the perplexity exploded into words: "Are you charging me with kidnaping?"

"Wait a minute," said Murchison, busy with his briefcase. He pulled out a tape recorder, checked the cassette methodically, turned it on and said: "This is William F. Murchison, interviewing David K. Yanami, on three January at"—he glanced at his wrist—"nine-twenty A.M. Dr. Yanami, can you tell me where you were on the twenty-third of October?"

It was easy enough for David to answer the FBI man's questions—where had he been? Drinking coffee in the restaurant at Lyman Field. What was he doing there? He had just put this Mrs. Rachel Chindler on the plane to Maui. Why was he doing that? Because he had agreed to serve as part of a search committee for a new head librarian at the university, and Mrs. Chindler had shown an interest in the job. Was it possible for him to be involved in the hijacking? Certainly not! . . . But that last question had not been asked, and yet the certainty that it was what was in the FBI man's mind sent David's pulse higher. How incredible that he should be asked such questions!

He shifted nervously in the narrow seat of the Honda, much too small for a man of his size. Murchison paused and, silently so as not to confuse the tape, indicated the window. It had been open a crack and David's right sleeve had a band of wet from rain coming in—he had not even noticed that it was raining! Then the next series of questions began, and they were even more unsettling: What was his purpose in attempting to overfly the Vulcan cluster of ships? But he had already answered that, exhaustively and repeatedly, for the CAA: it was just to show Mrs. Chindler what they looked like. Then a description of the woman who had passed him a note in the hotel lobby for her "husband." But he had answered that any number of times, too. Had he ever seen her before? No. Had he seen her since? No. Did he know what the message contained? No, it was in some foreign language. Ah! Why had he opened it? Damn it, he hadn't "opened" it, it was just folded over and he could see part of the writing—and what the hell did all these things have to do with each other, anyway?

The FBI man did not, of course, answer that. "Thank you, Dr. Yanami," he said formally, turning off the tape recorder. "That's all for now. If you go back to the lava tube, I am sure the Hilo police will drive you back home." And David Yanami, thinking bitter thoughts, hurried through the pelting rain to where Sergeant Chee was sitting in her car, waiting for him.

The young woman was looking tired and strained. Thinking back, David was not surprised. Apart from her regular duties, and apart from whatever personal involvement she felt with the kidnap victim, Sergeant Chee had been pulling a regular shift and devoting a lot of her spare time to trying to prevent from happening just what had happened to Rachel Chindler. She could not have had much sleep. She was not conversational. "We'd better get you home, Dr. Yanami," she said. "You'll catch cold in those wet clothes." And did not speak again until they were turning in toward the little house in Volcano, although she must have known that there, waiting for them on the lanai, was Captain Fielding. On the other side of the picture window was Kushi, placidly laying down solitaire cards, looking up only to beckon her grandson in to change his clothes.

By the time he was dry again the rain had stopped, the sun was bright, and everyone was waiting for him. Even Kushi had put away her solitaire cards and joined the others on the lanai, with the fresh pot of coffee she had been making.

What David wanted, out of indignation, was to know where the FBI man's questions had been leading. What Captain Fielding wanted, out of obedience to orders involving national security, was to tell David nothing, but to find out just what the FBI man had asked. "I'm sorry," he said shortly, "I can't comment on an ongoing FBI investigation."

"Investigating *me*?" David yelped, and Kushi hummed disapprovingly. "You think I had something to do with kidnaping Mrs. Chindler?"

"No," said the captain doggedly, "I don't. There's nothing in your background to suggest it."

"You've been investigating my *background*?"

"Dr. Yanami, of course we've investigated your background. It's all on public record. There's no suggestion of any complicity in any illegal activities—not counting buying an occasional bag of marijuana for your grandmother.''

"Now, listen—"

"No, Dr. Yanami, you listen. We aren't hassling you. This is a major investigation. Kidnaping is a federal crime. So is hijacking.''

"But what does this woman and her note have to do with either?''

The captain clamped his jaw. "If I knew the answer to that I probably couldn't tell you. Maybe nothing. Maybe Mr. Murchison knows something I don't know.''

"And my flying over Vulcan?''

"Same answer! That's a sensitive area, everybody knows that. If they know why, they don't tell me.''

Nancy Chee laid a hand on David's arm. "Please, Dr. Yanami,'' she said. He looked at her disgruntledly. "Our main interest is Mrs. Chindler,'' she said. "It appears your nephew is involved, so what we need from you is information about him and his associates.''

So for the next ten minutes, while the coffee that no one was drinking cooled, both David and his grandmother were asked to search their memories. People they had seen with Lono? People he had ever mentioned to them as friends or associates? Places where he stayed, or where those friends lived? Any trips off-island that they knew about, and where to?

David began to suspect that the questioning would never end, and perhaps it didn't. At least it was recessed, when the captain closed his notebook, nodded to Sergeant Chee, and left. David glanced at the young woman in puzzlement, and she said, "Do you mind if I stay here for a while, Dr. Yanami?''

"Do I have a choice?''

She said formally, "I'm supposed to keep your house under surveillance until relieved, Dr. Yanami. Surely you understand that. Your nephew may come here, or call. If you'd rather, I can wait in my car.''

"Stay here, Nancy sergeant,'' Kushi ordered. "What's matter with you, David?''

He said apologetically, "Of course she's right, sergeant. Are you going to arrest all those people?''

"Question them," she corrected. She hesitated. "Have you been listening to the radio?"

"When would I do that?"

She said, "According to the news broadcasts there have been more than forty arrests all over the islands this morning."

"Forty! You must have arrested everybody who ever heard of the Maui MauMau!"

"Unfortunately not. They've been busy. They've declared a hotel chain and a car-rental service kapu, also a couple of sugar companies. It isn't just talk. There have been two big fires in the cane fields, and somebody put a couple of pounds of arsenic in a syrup tank."

"Good God!"

"So they're not all under arrest, Dr. Yanami. And, of course, all that's just what has been on the radio, and those are just statements from the police. There are other agencies involved."

"Agencies? More than one? More than the FBI?"

She closed her lips. David said dazedly, "I had no idea there were so many people willing to take part in terrorism. And Lono—"

Nancy Chee hesitated, then said, "There's no harm in telling you, I guess, that we've established one thing about your nephew. He was definitely not on the hijacked plane; he was on the Kona coast that morning, at his job. He didn't leave until noon, and by then the plane was already taken over."

"Thank God," said David. "At least he didn't murder anybody." His mind was racing. "And if Mrs. Chindler went with him voluntarily, as you say she did, then I wonder if legally—"

Nancy Chee shook her head. "It's still kidnaping. I'm sorry."

"Even if she didn't object?"

"We don't know that she didn't object," Nancy Chee said firmly. "Even if she didn't, an implied threat of force is enough—how many rapes are there like that? Of course—but we're getting way ahead of the facts, Dr. Yanami. This is trial-lawyer stuff. Still, a lot might depend on how Mrs. Chindler testified against him—if she were released unharmed, for instance. What do you think of her?"

David was startled at the irrelevance of the question. "Why—a perfectly normal young woman. One who has been through a terrible experience but appears to have come out of it really well. She was quite outgoing and at ease when I was showing her around."

"Outgoing, yes. Laughed easily. Might have been any tourist."

"That's right."

"But she didn't identify Murray Pereira. You don't see many faces as mean as his. And I'm morally sure that she knew him."

"Now, that's ridiculous, Sergeant Chee! After all, the hijackers killed her friend. Would have killed her, too, except for the grace of God. Why would she lie if she really recognized him?"

"Why did Patty Hearst go along with the Symbionese Liberation Army?"

"Why—why—I don't really know," David confessed. "She was a young girl, badly frightened, subjected to terrible mistreatment. Naturally she was too frightened and confused to resist."

"But she didn't just give in, Dr. Yanami. Don't forget those bank-camera pictures. She was an active participant in the robbery."

David shook his head. "I don't see what you're getting at."

"I'm getting at why Rachel Chindler is behaving the way she is, Dr. Yanami. Have you ever heard of the Stockholm Syndrome?"

18

Hostage-taking has become one of the standard ploys of terrorist groups all over the world, from the Hanaafi Muslims in Washington, D.C. and the Tupamaros in Uruguay, through the American embassy personnel in Teheran and the Texas Penitentiary in Huntsville, Texas, to Croatian airline hijackers and Entebbe. What is astonishing in many of these situations is the incongruous response of some of the hostages. It is the terrorists who have put their lives at risk, made them captives, often subjected them to privation and sometimes physical harm. Yet in a surprising number of cases the hostages take the side of the terrorists, even against the police or soldiers who come to rescue them.

This response is called "the Stockholm syndrome" after the events of the last week in August, 1973, in Stockholm, Sweden. A lone robber with a submachine gun attempted to hold up the Sveriges Kreditbank. The robbery went wrong, and so for five days and seven hours four bank employees were held hostage, while the robber tried to negotiate his freedom. In the process the robber, Jan-Erik Olsson, demanded and got the release of another convict, Clark Olofsson, who joined him in the bank to share the guarding of the hostages; and over the long period of captivity the hostages began to identify with the cause of their captors. As one said in a telephone conversation with the Prime Minister of Sweden, Olaf Palme, "The robbers are protecting us from the police." When at last they were released, all four hostages tried to help their captors and one became engaged to marry Clark Olofsson.

The Stockholm syndrome is not limited to this incident, or to Sweden. Ex-hostages in many places have visited their captors in prison, or even contributed to defense funds for them. Ex-hostages, questioned in debriefings after a hostage situation, have said that in the event of an armed takeover by police they would have obeyed the terrorists' orders over those of the police. This is true even when the original crime had no political or idealistic motive behind it but was a simple bank robbery, as in the actual Stockholm case; it is even more so when the terrorists can make some principled case for their actions. For the hostages come to feel that they and the terrorists are actually in the same position, as victims rather than perpetrators. After South Moluccans hijacked a railroad train in The Netherlands in December, 1975, one of the freed hostages, Gerard Vaders, said: "And you had to fight a certain feeling of compassion for the Moluccans. They gave us cigarettes. They gave us blankets. But we also realize that they were killers. You try to suppress that in your consciousness. And I knew I was suppressing that. I also knew that they were victims, too. In the long run they would be as much victims as we. Even more."

Patty Hearst was not alone.

19

Because two jumbo jets were due in within half an hour, the usually relaxed parking regulations at the airport were temporarily being enforced. That didn't mean that David couldn't park his car at the curb as long as he liked. It only meant that he had to stay within eyeshot, so as to be ready to stroll back to it when the airport traffic cop approached on his little moped. He ventured in as far as the United passenger service counter and returned at once to Kushi, waiting in the car. "The flight is twenty minutes late," he reported. "If you'll stay with the car, I'll go in and keep an eye out for the boy."

"Okay," his grandmother said agreeably, "only we do it the other way. You stay here. I find kid wiki-wiki."

"You don't even know what he looks like," David objected.

"Huh! I know any kid, David. No huhu—also—I go in nice shiny toilet." With a look of sublime confidence directed at her grandson, Kushi sailed through the waiting throng. David retired under the roof of the overhang, out of the sun. Unsurprised, he saw that instead of turning left, toward the ladies' room, his grandmother turned right, toward the airport coffee shop. Even less surprising, he saw Sergeant Nancy Chee's little car roll to a stop a discreet distance away.

The policewoman made no effort to be inconspicuous. When she saw David approaching, she got out of the car and met him. "If you're here," David smiled, "I suppose somebody else is watching our house?"

She didn't evade or amplify. "Yes."

He nodded. "I guess I'm glad," he observed. Then, frowning, "I've been thinking about what you said. Is Rachel Chindler really taking the terrorists' side?"

"It's a possibility, Dr. Yanami."

"But that's so—strange," he said, looking for the word that would define this outré situation, and failing to find it. Then he answered his own implicit question: "I guess we live in strange times. Everybody's gone crazy and nasty."

"Not everybody, Dr. Yanami." The little police sergeant was looking up at him with warm approval. "You and your grandmother are really kind to take care of him. I should tell you that I'll relieve the other officer when you get home, so I'll just be down the street if you want me. But I don't want to confront the boy with policemen right away."

"I don't suppose you have any news?" But David didn't need an answer; certainly if there had been any she would have told him at once. He sighed and gazed around. He caught sight of his grandmother on her way from the coffee shop to the gate. She was nibbling at a Good Humor, with a second one ready in her left hand, still in its paper wrapper.

"I don't think any of us should blame Mrs. Chindler," the sergeant said suddenly. "I doubt any of us know what we would do in her position."

"I don't blame her! Not for anything at all," David declared sincerely. "She's a good person, Sergeant Chee. And I don't doubt this, what do you call it, Stockholm syndrome? It makes sense. With so many bad things going on in the world, we all have to admit that in some way we become accomplices to evil."

"Not you, Dr. Yanami," the woman said earnestly, then peered past him. "I think they're coming out now. I'll go back to my car and follow you home. Do be care—" She stopped and smiled at him. "I was going to say 'be careful.' Isn't that silly? I don't even know what I'm asking you to be careful about!"

What do you say to a boy whose mother has been kidnaped by deranged killers? Especially when one of the killers is your own nephew? But when the boy came through the gate into the

hot Hawaiian sun, clink, carrying a canvas flight bag with a
stencil of Huey, Louie and Dewey Duck surfing off Oahu's
North Coast, David didn't have to worry about what to say.
Kushi took over. She didn't say anything at first, either. She
just wrapped the boy in her thigh-thick arms, released him
to pound his back, steered him toward the waiting car.
"You, David!" she ordered. "We go now, wiki-wiki.
Kid"—hum—"kid starve to death on airplane food, we get
him something good at home!"

The boy shook hands with David and obediently climbed in.
He seemed much younger than David had expected—or
perhaps David had simply forgotten what an eighteen-year-old
looked like. Stephen Chindler wore a thin moustache, and that
made him look younger still. It was not a moustache which a
mature man would have allowed to be seen. David worried
over the moustache. It was the kind of thing a certain kind of
insecure teenager would grow to make himself look older; and
would such a person be able to relax under Kushi's huge
mothering presence?

He needn't have worried. On the way up the hill to Volcano,
Kushi was leaning forward, her head of scarlet hair between
David at the wheel and the boy, looking excitedly out the window. "You ever see Hawaiian lady like me before?" she
demanded.

"I don't think so," said the boy. "Maybe on TV. On
"Hawaii Five-O," and like that."

"We very"—hum—"big," Kushi conceded. "But we very
good people too, like your momma. You worried about her?"

"Yes," said the boy.

"Sure you worried! You crazy if you not worried, Stephen,
but don't"—hum—"don't worry *too* much, you know?
Everybody doing their best, you'll see. Now, look. Up there
ahead, after we turn off, that is Kilauea. That is volcano,
place where Pele live—very strong goddess, very bad to get her
mad at you."

"I wish I could see an eruption," the boy said wistfully.

"No you don't! Can be very bad if Kilauea erupts. You
nice-looking kid," she announced without change of tone.
"You got girlfriend?"

"Uh, well—sure."

"Naturally you got girlfriend," Kushi agreed. "Good thing to have girlfriend, get married, have kids—you do that, Stephen, don't be"—hum—"don't be like dumb grandkid David here, should be married, have son like you!"

"Kushi," her grandson said temperately, "I think Stephen wants to ask you something."

"Ask! What?"

"Well," the boy said, "I was just thinking—you said you were Hawaiian?"

"You bet, Hawaiian! Why not?"

"I just thought you looked kind of, well, Japanese."

"Japanese is good Hawaiian!" declared Kushi. "You know"—hum—"many hundred years ago, Japanese ship wrecked on Maui. You don't know that, hey? Captain name Kaluiki-a-Manu. Captain have sister name Neleike, and Neleike marry chief, Hawaiian fellow name Wakalana. So when they get married, Captain give Wakalana iron knife, first iron knife ever in Hawaii."

"That's a sword," David said, craning past the old lady to smile at Stephen.

"You shut up, you David," Kushi scolded. "Stephen knows iron knife is sword. Anyway, this prove Japanese blood in Hawaiian royal family, even, ever since!"

"Our own Japanese blood came quite a lot later, though," David grinned, and turned into the driveway. "Here we are, Stephen. Your room is all ready for you."

"Thank you, sir," said Stephen, a step ahead of David as they both reached to take his Disney World bag out of the trunk, polite, eager, as normal a young man on his first trip to the Islands as anyone could expect . . .

And how wrong that was! This poised and calm young adult could not really be so calm. When Kushi had retreated to the kitchen, her unshakable intention to feed this new nestling wiki-wiki-quick for fear it might die of starvation, David took the boy out on the lanai. "Stephen," he said, "I'm sorry we don't know each other better, because I am sure it is difficult for you. At a time like this. Among strangers."

"You're very kind," the boy said politely.

"We want to be. Let's pretend, Stephen. Let's suppose that we're family and you've known us all your life."

"All right, sir."

David felt a flash of irritation, suppressed it quickly. Then he had second thoughts and let it come out. "So let's not be so polite," he ordered. "This is a bad time. Your mother is in serious trouble. She has been kidnaped; she's been away two nights now, and nobody has any idea where to look for her. The police are working as hard as they can, but they haven't found her. And the worst part"—he took a deep breath—"the hardest thing for me to face is that the person who kidnaped her is probably my own nephew."

About that, at least, David had been right. It was the hardest part, all right. The reactions of Rachel's son went from puzzled incomprehension to shock, to anger, to as close an approach to tears as an eighteen-year-old young man could allow himself. But Stephen Chindler was not a breakable child. Things might be overwhelmingly bad, but he did not allow himself to be overwhelmed. He listened. He asked questions. He sat on the edge of the wicker chair and kept his eyes intently on David as David explained about Lono and the Maui MauMau and all the other young-firebrand groups, in all their various shades of violence.

Rachel would have been proud of her son.

David, leaning toward him as he spoke, put his huge hand on the boy's shoulder, and felt pride of his own. If only Lono had been as bright, as concerned, as steadfast as Stephen Chindler—

But, David thought, the terrible thing was that Lono was. He was all of those things; the disaster was that somewhere in his young life there had been a fork in the path, and he had taken his idealism and his courage along a way that led to kidnaping and killing.

Kushi came out with an opened can of beer for them in each great hand, listened for a second, then returned to the kitchen. The boy muttered a polite thank-you without taking his eyes off David. He missed nothing. When David paused for a moment, Stephen said:

"There's one thing I don't understand about my mom. Did she really have a chance to call for help? And didn't do it? Why?"

David shook his head. "I wish I knew. The police have a kind of theory—they call it the 'Stockholm syndrome.' It seems that sometimes hostages, victims of terrorists, even people who have been robbed or raped—they find themselves taking the side of the people who have harmed them." He told the boy about Rachel's failure to identify the terrorist in the lineup, and as much as he could remember of the lieutenant's explanation.

The boy absorbed it all, then looked up at David pleadingly. He looked younger then ever, the downy moustache comically out of place in the young face. "My mother wouldn't do anything wrong," he said definitely.

"No," David agreed, "she wouldn't. But sometimes it's hard to tell which thing is wrong and which is right. It's—it's almost the same with my nephew, Lono. He wouldn't do anything he thought was wrong, either—but, oh, Stephen, how badly people can go astray doing something they think is right!"

The boy nodded, puzzling over the irreconcilable dilemmas of the world. David let him mull it over, sipping the beer that had grown warm and flat in his hand. "Now," he said at last, meaning to get the conversation back on a practical level, "what we're going to do is stay right here until—"

But he didn't have a chance to finish the sentence, because he heard his grandmother's bellow from the kitchen: "David, Stephen! You come here wiki-wiki, look!" It was not like Kushi to be excited over nothing. David got up swiftly. Stephen was even faster; by the time David was in the kitchen the boy was ahead of him, standing next to his grandmother, flatfoot before the kitchen TV set. The volume was up high:

"—bizarre communication received from the group called the Maui MauMau, which appears to threaten the life of Islands visitor Rachel Chindler, just as it was delivered a few moments ago on the beachfront at—"

"Rachel?" demanded David, and the boy echoed, "My mom?"

"You listen!" Kushi thundered, as the announcer kept talking:

"—impromptu press conference was ordered, Miss Farrell said, by telephone. Here is the note as read by Miss Farrell just minutes ago."

The announcer's voice stopped, and the television picked up the voice of the young black woman in a brief bikini, standing on what looked like the diving board of a Waikiki hotel swimming pool, reading nervously from a piece of paper. The sound quality was fluctuating in the wind, but every word was audible:

"The haole woman Rachel Chindler has been tried by a Kamehameha People's Court for participating in the lynching of innocent Hawaiians. She is sentenced to death. The court has suspended sentence, however, and will release the woman unharmed under certain conditions. The American usurpers must admit guilt in expropriating and alienating Hawaii from its rightful owners. It must then agree to hold meaningful discussions with representatives of the Hawaiian people's liberation movement to set a timetable for complete withdrawal of all American restrictive forces from the islands. As an evidence of good faith, all political prisoners in the kingdom of Hawaii are to be freed and given transportation to a Polynesian destination of their choice. If these measures are carried out, the haole woman, Rachel Chindler, will be released. Otherwise sentence will be carried out tomorrow."

"My God," breathed David, as the announcer, looking grave, stepped before the camera.

"That is all we have at this time," he said. "We will bring you further bulletins as they develop. Complete details at six. We now resume our regular programming."

As the afternoon rerun of M*A*S*H returned to the screen, David cast a tormented glance at Stephen, standing stiff with Kushi's huge arm around him. Then David threw the front door open. He turned his body toward the end of the street, cupped his hands over his mouth and bellowed, "Sergeant Chee! Come in here, please!"

There was no doubt that the sergeant heard him—everybody on that block of the town of Volcano heard him—but she didn't respond at once. She was leaning forward intently. David saw her raise a microphone to her lips, speak, listen, speak again. Only then did she open the door and come toward him.

As she crossed the pebbled front yard of the neighbor David's rush of anger was dampened by the near tears in her eye. "They've threatened to kill her!" he cried.

She said, "I just heard the report on the radio. I'm terribly sorry, Dr. Yanami."

He held the door for her. "Come inside," he said gruffly. "If my nephew shows up, you can see him just as easily from inside the house."

His grandmother commanded, "Don't pick on little pak girl!" She hugged Stephen onto the living room couch and ordered, "Everybody sit down. Tell what is going on."

The sergeant sat down stiffly on the edge of a chair. "I don't know anything more than you've heard. Stephen? We're doing everything we can, but—"

The boy gently released himself from Kushi's arm. "I know you are," he said.

"And what is that, exactly?" David demanded. "Are you arresting all the members of the free-Hawaii organizations?"

"All we can find—almost all," she corrected bitterly. "It's not easy. There are half a dozen different organizations—not just the Maui MauMau and the Kamehameha Korps and the Order of Menuhene; there are social clubs that talk about Hawaiian nationalism sometimes, but mostly just play softball with each other. And the ones we want are the hardest to find—they know who they are, even when we don't, and they don't make it easy for us. We'll get them, Dr. Yanami. But there are just so many police on the islands. We can't be everywhere at once. And—"

She stopped. "And what?" David prompted.

She said reluctantly, "Some of them we've been told to leave alone. The Oahu section of the Kamehamehas—they're not to be bothered."

"Why?" barked David.

"I don't know why."

"But you can make a guess? Make it."

She said unwillingly, "I don't *know* anything. Some people might think that those particular people are infiltrated—FBI, maybe, or military intelligence people. That's not official information, of course—but," she added earnestly, "if it's true, it means we might be able to find something out."

Kushi stood up and sailed toward the kitchen. "Have not done much good so far," she declared over her shoulder. The sergeant didn't answer. It was not an arguable statement.

David said: "If you're so busy, why do you waste time watching us?"

"I volunteered for this, Dr. Yanami."

"Not just you! There's always a car down the block—if it isn't you, it's another policeman." Kushi came back in with two beer cans in each hand and stood listening as she popped each one open and handed them around. "This morning," David went on, "there was a Datsun where you park. Then when I went to the supermarket before I went to pick Stephen up, there was a blue camper at the end of the street; it was right behind me all the way down to Hilo, and when I came back I watched in the mirror. It parked in the exact same place again."

Nancy Chee shook her head. "That wasn't us," she said positively.

"Then who? The terrorists?"

She said evasively, "I doubt that, Dr. Yanami."

"You doubt it because you know damned well it was somebody else. The FBI? I don't like being followed this way."

"Make him so nervous he forget head," his grandmother corroborated. "Don't get salt, don't get Baco-Bits. Here," she added, offering the sergeant one of the beers.

Nancy Chee shook her head. "I'm sorry," she repeated, meaning either no beer on duty or nothing she could do about the FBI. And from the couch the forgotten son of the hostage said, "Will they kill my mother, Sergeant Chee?"

The question hung there for a moment. David was watching the sergeant's face. He saw the smooth skin around her eyes crinkle, not in laughter; saw her open her mouth to answer, then close it again, surely trying to make certain her voice was under control. It was not a question she wanted to answer, it was clear.

What was surprising to David was that his grandmother sighed and turned away. "I take car," she announced. "Get salt you forgot, you David." But that was so unlike Kushi! There could be little doubt, he thought, that it was not salt she was interested in; but his grandmother was not a woman to be afraid to hear truth, however bad the truth was.

If that were the case, both Nancy and Kushi were spared for

the moment. As Kushi turned she peered into her kitchen and froze. The neglected TV had stopped showing Radar O'Reilly walking the colonel's horse, because a blue and orange slide saying *Bulletin* had appeared. All four of them were suddenly in a knot at the kitchen door, peering at the screen.

The announcer was talking to the young black woman who had delivered the terrorists' message. Someone had provided her with a plum-colored beach jacket, so she no longer looked quite as much like a page out of *Playboy*. Her expression was serious, even frightened, as she listened to the broadcaster briefly recapitulate the message she had read. David put his arm around Stephen's shoulders, awkward but comforting; the boy kept his eyes on the screen.

"The message," the announcer was saying, "was delivered by Eloise Farrell, a visitor to Waikiki, who is with me here now. Miss Farrell, as I understand it you were in your room when you received a telephone call. Can you tell us what it said?"

The young woman's voice was husky and she was obviously nervous, but she spoke up clearly.

"It was a man's voice, real businesslike, you know?"

"Could you recognize the voice?"

"Oh, no. He said I wouldn't know him. He said he needed to hire a model for an hour's work. I'm a dancer, not a model, but he said two hundred dollars, and I could do it without changing my clothes. Well, he must have known I'd just come up from the pool in my bathing suit, you know?"

"Did he say what the work was?"

"He said I'd get instructions. Well, I thought, you know, he was one of those kinky guys, but he didn't really sound that way. He said he had arranged a press conference. All I had to do was go back to the pool. He said there would be news-people there with cameras, and I just had to read a one-minute statement for them. Actually, it sounded kind of interesting."

"Did you ever see this man?"

"Oh, no. No. Unless he was one of the gang around the pool, you know? There was a whole bunch, I guess because of the TV crews and all. Anyway, just about a minute later there was something under my door. I looked, and there was this envelope on the floor. So I opened it up. There were two hundred-dollar bills in it, and a driver's license—"

"A driver's license?"

"It was the lady's, I guess. Anyway, on the back it had written something—"

The announcer glanced down. " 'Please help me.' And it was signed Rachel Chindler. Is that it?"

"Yeah. And there was a note, and another envelope. The note said I should go down and get up on the diving board, and then open this other envelope that was inside and just read what it said for the reporters."

"Is that what you did?"

Eloise Farrell hesitated. "Well, when I saw the TV crews I got a little nervous. So I opened it up first while I was still on the sidelines, like."

"And then you did as instructed?"

"Well, I didn't know what else to do. I was scared, too. I didn't think I was going to get into a kidnaping here, you know."

The reporter opened his mouth to continue the interview, then put his hand to his ear. "I understand the police want to ask you a few more questions, Miss Farrell, so I'd better let you go. Thank you for being with us." The girl licked her lips and nodded, as the reporter turned full-face to the camera and said, "That's what we have learned here at the poolside about the kidnaping and threat to Mrs. Rachel Chindler. Now we will return you to the programming in progress. There will be bulletins as they develop, and full details on the six o'clock news."

The frozen tableau in the doorway began to melt. No one had moved. No one had seemed even to breathe as they watched, until David went to turn the sound down and Kushi exhaled a long, soft sight. Nancy Chee shook herself. "May I use your telephone?" she asked, and disappeared as soon as David gestured toward the phone in the hall.

"Stephen," David ventured, "I know it looks pretty bad, but don't give up hope."

The boy thought it over before he responded. "You know," he said, "on the plane coming out here, all the time I kept wondering if the police were really bringing me out here to identify my mother's body, and just didn't want to tell me. I—*want* to hope. But—"

He didn't finish.

Kushi hummed to herself for a minute, then demanded, "You want 'nother beer, Stephen?" The boy shook his head. "Then eat!" she ordered. "Got nice cold pork, hot bake beans, plenty fruit—all on table. Come!"

Stephen knew the voice of authority when he heard it. He followed Kushi to the table, already laid out with one place, and the beans bubbling softly in a pot on the stove. There was a halved papaya on one plate, and slivered raw carrots and celery on another. Kushi fetched milk out of the refrigerator and ordered her grandson to dish out beans, and Stephen did as told until Nancy Chee came back. "Any news?" David demanded.

The sergeant hesitated. "Not really," she said. "Forensic is going to go over the letter and the envelope, and they're trying to track down the person who delivered it for Miss Farrell. The only thing—"

"Yes?" David encouraged.

"Well," she said, "what strikes me is that this is all so *professional*. I don't know if you noticed, but whoever sent that message knew a lot about how the news media work. They kept it short, so they could get the important parts in what they call a 'sound bite'—about half a minute air time. They called the TV stations and the newspapers and had them waiting at the pool when Miss Farrell showed up. And"—she glanced at her watch—"look at the time. It's prime time all over the forty-eight, and even if they don't get a bulletin they'll make the late night news everywhere." She looked uncertainly at David. "Do you see what I mean?"

"Our beachboys have been getting a lot smarter," David offered.

"Or else they've been getting some high-powered help. Technical help."

Kushi hummed to herself and breathed, "Kanaloa."

"Well, him, too," Nancy Chee conceded. "He was an Air Force helicopter pilot once, and I doubt they could have done the hijacking without him, but I mean *outside* help. Somebody had to put up ten thousand dollars to get him out on bail—where did they get it? And the way they stage-managed that thing with Miss Farrell?"

"So who?" Kushi demanded.

"There was a report," the sergeant said slowly, "that there was some Weather Underground person on the Islands a month ago. And that scares me. It's bad enough when every little terrorist group is doing its own thing . . . but if they start working together . . ."

She shook herself. "Anyway," she said, "we're doing everything we can." She looked down at Stephen Chindler, chewing dutifully, listening to every word. "We'll do our best to find your mother."

"Sergeant Chee?" he asked. "What about those demands? Are they going to get them?"

"I don't think so, Stephen."

The boy put down his fork. "I don't, either," he said. "I bet the kidnapers don't think so, too. So do you think my mother is still alive?"

For a moment the only sounds in the room were the whisper of the TV set and Kushi's faint humming. Then the old woman stood up. "Is pretty bad, Stephen," she said solemnly. "You hope for best, though. I go get salt David forgot."

Although Kushi considered herself a good driver, her grandson did not. It was a measure of how worried he was that he handed over the car keys without protest. As she turned into the highway, she saw the blue camper waiting on the shoulder, and was not surprised to find that it started up after her. She hummed to herself thoughtfully, then drove straight for the shopping center. She did not drive fast. She was meticulous about stopping for lights as soon as the color changed to amber, making one or two other drivers blow their horns. She was as easy to follow as any very old woman should be.

The shopping mall occupied a full block, the core of stores surrounded by acres of parking space. She entered across from the big hotel on the hill and ambled slowly through the lot, pausing at every parking space as though in doubt, then moving on. In the rearview mirror she saw the camper following, a good distance behind. When she was halfway around the mall she speeded up, pulled out of the lot and across the street in the teeth of oncoming traffic. She raced around another corner, turned into the hotel lot and pulled dexterously into a space next to a large delivery van.

Humming to herself, Kushi watched the blue truck appear around the corner of the shopping center. It hesitated, then screeched away back the way they had come. As soon as it was out of sight Kushi backed out of her place of concealment and drove off in the opposite direction. She hummed contentedly. All those hours watching "Hawaii Five-O" had not been wasted!

Her first stop was the Buddhist temple, on a residential street a few blocks away. It was not a place Kushi visited often. In twenty years she had been there only for funerals as old friends and relatives died—would be there again, most likely, only for her own, whenever that happened—but there was a monk almost as old as herself. In some sense he was a relative, too, or at least their respective mothers had thought so, long ago.

He sat silent under the great figure of the Redeemer. One hand of the statue was upraised, the other open on his lap—saying, jokers pretended, with the one hand, "Wait a minute," and with the other, "First pay!" Kushi didn't pay. In a mixture of Kanaka and Japanese, half creoled into English, she asked after her great-grandson.

The old man shook slightly. He was laughing. How would he know anything about a boy of twenty? A boy, moreover, who belonged to the Maui MauMau? Did Kushi not know that the MauMau disliked the Buddhists almost as much as the haoles? Of course she did, she told him patiently, but the parents and relatives of those kids must have worries about them. Hadn't some of them ever talked to him? Where did the kids hang out? Were there any names he could give her?

Reluctantly the old man quarried his memory. There was a hippy commune where some had lived. There was a young woman who had been jailed for selling drugs, though drugs, her grandmother thought, were the least of what she had been into. There were two boys on the welfare, unemployed because they had beaten up their boss in a quarrel over Hawaiian rights.

It was a meager harvest, but better than none. As Kushi rose to go the monk reached out a hand to detain her. "Why they talk about Hawaiian?" he asked. "Who Hawaiian today?"

"Go back to sleep, old man," said Kushi gently, because it was, of course, the only answer anyone could give. Who was

Hawaiian? Not very many. Certainly not her great-grandson Lono. At most an eighth of his blood was Hawaiian, and that was giving the benefit of the doubt to an unknown grandfather on his father's side.

Kushi herself was exactly one-quarter genetic Hawaiian. The rest was Japanese. In fact, the Japanese strain in Kushi went back as far as there were Japanese in Hawaii at all—at least if one discounted the semi-legendary sailing ship captain with the iron knife—to 1868, when the first load of Japanese cane-field workers were imported by the planters. She knew those forebears by name. One of that levee, Shinko Yamayashi, got pregnant her grandmother, the daughter of the Hawaiian luna, or foreman of the plantation. The girl had been pregnant before, and was to be again, but this was her only half-Japanese child: Kushi's mother.

In 1886 a new Japanese laborer, Hideo Shiroma, married the daughter—perhaps thinking that he might become luna himself when the girl's grandfather died. He had no such luck. A Portuguese got the job. But they had seven children. The third was a girl, Kushi.

Kushi claimed, and sometimes even thought, that she remembered seeing Queen Liliuokalani and King Kalakaua. It was at least a possibility that she could have, if they had visited the right parts of the Big Island at the right times. She was born at the time of the ill-fated Red Shirt rebellion in 1889; was two years old when King Kalakaua died of a stroke in San Francisco and left the monarchy tottering; was four when Kalakaua's sister, Queen Liliuokalani, ended it by abdicating under the guns of the U.S.S. *Boston*. But Kushi had been alive in the days when Hawaii was an independent nation, ruled by its ancient line of kings.

That was unquestionable. It was also unquestionable that she did not want those devious, arbitrary and hard-drinking people back. Neither did anyone else she knew—except, it seemed, her foolish great-grandson, Lono.

How right it would serve him, she thought grimly, if he got what he wanted!

The nearest address was the "hippy commune," near the public beach just west of Hilo Bay.

It did not seem to be exactly a commune any longer. The old

monk's information was out of date, perhaps by many years.
But Kushi parked her car and waddled toward the nearest of
the three tumbledown houses on foot. There were "This Prop-
erty Condemned" signs in the littered yards, untended for
years, but the houses seemed still inhabited. A bare-bottomed
little boy played among the old auto parts and broken washing
machines. When Kushi bent ponderously down to talk to him,
the child stared up in terror at the red-haired old woman, and
a female voice called, "Hey, you! Leave the kid alone!"

Kushi elevated herself once more to her feet and walked up
to the woman. She was skinny and belligerent, secure behind a
screen door with the latch hooked. "I am looking for great-
grandkid Albert, they call Lono," she said politely. "Used to
live here, I think."

"Never heard of him."

"I am not police," Kushi declared indignantly. "Is all right
to tell me."

The woman looked scornful. Then she didn't look anything
at all, because she wasn't there. A shape loomed up behind her
and pushed her out of the way. It was a man as big as Kushi,
sallow-complexioned, obese. He wore dungarees held just
under his belly with what looked like a length of clothesline,
and nothing on top but an acre or so of bare, maple-syrup-
colored skin. He studied Kushi appraisingly. "No, you ain't
police," he said, "but we don't know nothing."

Kushi sighed and rummaged in her straw totebag. What she
pulled out was a twenty-dollar bill. "You talk serious," she
scolded. "I don't make no huhu for nobody, but I need to
know!"

When Kushi pulled away, the giant was standing on the
rickety porch watching her, and she had acquired a couple
more addresses.

Kushi hummed to herself dispiritedly, sitting behind the
wheel as she crept toward the intersection. There was a certain
problem in her belly, and she wondered, for the first time, if
she weren't getting just a little elderly for this kind of thing.

If so, there was nothing she could do about it. Instead of
heading directly for the next address she turned down to Banyan Drive, parked in a hotel lot and imperiously crossed the
lobby to the ladies' room. Such were the penalties of two hun-

dred and seventy pounds of constantly metabolizing flesh.

On the way out an idea struck her. She rummaged for coins in her totebag and made a telephone call. She didn't call David, because she didn't want to hear any arguments from him. She dialed police headquarters. "Have message for Sergeant Nancy Chee," she told the duty officer. "You write down. Nancy Chee tell David Yanami not to worry about Kushi, she visiting old friends. Okay? Thank you!" and hung up on the questions.

She did not want David to tell her what that nagging little voice inside her had already said, that she had no business trying to find Lono by herself. It was a personal matter. She intended to try to deal with it personally.

Kushi had listened intently when the sergeant had said that Lono could not have been on the hijacked plane. But the sergeant had not said that the boy couldn't have been at Kamuela to help the hijackers escape, and therefore indeed a guilty accessory to the mass murder.

20

On the 18th of January, 1778, Captain Cook sighted the island of Kauai. It was the first recorded encounter of a European with the Hawaiian Islands. Over the next ten days landing parties from Cook's two ships went ashore, to investigate the new lands and to barter iron nails for coconuts and pigs. No English sailor stayed ashore at night. Cook forbade it—until the night of January 29th, when an officer and twenty men could not get back through the rising surf before nightfall.

Cook had not wanted any of his men to do that, because he was a—more or less—well-intentioned man, and he knew what would happen when his deprived sailors had a night's freedom in the presence of native women. It happened. A day or so later he sailed off on his fruitless mission to seek a Northwest Passage.

At the end of the year, when cold weather again drove him south through the Bering Strait, no passage having been found, he made landfall on a different island of the same chain. He was not surprised that the Hawaiians who greeted them there already bore the sores of venereal disease. From then on, ship captains might try to keep their crews aboard for protection—but it was the sailors they wanted to keep uninfected; for the islanders it was too late. In less than a year, syphilis and gonorrhea had become epidemic.

The Hawaiians who, in February of the next year, stabbed Captain Cook to death in the surf of Kealakekua Bay were not avenging themselves on him for adding a new care to their sexual pleasure, but perhaps some might think they had that right.

Within a century the Islands had changed unbelievably. The institution of "kapu" was gone. So women no longer feared to eat at the same table as men; subjects no longer had their eyes gouged out for stepping on the shadow of a king; commoners were allowed to own land. (Unfortunately, this implied that they were allowed to sell the land they owned, so that more and more of Hawaii fell into the hands of sharp foreign traders.) The warriors who had once waged war with flint-studded clubs and sharpened wooden spears moved up to knives, then to muskets. The chiefs' double-hulled dugout war canoes were replaced by cannon-bearing schooners. The art of weaponry advanced a thousand years in every generation, and, predictably, the new weapons did almost as much as the new diseases to wipe out the native Hawaiians. Whatever weapons the Hawaiians acquired were only practical against each other, for the Europeans always had better ones. No shore city could stand up against a foreign warship. Russia, France, England, the United States—they all sent naval vessels from time to time to make sure their subjects on the islands were fairly treated. Fairness, unfortunately, was often construed to include the right to steal what they chose and swindle what was left. Hawaii was not fortunate in most of its foreign visitors. Some came through idealism and religious fervor. Others found the civilized world too hot for them and set out to try their luck at defrauding the innocent savages. The visitors who came to do good proved all too frequently corruptible, and most of the others were corrupt already.

Fewer and fewer native Hawaiians were in a position to resist. On February 10, 1853, the *Charles Mallory* brought smallpox from San Francisco to Hawaii. Typhoid and typhus were earlier imports. A few years later, leprosy (the "Chinese disease" it was called, though no one could honestly say whether it came from China or any of a dozen other places) began to spread, and the Hawaiians had to open a quarantine colony on Molokai. Not all the imported diseases were bacteriological. Alcoholism (the Hawaiians had never learned to make alcohol) and prostitution were also epidemic. There was no such thing as sex for money in pre-European Hawaii;

and there was no need for it, for the Hawaiian women had
never had many moral qualms about "sleeping mischie-
vously." The Europeans taught them to put it on a paying
basis—so well that the average annual income for Hawaii's
colony of whores, about a hundred thousand dollars a year,
just about equaled the government's average annual revenues.

By the time Kushi Shiroma was born, in 1889, the Hawaiian
government was no longer very Hawaiian. Kalakaua, the last
of the Hawaiian kings, was still on the throne; but the con-
stitution the kings had been forced and tricked into accepting
gave all real powers to the ministers of state—almost all
Yankees. Kalakaua did not enjoy that. He even tried, among
other things, to start an underground secret society, Hale
Naua. Only males of provable Hawaiian ancestry could join.
The rituals were complex and bizarre, the purpose—probably—to counter foreign force with dedicated resistance.

But the resistance did not effectively resist, and in 1893 the
last of the line was forced off the throne. Kalakaua's sister and
successor, Liliuokalani, was the first reigning Hawaiian
queen—and also the last and the only.

By a century after that the wishes, deeds and trappings of
the Hawaiian kings were of interest principally to tourists.

21

Before daylight Lono made Rachel accompany him to the parking lot of the Volcano Hotel, where he stole a car. By the time the sun was high they were down the mountain and into the condo developments above Hilo. They didn't park there. Lono parked the car a good mile from where they were going, and they walked together in the morning sun, arm in arm. Like lovers. Like, in fact, the kind of lovers they were. Lovers with the immediate history of physical intimacy that was not reflected in warmth of eye or tenderness of expression. "Look at me," Lono commanded as they walked. "Keep your eyes straight on me." Rachel obeyed dreamily, her body aching, her mind drugged from lack of sleep. They walked arms-around-waists, with their faces turned toward each other. No casual observer could get a good look at either face that way.

The knife in Lono's hand was concealed by Rachel's arm.

Rachel knew it was there. Sometimes when their footing faltered she felt the sting of its point, very close to her breast. "You're hurting me," she pointed out after the second or third time. "You don't have to. I won't run."

But he kept the knife grimly where it was. Rachel did not object again. She had no intention of objecting, to that or to anything else. Rachel Chindler had abandoned all thought of independence of action. What Lono told her to do she would do. She had no other plan. It puzzled her to know that this was so. That wasn't bad, either. It gave her something to think about, while they strolled up the slope, past a 7-Eleven and a filling station, high enough over the town of Hilo now that they could see the warm Pacific in the morning light, into a cul-de-sac of condominium homes.

When they turned into a driveway, still face to face, Rachel relinquished the puzzle, still unsolved. Curiosity stirred. It almost made her turn her head to look at the house they were approaching, but Lono forbade it. "Hold still," he commanded, his eyes flickering from side to side, to see if they were observed. "Now, just up that step. Yes. Now I ring the doorbell. Now we wait . . ."

They did not wait long. The door opened almost at once. The woman who opened it did not waste time in greeting them. She swept them inside, peered out into the street, closed the door and locked it. "Did anybody see you?" she demanded.

"Dozens of people saw us, Pele," said Lono. "But I don't think anyone will remember. Have you something to eat, for heaven's sake?"

"In the kitchen," said the woman. She put one hand in the pocket of her apron, pulled out a small revolver no bigger than a toy, and when she was sure Rachel had seen it put it back. She studied Rachel's face. Rachel gazed back until the woman said, "Do you know who I am?"

"Yes," said Rachel. "You were at David's party. You're the librarian who quilts rugs. I think your name is Meg Barnhart. Only," she added, "your hair was dark and pulled back then, not blonde and curly. I guess you're wearing a wig."

"Quite right," the woman said, glancing at herself in a wall mirror. "You recognized Ku, too, didn't you?"

"If that's the man I saw day before yesterday," Rachel said, "yes. The police couldn't find him afterward, though. They said his name was Oscar Mariguchi."

"You're very good at faces, Rachel," said the woman. "It's a pity."

Rachel did not find anything to say to that. She looked around at her surroundings. It was quite a nice house, she thought, at least for, say, an elderly couple seeking to warm their later years in the Hawaiian sun. It did not seem appropriate for a radical revolutionary gang. The living room had a cathedral ceiling and a wall hanging of woven cloth.

There was a fireplace—gas and ceramic logs, but still pretty. There was no wall-to-wall carpeting, but simple rugs were by the chairs and couch. It looked as well bred and reassuring as Meg Barnhart herself, not counting the blonde wig.

And not counting the gun.

Lono had stopped halfway to the kitchen, watching them. "Well?" he demanded.

"Oh," said the woman. "You want to talk. Then put Mrs. Chindler upstairs, and I'll get the sandwich stuff out for you."

Wistfully Rachel thought that she wouldn't mind a sandwich herself. No one offered, though, and her passivity extended far enough even to override her hunger. The upstairs room Lono conducted her to had the look of someone's music chamber, disordered and incomplete, as though that someone had been interrupted in the process of packing to move. There were giant speakers on the walls, though there was no visible record player. The windows were double-glazed—incredible in balmy Hawaii—and there were shelves of records along one wall. Tschaikovsky and Stravinsky and Del Tredici and John Cage were mixed up with Corelli and Mozart and Palestrina, and on another level were Kiss and Michael Jackson and the Grateful Dead. The word that came to Rachel's mind was "eclectic," as far as the taste of the owner was concerned. As to his, or her, provisions for comfort, the word might have been "inadequate." There was no flat surface to lie on, neither couch nor bed; there was not even a comfortable chair, only a straight-backed kitchen thing. "Sit," ordered Lono, and when Rachel obliged, she felt her hands pulled behind her, quite roughly, and something being tied around them tightly enough to hurt.

Lono stood back and looked at his bound captive. "If you want to yell," he said, "no one will stop you, but nobody will hear you, either. This room is soundproof."

"I wasn't going to yell," she said truthfully. In fact, the idea had not even occurred to her.

He looked at her wonderingly for a moment. Then he shrugged and turned away. "I'm sorry," he called over his shoulder, as he closed the door.

A moment later she heard it lock from the outside.

• • •

Although she had not slept for more than minutes at a time in the complicated night before, Rachel was no longer sleepy. She sat straight in the straight chair, gazing at the wall of record albums and the window. She tested the rope around her wrist more out of curiosity than any intention to get free of it. It seemed secure, and twisting against it was uncomfortable.

On the other hand, nothing else was very comfortable, either. Her joints ached. Probably from the night in the damp lava tube; possibly from prostaglandins flooding her body. She tried to count back in her mind to see if she was due for a period. It was hard to remember. Also it was not very enjoyable to do. Thinking about when her period was due was like thinking about whether she was going to be pregnant or not, which in turn was too much like worrying about the future at all. That she had given up. What happened would happen, and her only emotion about it was annoyance that she had to wait around for it. Whatever "it" would turn out to be.

Meanwhile she sat upright in the straight chair, her mind separated from everything that was threatening—which is to say, nearly everything in her environment.

After an hour or so the door opened and Meg Barnhart appeared, still in the blonde wig. "You probably need to pee," she said politely, untying Rachel's hands. As soon as the hands were free she stepped back, alert. Rachel rubbed her wrists to start the blood flowing again, and noticed with interest that now the woman had a gun slung over her shoulder instead of a pistol in her pocket. It looked to Rachel—who knew nothing of guns bar what she was learning from one terrorist or another—like the kind of rapid-fire weapon American GIs had carried in Vietnam. Barnhart stayed considerately in the doorway, eyes averted while Rachel used the toilet. "Hungry, honey?" she asked then. "You'd better eat while you've got the chance." And she escorted Rachel to the kitchen.

Barnhart didn't make the meal for her. Barnhart stood in the doorway again, amiably offering directions and suggestions. Eggs in the refrigerator, also butter. Skillet under the sink. Bread in the bread drawer, toaster on the counter, plates in the cupboard. Knives in—

But then Barnhart had second thoughts. She didn't offer

Rachel the use of the silverware drawer, but opened it herself and took out only a salad fork and a butter knife.

When the scrambled eggs and toast were eaten, Rachel dutifully rinsed and stacked the dishes and was escorted back to the music room—with one small detour when she remembered to tell Meg Barnhart that her period seemed about to start. So then she was back in the chair with a box of Tampax at her feet—and her hands still tied. Now, really, she thought to herself, almost amused, what am I supposed to do with them when I'm like this?

It was almost a comfort to realize that the terrorists were not supernaturally prescient in thinking out every detail in advance.

Being a hostage was never fun. On the hijacked plane at least she had had company. Not to talk to, no; no one dared conversation. Not for the hope that one of her fellow victims would miraculously pull out a hidden machine gun, strike down their captors and set them free—certainly not that. But at least there had been someone to share the misery and fear . . .

On the other hand, she told herself to be fair, at least in the present situation she didn't have to worry about anyone but herself. No other person would be harmed by whatever happened to her here.

But that wasn't true.

Someone else would be harmed. Stephen would.

It was only then that Rachel began to cry.

When the sun went down, the music room was wholly dark, except for a faint yellowish glow from the street lights outside. Cars had driven up and away once or twice during the day, and Rachel had heard voices from below. Whose voices they were she could not say, nor what it was they were saying; but sometimes they had been loud.

When the door opened without warning she was for a moment frightened. The voices had been quite angry just a moment before. But it was only Lono. He didn't look upset or dangerous. He looked exactly like the attractive young boy who had been at David's party, eons ago. He had bathed and shaved, Rachel noticed with approval, although the darkness under his eyes suggested he had not slept. While he was bent over to untie her hands he glanced up at her almost with a smile, but when she smiled instinctively back his smile vanished. "Eat," he said, pointing to the tray he had set down on the floor, and retired to the doorway to watch her do it. "I don't want to talk," he said clearly when she offered a remark; and he stuck to it.

The meal was actually rather good. There was a sliced fresh papaya on the tray along with the chop, the tiny boiled potato and the salad. Rachel was allowed to use the bathroom again, this time even to shower, even to rinse out her underwear and hang the bits up to dry. Lono didn't take her back to the music room. He took her to a bedroom, an attractively wall-papered room with golden drapes hiding the windows and a king-sized bed, neatly turned down. The room was a bit too small for the bed, Rachel noticed, so it had been pushed against the wall; you could get into it from only one side, and it was undoubtedly an annoyance to make up. "We'll sleep here," Lono said, motioning Rachel to get in first. She obeyed without speaking, slipping her dress off and climbing in naked. She watched the boy undress and then, as bare as she, slide in beside her—then quickly out again, because he had forgotten to tie her hands. When that was done he got back in, still without speaking.

Rachel wondered if her period might start in the night, and thought apologetically of what a mess she might make of the bedding. Then she wondered, since it hadn't started already, if Lono was going to make love to her again. He didn't. In the huge bed they did not touch, but she could hear his breathing become regular and deep, and peacefully she too went to sleep.

She woke up while it was still dark.

She was lying with her face to the wall and, in his sleep, Lono had thrown one arm over her, holding her belly, while one of his knees pinned her legs. It was not comfortable for her, but she thought that to move would wake him. She lay quietly, listening to him breathe, feeling the warmth of his body against hers. There was a pleasant scent of male body and last night's soap. She lay as still as she could for what she thought must have been an hour. The window in this room was screened and open, and interesting floral scents came in with the warm breeze. She was, after all, Rachel thought, in Hawaii. She tried to remember what Hawaii had been like for her before it became a nightmare: the whaling museum at Lahaina, the toppled U.S.S. *Arizona* with its dead crew still entombed, the hotel roof where McGarrett greeted the "Five-O" television audience, the flowering ginger that always made her sneeze, the sunsets that almost made her cry, the fish, the fresh fruit, the tourist cocktails with their little paper parasols or their tiny floating orchids—

And then, at the end, the horror.

It all seemed very remote, and no longer important at all.

Rachel felt quite peaceful. She realized that the pressure she had begun to feel in the small of her back was Lono's penis —the boy had an erection in his sleep. She remembered how it had been to have him inside her, and wondered if he had thought their lovemaking in any way special or important. She wondered if they would make love again, perhaps when he awoke, if he had another of those involuntary nighttime erections. Then she wondered if she would ever make love to anyone again. But that led to wondering if she would be still alive long enough for that to be important, and that thought disturbed her tranquillity. So she went back to sleep.

By midmorning the next day Rachel was back in the music room, fully dressed again, alone, un-made-love-to . . . and untied. The way it came about that she was untied was that shortly after she was left there, she became aware her period had started; so, patiently she picked at the knots until she was free and could insert the Tampax.

Rachel strolled around the room, wishing that they had left the record player in it. All those records, and nothing to make the music come from them! There were no books in the room and, though she tried reading record jackets for amusement, they were not in fact very amusing.

Looking outside was only slightly more interesting. There was not much to see. The window of the room was locked. It was a louvered window and she could not have squeezed through it in any case. It did not seem to her (she thought academically, to pass the time) that she could have managed to open it, and then break the outer pane, even to yell for help (of which she had no intention anyway). So as a means of escape or summoning assistance, it was no use at all.

As entertainment, not much more. She could see the street outside but there was not much to see on it. The condominium was in a cul-de-sac. No cars entered that had no business there. In more than two hours of watching, there were fewer than half a dozen vehicles—a telephone company truck, the mailman on his little scooter, a motorcycle that paused across the turn-around loop long enough for a girl to appear and clamber on the back. Rachel stared almost enviously after them. She had not been on a motorbike since Stephen was small and she a fresh divorcée and her first serious date after the divorce an advertising executive who spent his weekends dirt-racing. Not a bad man, she reflected. She'd given him up when her lawyer pointed out that if she were to continue riding a motorbike it might easily cause the custody-case judge to think her a little careless of Stephen's security. That was the first man she'd given up. There had been others, including some who looked really promising for a while—two who were nice looking, one intelligent, one kind and caring. Unfortunately, no two of the qualities she prized had turned up in the same individual, so nothing had come of any of them in the long run.

It did not now seem that anything ever would.

It was curious, she reflected, that if she were going to die now her last lover would have been a murderous boy half her age. It could have gone the other way. It could have been a gentle old Oriental college professor twice her age, or almost. And if that had happened—if she had responded to the bashful interest David Yanami had shown—why, then she might not have been in Frank Morford's office and Lono might not have been able to entice her away. She might, in fact, not now be under sentence of death at all. Pleased with the new subjects to think about, her mind went on inventing permutations and consequences. Then, she thought, she might have confided in David that she really had recognized the terrorist they called Kanaloa. Might even have gone back to the police station to say so; might have testified in court and seen him tried and convicted.

And none of this would have happened . . .

But all of this, she thought, did happen, and so perhaps it was meant to. It was not a frightening thought. It almost contented her.

What frightened her was when she heard another car climbing up toward the turn-around loop and peered out. A young man was driving, someone unknown to her. Next to him was a woman, a huge one with bright blonde hair, a floppy hat and a bright red blouse. She could barely see either the driver or the passenger, because of the angle. But then, just as the car entered the breezeway, the passenger looked up, and she was no she; those eyes could not be mistaken; wig and padded bra could not disguise the fact that Kanaloa himself had just come back into her life.

When Lono came to get her half an hour later he made no reference to her untied hands, unless another of those half-smiles was a reference. She was taken back downstairs to the kitchen. "Sit down," said Meg Barnhart, pointing to a chair at the table, where someone had left her a plate of sandwiches and a glass of milk. Lono went over to the window and stared out of it, moodily smoking a cigarette. Of the young boy who had driven the car there was no sign, but his passenger was there. No more wig. No woman's dress. Just Kanaloa himself.

He got up and came over to her. She stopped eating as he stood over her—to look her up and down, then reach out and touch her face. It was not a loving gesture. It was not in any way sexual. It was as though one of the buyers at the fish market in Hilo were poking a finger into the gills of a tuna, to make sure it was fresh enough for his sushi customers.

He let go of her and studied her broodingly for a moment. "Why didn't you I.D. me?" he asked, the organ voice as deep and remote as ever.

The only answer Rachel could truthfully offer was "I don't know." It seemed to satisfy Kanaloa. He glanced at Lono and nodded, as though agreeing to something previously discussed, and let Meg Barnhart take over.

"Rachel," she said kindly, "in case you don't make it out of this, you ought to know that none of us bears you any ill will at all." She paused, almost as though waiting for a thank-you from Rachel. Rachel only gazed back at her, chewing. "We would prefer not to kill you," the woman amplified.

Again Rachel thought some response was wanted from her, but all she could think of was a nod.

"Let me explain what we are doing," said Meg Barnhart, in the polite, precise tones of any librarian explaining why some periodicals could be taken out on loan and others not—but that was the wrong way to think about her, Rachel warned herself. This wasn't a librarian named Meg Barnhart, who quilted rugs for tourists; this was a murderess named Pele. "We are trying to prevent a crime against humanity by the fascist power elite," said Pele.

Rachel drank the last of her milk to cover what might have looked like amusement. What archaic and formal words these people used, she thought detachedly. Objectively. Yes, and that other quality that had seemed to dominate her behavior for the past few days, passively.

But then, as the woman went on, Rachel could not be entirely passive any more. The change made her tingle painfully, like a numbed hand coming back to life. "An H-bomb?" she whispered. "Going to blow up the whole world?"

"No, no," said Pele, impatient as a librarian who had to explain the whole thing over again, "not blow it up, freeze it. Freeze a lot of it—don't you remember? You saw the computer simulation yourself; you told Lono about it."

"But that wasn't a bomb, was it? I thought it was about some make-believe volcano erupting."

"Both bomb and volcano," rumbled Kanaloa pleasantly, "and not make-believe."

"So that is the thing we're trying to prevent," Pele said. "Do you understand what we have been telling you?"

Faintly, "Oh, yes, I think so."

"Do you have any questions?"

"No. Well, yes," Rachel corrected herself, thinking. "You didn't know about this Project Vulcan thing until just now, did you? But it was last December that you killed all those people on the airplane."

Pele frowned severely; the librarian had caught a teenager leaving with a book under his jacket. "You don't understand at all, Rachel," she said sharply. "The struggle against the fascist militarists did not begin yesterday. It has been going on forever. This is merely one more manifestation."

"A hell of a big one," Kanaloa said softly, seeming to enjoy himself. "Get on with it, Pele."

"I am waiting," she said, "for Rachel to answer what I have just said."

There was a sound from Kanaloa. It wasn't a growl, exactly. It was like the purr of a great, predatory cat. Lono turned from the window to watch. Meg Barnhart looked up apprehensively.

"You're wasting time," Kanaloa rumbled. Barnhart nodded almost appreciatively, as though thanking him for some constructive suggestion. He came back to stand over Rachel. "Little haole bitch," he said pleasantly, "do you want to make a deal? Right now you're an asset. We've offered to trade your life for something we want." Rachel flinched, but he went right on. "If they meet our demands, we'll give you back to them—that's a fair arrangement, with profit for both sides. But," he added, in his soft organ voice, "if they don't do as we ask, then we should kill you. Your death would be a kind of asset, too. It would show that we are serious, so next time perhaps they won't be so hard to deal with."

How long-winded they all were when they chose to be, thought Rachel as she waited to hear the "deal." But she only nodded encouragement to go on.

"That's a sort of accounts-receivable asset," he explained. "Your death, I mean. But you could be a current asset for us."

He paused expectantly. Trying to do what was apparently wanted of her, Rachel ventured to ask, "How can I do that?"

"By becoming one of us," Kanaloa purred.

Rachel looked around the room to see if they were joking. It did not seem they were.

"You kill people," she pointed out.

"In the cause of revolutionary jus—" Pele began, but Kanaloa cut her off.

"Yes, we do," he agreed.

Rachel shook her head. "I couldn't kill anybody," she said. From the window Lono put in, "Not even to save your own life?'' His voice was shaking, Rachel noticed. Obviously this was not easy for him.

She said apologetically but firmly, "I won't be part of killing anybody, no matter what."

"Rachel!" he cried. "What about your son? He's here, you know. It said on the TV they were flying him out. Do you want him to have to identify your body in some ditch?"

"Shut up," said Kanaloa softly, studying Rachel's face. Rachel almost thanked him; the studden stab of the thought of her son had been more than she was prepared for. Stephen, *here*? The picture Lono had suggested to her ran vividly across her mind, but she shook her head.

Kanaloa turned to gaze at the boy. "This is what you thought could be our Tania?" he asked. He seemed to have grown even larger, and Lono put out a hand to him, palm first, as though warding him off. But the boy said doggedly: "This is an evil thing the government is doing, Mrs. Chindler. Don't you want to help keep it from happening, when it means you can go on living?"

"I don't want to be part of any evil thing," she said sadly, and added, "and you're all evil."

That was the end of Rachel's participation in the conversation.

The others went on as though she were no longer present. "Ku should be back by now," said Pele, planning. "He'll have to make the drop."

"Not in that thing of his," Kanaloa said contemptuously. "It doesn't have enough of a trunk. He'll have to take your Rambler. What about the radio link?"

Rachel shivered, understanding how quickly her future had been determined. She hardly heard the next part:

"The best thing," said Pele judiciously, "would be for all three of us to go up the mountain and set it off."

"What if it's already fused to the H-bomb?" Lono demanded. His voice was still shaky, and he was avoiding looking at Rachel.

"I don't think they've done that, but if they did—" Pele's eyes gleamed, but she shook her head. "No. At least we'll blow their fusing, though. That should look good on the TV news! We can alert the media, have them flying nearby to take pictures—"

"You talk like a fool," Kanaloa observed softly. "We don't know the codes for the triggers."

"You said you could get them by trial and error!"

"I can. But not in five minutes. It could take an hour or more, and if we tell the papers they'll be flying over us, too. Then what, fool?"

"We have guns! We'll hold them off if they come!"

"Fool, fool," sighed the organ voice. "No. We can't get media coverage this time. We'll just have to do it. Call Ku and make sure he's on his way; we'd better get moving."

As Pele went for the phone he gazed amusedly at Rachel. "Are you following all this?" he asked.

She asked boldly, "How do you know so much?"

Kanaloa looked at her, the black eyes fond. "There's a Russian fellow that the Kamehameha Korps picked up for the feds. They're hand-in-glove with the CIA, but not all of them have finked. There's one that still reports to us. Have you changed your mind?"

She shook her head, and Kanaloa dismissed the captive and her foolish questions from his mind. "What's your trouble?" he asked, looking at Lono.

The boy said steadily, still not looking at Rachel, "You're doing this all wrong, Kanaloa."

"Oh?" The purr was deep and somber.

"It won't work," said Lono firmly. "If we're up there on the mountain for an hour, someone will see us. Someone from one of the telescopes. Some repairman or something coming up to check out circuits or something; there are people up and down that road at any time. Even tourists."

The phone rang. Kanaloa frowned, and looked questioningly at Pele, who shrugged to say that the number she had called had been busy and she was just waiting to try it again. As she picked up the phone to answer, Kanaloa turned back to Lono.

"It could be that way, yes," he said, and thought for a moment. "All right. We'll keep the wahine alive and take her with us up the mountain; she could be an asset if we need a ticket out.''

Lono shook his head. "Still wrong," he said doggedly. "Not in broad daylight. We should wait until it's dark, at least, and then—"

He didn't say what "and then." Pele had hung up the phone with a sharp, small clatter. "What is it?" Kanaloa demanded.

Pele said, "That was Hina. She says they've picked up Ku and Akea—it's a roundup—and she says there are cars coming into her driveway now."

"She's gone," said Kanaloa decisively.

"We're gone," said Pele. "Hina knows me and she knows this house. She'll talk."

"No more discussion," Kanaloa ordered, his voice sweet and joyful. "We'll go up the mountain right now, and this woman—"

He paused, looking thoughtfully at Rachel. Then he nodded. "We'll take her with us," he decided.

It wasn't until all four of them were in a car, Lono driving, that Rachel realized how close she had come to being left in that condominium house above Hilo, the tardiest of the victims of the hijack murderers.

And where the private condominium road entered the city streets, a little Toyota was parked on the shoulder. Kushi sat behind the wheel, eternal and immovable, watching.

Meg Barnhart's name had come, unexpected but terribly right, from one of the kids the Buddhist monk had given her. The house had looked innocent enough when she dared to peek at it from a neighboring back yard—expecting a householder to challenge her, ready with a flood of pidgin to fend him off. But then she had seen the car with the huge blonde woman in it, and it would have needed more than a wig and a bra to disguise Kanaloa from her.

When she saw Lono's car, she slipped the Toyota into gear and followed. She drove carefully and confidently through downtown Hilo, made the left turn past the library, out onto the Saddle Road. Miles later, with the other car just in sight far ahead, she saw it turn off to the right.

It was the road that led up to the summit of Mauna Kea.

Kushi pulled her car over onto the shoulder and watched for a while. It wasn't until she saw the distant glint of reflected light from a window, as the kidnapers' car turned onto the gravel road up the great bulk of the mountain, that she felt sure she knew where they were going.

From that point, there was no choice.

She drove quickly to a payphone at the hunters' station just across from the access road, made a phone call, then turned toward the slow, tricky climb up the mountain.

22

As the visitor approaches the road that leads to the top of Mauna Kea he is confronted with a sign that says

WARNING!
Four-wheeled vehicles only. No shelter. No services. No toilet facilities. No turn-around. Persons suffering from respiratory or circulatory conditions should not attempt this road. Visibility may be impaired by fog, cloud or storm. Wind may make driving treacherous. Proceed at own risk.

Not a word of the sign is exaggerated. Mauna Kea is the tallest mountain in the world, figured from the base at the sea bottom to its peak. Even the part exposed above sea level is two and a half miles high. The person who bravely drives past the warning sign has actually begun quite a long journey. It begins in the tropical warmth of sultry Hawaii. It ends on a windswept peak with arctic temperatures.

To drive up Mauna Kea is to drive beyond much of the Earth's atmosphere and a major fraction of its water vapor. This makes the summit uncomfortable for human beings but wonderful for telescopes. Along with one or two other ocean islands and a few mountains in the Southern Hemisphere, it is the world's best place for astronomical observatories. They cluster there, infrared and optical, run by consortia of institutions from many countries.

There is no other good reason for anyone to spend much time there, except one.

When the University of Hawaii's ship *Kana Keoka* took its Angus camera pictures of the baby underwater volcano Loihi, when the Navy's *H.H. Hess* and NOAA's *Fairweather* and *Rainier* did their bathymetric surveys in the same location, the persons aboard could look northward and see Mauna Kea's peak rising above the sea.

Mauna Kea's height commands a wide horizon. A person standing on the peak can see, or a line-of-sight radio communication from there can reach, more than a hundred miles out into the Pacific—certainly as far as the submarine volcano, Loihi, to the southeast.

23

Of all the unlikely places in the world for Arkady Bor to be kidnaped to, the dormitory ship *Hermes* was the most preposterous of all. How ludicrous and improbable it all was! First to be trapped by the KGB. Then hijacked by those aboriginal brutes who called themselves the Kamehameha Korps. Then transported to Military Intelligence at Fort Shafter with whom the Korps, it seemed, was working hand in hand. Finally the long nighttime flight—in one of those nasty, bumpy Army helicopters, with himself and the KGB woman and three of the beachboys all tumbled together— right back to Project Vulcan . . . why, with all the kidnaping and hijacking, he was only back where he had started!

But that was not to say that things were the same for Arkady Bor. They had changed, and by no means for the better.

But that, Bor told himself bitterly, was no real change, at that. For Arkady Bor, every minute from New Year's Eve on had been a downhill slide.

The only difference was that now, at last, he seemed to have reached absolute bottom.

He was no longer in his comfortable stateroom—so he remembered it now, nostalgically, forgetting how cramped and undesirable it had seemed just the other day. He was, in fact, in the brig. Bars were on the door. In the cell next to him was the KGB woman, snoring loudly in her drugged sleep, and at least one of the beachboys a little farther away, also apparently asleep—at least the noisy yells and giggles had stopped some time earlier.

Bor almost envied them. He himself had not been allowed to sleep. First there were the hours of interrogation and denunciation at Fort Shafter. "Why did you see that KGB woman if you weren't going to spy for her? How long have you been passing her information? What have you passed? How does she pay you? What is it, Bor, a Swiss bank account? Roubles? A dacha? A secret general's commission in the KGB?" And all of his protestations in answer received scornfully, or in stony silence. And then, even after that ordeal was over and they reached the *Hermes*, dawn light just breaking over the sea, there was no chance to sleep. This was not a deliberate plan on the part of the Americans to crack his spirit and loosen his tongue, as the Chekists would have done. *Had* done, more than once. No. This deprivation of sleep was peculiarly American. His head down on the mingy pillow, his eyes just closing, then was the first interruption: Bor must sign a receipt for the contents of his pockets, which had been taken away from him hours before. Back to the pillow; then, just as he was trying to turn over to a more comfortable position on the narrow steel bunk (a hopeless attempt; no position was comfortable), the second interruption: to sign a "travel voucher" for his helicopter flight! The third was to demand his Social Security number, which had been accidentally omitted from the travel form. The fourth was purely a mistake. One of the Hawaiians was to be released, and somehow Bor's cell number had been put down in error. So it was Bor, not the Hawaiian, who stumbled groggily to the guard cubicle to be put through the flip side of the booking procedures—sign for the return of the personal possessions, take off the brig slippers and put shoes back on—it was when Bor found the cowboy boots swallowing his tiny feet that he complained and the mistake was discovered . . . and by that time it was broad daylight. Forget sleep for that night. Think instead of breakfast. Bor was willing to think hard about breakfast, too, for the curried beef in Sam's All-Nite Drive-Inn had been a waste, and a long time past anyway. Appetizing smells of fried eggs and coffee began to waft through the bars.

So of course it was at that moment that the Marine guards came for Bor again.

They marched him to a "conference room" three decks up. The difference between a "conference room" and a cell was that the conference room had a door instead of bars, and a table and chairs instead of a cot; but the door had no knob on the inside and the porthole was welded shut.

They left him there, untended and unfed, for another hour and a bit, until Mr. Jameson Burford had had comfortable time to finish his own breakfast and join him.

No sleep. No sensible discussion. No food. It was precisely what the Chekists would have done, except that the Chekists would have done it all on purpose.

When Jameson Burford was ushered in by the guard, hair moussed and blow-dried, khaki shorts neatly creased, smelling of breakfast and men's cologne, Arkady Bor summoned up his courage and his indignation: "Jameson! I have had no sleep and no food! I have been treated like a common criminal! I have—"

He stopped, because Burford was shaking his head regretfully. "That's not important," Burford explained. He sat down and faced Bor, his expression almost sympathetic. "What's important," he said regretfully, "is that you've really fucked the fowl this time, old boy. I didn't think you'd do it. When they told me you were sneaking off to Waikiki, I didn't tell them to stop you. I said, 'Shit, let the poor bugger get his rocks off if he has to. What's it to us? If he wants to suck a cock so badly he's been bothering the crew, let him get it out of his system.' It's only the kind of thing I expect from somebody like you, Bor."

Bor said, quailing, "But I assure you, Mr. Burford—"

"No, don't do that," Burford ordered. "Don't assure me of anything, Bor. I was wrong. They were right. I'm man enough to admit it when I'm wrong. Let the Kamehameha Korps keep an eye on him, at least, they said. Some of them are double agents—shit, who knows, triple agents if they can manage it. One of them will finger him to the KGB, and then we can pick up the Russky too. So I went along with that," said Burford, shaking his head regretfully, "but, honestly,

Bor, I didn't think you'd fall for it . . . and I was wrong." He gazed reproachfully at Bor. "Now what are we supposed to do with you?" he asked.

Since Bor had not expected to be asked any questions, at least not any that might have sensible answers, it took him a moment to shape his mouth for speech. "Why—why, return me to duty!" he managed. Burford looked amused. "But of course, back to duty, what else?" And then the rage rose up in him. "You endangered me!" he cried. "You used me for bait, which is—what is it? Yes—which is entrapment, do you see? Illegal under your own laws!"

Burford laughed out loud. "How fast you people learn," he commented. "Next thing you'll be wanting to call up the ACLU."

"No, really," Bor insisted. "Such behavior is simply not acceptable. If you do not trust me, how can I continue to be of value to Project Vulcan?"

He bit off the end of the sentence. It was a dangerous question; Bor did not like the possible answer he saw in Burford's smiling eyes.

However, Burford only said pleasantly, "I have a few questions for you, Bor. I want you to tell me exactly what your relationship is with that old gook professor, David Yanami, and his nephew, the terrorist called 'Lono,' and Mrs. Rachel Chindler."

"Nothing," Bor whimpered. "None of them. I know nothing of any of them except that you have asked me such questions before."

"I see," said Burford regretfully. "It's a pity." Then he said, as though the previous conversation had not happened at all, "The implantation went smoothly. Very smoothly indeed."

"That's good," said Bor eagerly.

"So perhaps your job is nearly ended anyway," smiled Jameson Burford.

Back in his cell there was still no sleep. Under the eyes of the Marine guard, Bor made up his bunk, and understood well that it was not to be unmade until lights out that night; yes, he might sit on the edge of it, since he had no chair, but *no sleeping.*

It did not really matter. Bor could not have slept anyway.

How had things got so very bad? He had done nothing, after all! Well, nothing except, perhaps, certain sexual things that were really no one's business anyway, in this country which claimed to be free in such matters!

And yet here he was. And they went on asking him questions, questions. Questions to which Bor had no answer. Certainly not any honest answer that would placate them. Not even a useful lie that he could find, though he searched and struggled to invent one.

And the consequences—

The consequences were even worse. Because the KGB woman had been caught, her superiors back in the little gray building in Moscow would naturally do what they had threatened. They would take reprisals against Serafina. That was a great pity, thought Bor. Of course, that was her problem and no longer any of his, for she was a grown woman—but how awful that it should come about through no fault of his own! He had not *tried* to betray the KGB operative to the Americans! If they had been properly alert they would have forestalled the kidnaping! So Bor's conscience was not hurting, to the extent at least that he could be said to have one.

What did hurt was his own predicament.

He had been caught, caught in private with an agent of the KGB. Even if he had been trusted at all before that, which was not really very likely, he would never be trusted again. Would never be rewarded in the ways in which they had promised to reward him. Would not be given the security protection and the open, civilian, unafraid life he had desperately yearned for. Would never have that American pension paid into a blind bank account every month. Would have no friendly phone number in Washington to call any time he saw a suspicious car or needed some new fake document. Would never have any of the things defectors defected for—ever!

Meanwhile—

Meanwhile he was in this cell, with the KGB woman no more than two meters away, still snoring so violently that she might have been in Bor's own bed—God forbid! At least she had no fears, Bor thought bitterly. A show trial. A terrible sentence, maybe even a sentence of death for espionage—but commuted, of course, so that in a few months, a couple of years at most, she would quietly be exchanged for some unlucky American CIA man caught in Kiev or Sofia. If only he were that fortunate! What did he have to look forward to? After he got out of this place where, when he wanted to urinate, he had to knock for a guard to open his door? Oh, yes, the few thousand dollars already banked—they probably would not take that away from him. Perhaps they would give him a handful of sleazy forged identity documents and a ticket to—where? Where was there a place on the face of the Earth where Arkady Bor could live a life without fear?

Perhaps, he thought with the first glimmerings of hope, the KGB might find him too unimportant to bother with, once the Americans had squeezed him dry. Perhaps they would leave him alone after all, so that although he would be broke and friendless and alone, he would at least not have to run from every shadow—

Perhaps.

Perhaps also, he thought, hopes fleeting, the workers' revolution would at last go the way Marx and Lenin had promised, and the Fatherland of the Working Class would turn into the proletarian paradise, no police or camps or vengeful assassins, that would welcome an errant comrade back with open arms . . .

Or perhaps God Himself would reach down and take Arkady Bor bodily into heaven. One was no more likely than any of the others. What was likeliest was very unpleasant indeed.

It wasn't God that got Arkady Bor out of his cell. It was the closest thing to an angry deity the ship could provide, though. It was Jameson Burford, and his aspect was terrible and avenging enough. Bor's flesh crawled when the Marine guard hastily unlocked the cell door and Burford hooked Bor's elbow and dragged him forth.

"You've really screwed things up," Burford observed. His

tone was pleasant enough, but the grip on Bor's arm wasn't pleasant, and neither was the pace at which the big man hustled Bor along the passage.

Bor stumbled and staggered, dragged like a schoolboy to the headmaster's chambers. "What—" he gasped. "What—"

But Burford only grimly squeezed his arm. The man had fingers like steel! Bor yelped, stumbled, was dragged erect and found himself at an open landing stage. Frail looking steps led down to a float secured to the side of the *Hermes*, and Burford was practically shoving him down them. "The launch, God damn it!" Burford yelled. "Get the fucking launch over here?"

Clinging to the rope rail of the steps, the swell of the Pacific making the float surge and sway under him, Bor begged, "What is it?"

"Shit," said Burford. "Do you know what the radio room tells me? They tell me we've been getting coded radio signals from the top of Mauna Kea for the past twenty minutes. Different code every time. Right on the channel frequency, though. Does that suggest anything to you?"

Bor shrank back against the gangway. "But—but—"

"But yes, asshole," nodded Burford grimly, and roared to the incoming launch, "You there! Get your ass over here!"

"But that's the trigger frequency for the detonator," Bor whimpered. "Jameson! Why do you tell this to me? Pritt, Stevens, the fuse crew—"

"If any of them was here, do you think I'd bother with *you*? Get in the launch! Get over there before whoever the hell's trying to set off your bomb gets lucky and hits the right combination!"

The launch did not simply ride up and down over the sea swells. At speed, it splatted across the tops, each one a solid smack that transmitted itself to Bor, fidgeting in the stern of the little boat. As they raced toward the buoy, reversing thrust to stop as close to it as possible, Bor saw that the three-meter whip antenna had been chopped off; bolt-cutters lying on the seat beside him told him now. That was a good emergency measure, Bor saw; but probably not enough. The transmitter on the Big Island had unfortunately been designed with typical American overkill in mind, and even the stub might pick up just enough signal to—

To do the job Bor had designed it for. He wrenched his mind away from that.

Fortunately someone had had the wisdom to bring along the special socket wrenches in the fuse kit; the fittings were designed to be ocean-tight. Also fortunately, no one had tried to open the receiver buoy himself, since an unskilled mechanic could very easily set it off by accident.

That was as far as fortune seemed willing to go for Arkady Bor. Sweating, empty stomach surging ominously with the surge of the launch and the buoy, trying not to be sick, Bor found it almost impossible to get at the fuse shell from the boat. He muttered to himself, closed his eyes for a second and then jumped, clinging precariously to the buoy itself with one hand, while he scrabbled at the fittings with the socket wrench in the other.

What Bor told himself was that it would be an incredible stroke of luck, very bad luck, if whoever was trying to detonate the fuse happened to hit on the right combination of pulses. The odds, he calculated to himself feverishly, had to be a million to one against—well, no, not a million—thousands to one, though, anyway? Hundred at least? But there were only a finite number of bits of information in the triggering code; the sequence lasted just eight-tenths of a second. If the broadcaster were varying the sequences randomly he could try, let's see, nearly eighty a minute—they'd been going for twenty minutes—no, make that nearer thirty-five by now— that meant they'd had a chance to try nearly three thousand combinations—

Bor tried very hard not to be sick. It wasn't the motion of the buoy as much as the knowledge of what lay below him.

At least, he told himself as he got the last bolt open and began to slide the wet, slippery cylinder out of its receptacle, they wouldn't have inserted the detonator package into the bomb itself yet. There would be only a chemical explosion, not a nuclear one. It was very unlikely—oh, it was quite impossible, Bor told himself—that the chemical explosion would set off the nuke itself.

If it did, of course, he would never know it. The 3200 meters of sea water between him and the top of the Loihi mount would turn into plasma. And so would he. There would be nothing more left of Arkady Bor than a scattering of dissociated ions, floating around in the air of all the world; and it was no consolation, either, to think that a lot more people than Arkady Bor would die.

When he finally got the antenna plug out and rendered harmless, he had just time to toss it to the crewman in the waiting launch before he lost his grip on the buoy and slid off into the sea.

They rescued him with boathooks, draped him over a seat, pressed the sea water out of his lungs. He was a sorry sight when they got back to the landing stage, but alert enough to be indignant. "This was extremely irresponsible," he told the waiting Jameson Burford. "If that had gone off, the chemical explosion itself could easily have damaged the bomb beyond repair!"

Burford stared. "You mean you didn't know it was fused to the nuke already?" He shook his head angrily. "Be glad we're all still here," he told Bor, before ordering the waiting Marine to take him back to his cell.

24

There is a story about a terrible time when death stalked the surface of the Earth. The story goes like this.

About sixty-five million years ago (the story says), a wandering body, perhaps an asteroid of eccentric orbit, perhaps the nucleus of a particularly massive comet, encountered the Earth in its path. This body was probably about five miles in diameter and, when it struck the outer fringes of the Earth's atmosphere, may have been traveling twice its diameter every second.

As it penetrated the tenuous beginnings of air, at the edge of space, it collected the air molecules before it, compressing them, heating them. It became a very bright fireball, brighter by far than the sun at midday.

By the time it was in the dense atmosphere where planes now fly and animals breathe, it had acquired a film of squeezed air molecules before it that contained almost every bit of oxygen, nitrogen and trace gases it had encountered —for it moved too rapidly for them to get out of its way—but so compressed and heated that the molecules broke down into atoms, the atoms had electrons stripped away, the gas was ionized and hotter than the surface of the sun.

This fireball (in one version of the story) struck the North Atlantic Ocean. The object itself was vaporized. The energy released by the impact scooped out a volume of sea and sea-bottom rock (and perhaps a volcanic island or two) as much as sixty times as massive as the object itself. That material, too, was hurled into the air as plasma and water vapor and dust.

At that time, sixty-five million years ago, the North Atlantic was still spreading. A land bridge existed from what is now northern Canada and Greenland to what is now Scandinavia and the British Isles. The ocean itself was shaped like a triangle, point up.

The hydraulic ram created when the object struck hammered southward through the ocean, crushing everything in its path. The shock in water produced huge tsunamis that swept over the sea coasts of the continents surrounding, and they drowned and scoured everything they touched. The shock through earth produced quakes of measurable intensity all the world away; nearer, they shook down cliffs and started landslides—there were no buildings to collapse. But it was not hydraulic hammer or tsunami or earthquake that made this event the supreme killer of history. It was not the explosion itself (greater than all the world's stock of nuclear weapons by orders of magnitude). It was not the heat, or the violent storms that followed.

It was dust. Billions upon billions of tons of dust.

The plasmas, gases and dusts which were exploded up out of the primeval North Atlantic had to go somewhere. Some were accelerated so violently that they were lost in space. Some, the parts from the fringes of the event, were in the form of fairly large particles that fell fairly quickly and nearby. But a great part of them became aerosols floating in the air.

It took perhaps five years for the dust cloud to dwindle away and let the sun shine on the Earth's surface again, and by then the world was very different.

Plants had died from lack of sun; so had the animals that fed on the plants; so had the animals that fed on those animals. Of all the known species alive at the end of the cretaceous period, three out of four disappeared. The largest animals were the most severely affected. Almost no creature weighing more than ten pounds whose bones appear in the Cretaceous beds left a skeleton in the layers that followed.

Did this really happen the way the story says?

No one can say for sure, but there is a fact—at least an interesting coincidence; perhaps evidence that the story is true.

At about the same time, some sixty-five million years ago, a thin layer of sediment was laid down which is about thirty times richer in iridium than the deposits that appear just before and just after it. Whatever caused this seems to have been worldwide. The layer appears in at least a dozen places, from Texas and New Zealand to Denmark and Spain.

A man named Luis Alvarez, with a number of other scientists, studied these matters and came to the conclusion that it was a meteorite, rich in iridium as meteorites often are, which struck the Earth then and caused that extinction.

One objection to this theory is that a meteorite (or any other falling body) large enough to do all that should have left a crater somewhere. No crater of the right size and age has ever been found. Of course, it might have struck the sea. There's much more ocean area than land to be struck, and always has been, however the continents may wander. In that case, the effects would have been much the same but there would be no visible crater on land.

Or it might have struck where its footprint was later covered over. There are places like that—places where volcanic activity, for example, is so frequent and large-scale that nothing now survives of events that took place so long ago.

Iceland is a place like that.

If, as the variation on the story goes, there were a new volcano at that time in the part of the proto-Atlantic that is now Iceland—if the object struck it and released an eruption—if the lava and magma that poured out obliterated all traces—

There are a great many "ifs." But in infinite time all "ifs" become facts. Perhaps they did on that day 65,000,000 years ago. The volcanic eruption could have added much to the disaster, through synergy. Even an unaided volcano can seriously affect the Earth's weather. Mount Tambora did in 1815 when it erupted. In the following year crops could not ripen in much of the Northern Hemisphere because there was not enough sunlight; New Englanders called 1816 "the year without a summer." Mount Saint Helens, in 1980, was getting ready to erupt anyway when a landslide on its slope lanced the abscess. Its force was released far more violently than it would have been without the sudden opening in its cage. A meteorite striking a volcano poised to erupt would produce an event far more violent than either happening would be by itself; and in the violence of the eruption all trace could be obliterated.

So perhaps the story is true . . .

But even if the story is wrong, volcanos are a fact, the worldwide iridium layer is a fact—most of all, the extinction of most living things some sixty-five million years ago is a fact.

Such times of extinction are real, and there is more than one of them.

Half a dozen times at least they have occurred, in the long history of life on Earth. Over and over, *something* has killed off major fractions of all the living things there existed at the time, whether soft-bodied blobs or giant dinosaurs. If it was not an asteroid strike, it may have been a shower of comets wrenched out of their distant Oort-cloud orbits by an approaching star. Or by wobbles in the sun's orbit around the core of the galaxy. Or by patches of gas between the stars. Or by a distant (but not very distant) star exploding into a supernova and drenching the Earth with lethal radiation; or by a change in climate brought about by a long-term wander in Earth's own orbit (or by a temporary dimming of the sun's radiation) . . . There are any number of possible explanations.

The fact that needs explaining is still there.

Every now and then, at intervals of tens of millions of years, something works mass murder on the Earth—as a householder might, now and then, spray a garden to cut down the number of insect pests.

Of course, the pests will always come back.

Of course, life on Earth has always come back, too.

When the dinosaurs died off, they gave mammals a chance —in the long run, gave us a chance. When any dominating taxa have disappeared, other families of living things have quickly changed and expanded to fill the gaps.

There is a notion among some scientists that life always has survived and flourished, whatever the scope of any disaster, and that it always will—that the life that inhabits the Earth somehow creates a sort of feedback effect, a homeostasis, so that no matter what happens life will survive and proliferate.

This is called "the Gaia hypothesis."

25

When Nancy Chee rapped on the lanai door to tell David that an invasion was on the way, David was furious. "Television reporters? Newspeople?" he raged. "Who gave those people our address? I don't want Stephen bothered like this!"

Neither did she, Nancy Chee explained; the police hadn't told the press about Stephen. Probably it was an airline stew, or maybe one of his fellow passengers—Chindler wasn't exactly a common name, and no one had told the boy to keep his identity a secret. "None of us wants them to disturb the boy," she said forcefully—including Stephen in the "us," though no one had asked him.

Stephen might have surprised them. He'd done that already simply by being tearless and, as far as they could tell, quite poised about the situation. When he was taken to David's house he mentioned that, if there was nothing else pressing, he wouldn't mind getting some of that he-man Hawaiian tan; so he had changed into ragged cutoffs and was sunning himself quietly enough in David's back yard. When spoken to, he responded alertly and politely. When not, he lay with his eyes closed like any Waikiki tourist.

It worried David that the boy seemed so calm. He fussed around for things to offer him. Stephen had declined a game of chess, didn't think he'd like to watch television, asked only to be called as soon as either David or Nancy Chee heard anything. Fretfully David invented excuses to bring him Cokes or bags of highly flavored potato chips out of Kushi's private stock; each time Stephen thanked him nicely and returned to his tan.

But now he would have to interrupt his sunbathing. They couldn't stay in the house, David was sure of that, but where could they go?

It was Nancy's idea to take him up to Volcano Park. The boy's eyes gleamed. "Mom said that was great," he declared, and found a Madonna T-shirt in his bag to put on for the trip.

So they drove the great crater trail clockwise from the hotel—where (no one mentioned) Lono had stolen a getaway car. Nancy Chee drove. David leaned forward from the cramped back seat to offer commentaries, got out with Stephen at the overlook point where the vast crater lay before them. The boy snapped pictures with a little camera, listened with fascination to what David said and asked only questions David was glad to answer. He did not, for example, ask about the Thurston Lava Tube when they passed the signs for it without stopping. Perhaps he didn't see the signs. Or perhaps he knew why they didn't stop.

They paused at the point overlooking Kilauea's summit caldera, called Halemaumau. David and the boy left Nancy in her car, with the radio; and when David pronounced the name of the caldera he felt the boy stiffen. "It isn't MauMau after the Africans," David said quickly. "It's just an old Hawaiian name that sounds the same."

The boy nodded thoughtfully, snapping pictures of the constantly rising volcanic steam. He coughed as he caught a whiff of sulfurous steam and looked up at David.

"Is this where they took my mother?" he asked.

"No," David said unwillingly. "At least, I don't think so. The only place we're sure of is back farther, off the road."

"There wouldn't be anybody around there at night if she called for help," the boy commented.

"No."

"But if he stole a car at that hotel, she could have made some noise then, couldn't she?"

"Well, you would think so," David conceded. "Of course, we don't know. He might have had a knife at her throat or—" David swallowed the rest. The words didn't seem to come out reassuring, no matter how he tried.

The boy was looking absently through the viewfinder of his camera. "Mom said—" he began. David waited, tense. But when the boy finished it was only, "Mom said there were two kinds of lava, pahoehoe and aa. Which is which?"

Gratefully David began to explain. The boy had a good ear and a quick mind—he had even pronounced them correctly, *p'hoyhoy* and *ah-ah*. He was well launched into a description of the fudgy, flat pahoehoe and the crumbly, cindery aa when Nancy Chee came over to suggest that they move on because they seemed to be in a radio dead zone and she was having trouble getting a signal from her headquarters.

In the car, David felt a sense of relief, as though he had escaped something. Well, he had. He had escaped a potentially emotional, possibly even teary scene with the boy as at last Stephen opened up and released his feelings about his mother's plight . . .

But wasn't that exactly what he wanted to encourage?

And yet it was not an unpleasant experience, not unpleasant at all, to be showing Stephen Chindler around the volcano. After that one question they did not refer again to the circumstances that brought him there. Stephen got out with David, clicking busily, as they reached Devastation Trail and he tried to get a picture of the tiny green shrubs that were just beginning to try to find a life for themselves in the hardened lava that was still red hot and liquid just a few yards down. Steam vents puffed out here and there; the sulfur smell was strong. "Wait till my girlfriend sees these," said Stephen, grinning. "They'll make her Yellowstone Park slides look sick!"

When David and the boy got out of the car, Sergeant Chee stayed behind to fuss with the radio. When they were all together, Nancy Chee was as good an audience as Stephen. As they approached the U.S. Coast and Geodetic Survey observatory, David told them about his early apprenticeship to one of its seismologists, and how it changed his life. "He was a wonderful man," David said. "Do you know anything about seismology, Stephen?"

"Not really," Stephen conceded, and Nancy Chee gave a quick, encouraging nod of her own.

"Well," said David, with pleasure, "under the surface here there are huge pockets of molten magma. Think of them as storage tanks of molten rock, with big ones maybe a quarter of a mile down. They fill up as magma seeps up from the core of the Earth. You can tell they're there, sometimes without even instruments, just the naked eye, because they make the surface swell upward, almost like a balloon. Usually the change is too small to see without careful measurement, but you can detect their presence with seismographs. It's almost as though you put a stethoscope on somebody's belly. You could follow the course of what he ate by the sound as it moves. First it's here in the stomach, then in the duodenum, then it's in the small intestine—"

The boy was actually smiling. "And pretty soon it's going to erupt, right?" he grinned.

David smiled back. "It's a little more complicated than that," he said. "The magma doesn't flow through pipes underground. There aren't any pipes. It seeps through crevices, or sometimes there aren't even crevices, it's just that one body of magma is a little hotter than the stuff around it, so it rises while the other descends . . . You'll have to excuse an old professor," he apologized. "It's an occupational disease."

Stephen said happily, "My girlfriend's father is like that. I really like it when he explains things to me."

"I like it too, Dr. Yanami," said Nancy Chee, and she parked in the visitors' lot at the vulcanological observatory so David and the boy could get out. She was right behind them. Still having radio trouble, she disappeared into the building to borrow a phone while David and the boy walked to the edge of the caldera and looked down.

"This is Uwekahuna Bluff," David told Stephen. "My ancestors used to throw sacrifices over the cliff here for Pele, the goddess of the volcano. Sometimes they threw human beings."

"Gee," said David, impressed. Then he pointed at a litter of Coke cans and Big Mac wrappers on the steep slope. "Maybe they still do," he grinned.

"Only now," David grinned back, "the rangers have to climb down there and pick them up." Without thinking he threw an arm around the boy's shoulders, and Stephen accepted it comfortably. Chuckling together, they walked along the rim of the crater.

This was indeed a likable young man, David told himself, exactly what he would have expected from a son of Rachel's. If the father had been moody and hard to live with—well, no matter what the father had been, or who, it was Rachel who had had the raising of the boy, and the result was a son to be proud of. He thought of Kushi's naked hints. It was too bad that, after all, they could come to nothing. Rachel was a sensible woman and certainly not a child, but David could not convince himself that she would take an interest in a man of his age. The very thought was preposterous. Although, David admitted to himself, if by any chance she might not laugh at any advances he might make, that would certainly be a good thing—

Tardily David realized that Nancy Chee was calling to them as she hurried from the observatory to her little Honda. The young woman seemed almost distraught. At first David could not understand her words.

Then he did. "The terrorists?" he repeated. "On Mauna Kea? My grandmother?" And then the words arranged themselves into sense. "My God!" he cried. "Stephen, get in the car. We'd better go there right now!"

David's weight made the shock absorbers of the little car bottom out as they bumped across the cattle guard and started up the mountain. "We should have four-wheel drive," Nancy fretted. "Maybe we should wait for the backup cars—"

But she didn't wait for an answer, or expect one; none of them wanted to wait. Probably, she told herself, the police cars were well ahead of them by now, though it was worrisome that she'd lost radio contact again. When they were well up the mountain, there wouldn't be any problem, though—

At least, she corrected herself, not with the radio.

Stephen was gaping at the warning sign by the side of the road, threatening dire conditions and serious consequences for the traveler who ventured past. "It's like *The Wizard of Oz*," he marveled. "No food, no toilets, no turn-around—they really don't want us up here, do they?"

They really didn't. The little car didn't much want to be there, either; it bounced stiff-legged on the narrow gravel road, the slidy surface making the rail-less drop to the side look even more dangerous than it was. Nancy didn't answer the boy, but darted a quick look at David Yanami. The old man didn't answer either. He was hunched to the side of the little car, neck craned to peer up at the peak, bright in the sun still, though the lower parts of the island were already beginning to be in shadow.

David Yanami was more tense than she had ever seen him, Nancy Chee realized. Afraid of what they might find? Scared by the drive up the treacherous road? Concerned for the boy with them? More than any of those, she thought. It was Rachel who was in his thoughts, not with just the natural concern of a householder for a guest and friend, more like the anxious fears of—a lover? Was that possible? Once you looked past the snowy hair and eyebrows, David Yanami was by no means a fossil, but still, the difference in age was—was about as much, Nancy thought, as her own whole life span.

Those were interesting thoughts, and a lot pleasanter than any of the others that crowded through her mind, but Nancy Chee really had no time for reveries. The car required as much attention as she had to give. They jolted around a switchback, the loosely compacted rocks and lava cinders slithering randomly under their wheels. The road was a pretty impromptu affair at best. The gravel was sometimes good-sized rocks, and now and then a chunk a foot long that Nancy had to swerve to avoid—with her heart in her mouth, as each swerve slid them toward the downhill side. "Downhill" here meant *steeply* downhill, sometimes a plunging fall of several hundred feet. And still no guardrail.

As the winding of the road hid the peak from sight, David Yanami turned from the window and blinked at the other two. He seemed to realize that both were nervous. He smiled that great jack-o'-lantern smile and began to lecture. "This road," he announced, "used to be even worse, if you'll believe it. When I was a boy—"

And he began a long story about his membership in the Waimea Astronomical Federation, pompous name for a dozen callow kids with their laboriously hand-ground three-inch reflector that they'd carried halfway up this mountain to watch the stars. And other things. "Sometimes," said David, "we called it the W.A.F.—Whales And Frails, because if we came up before dark we'd use it to look at the ocean and the girls sunbathing on the beaches—"

He didn't stop talking, the whole way up. For that Nancy Chee was grateful; it helped to keep them all from thinking too much about what they might find. She kept her window down, hoping (or fearing) to hear something from above—a fusillade of gunfire, maybe, as the police cars got up there. But of course there was nothing. Distance and the wind made it impossible to hear anything, even if there had been anything to hear.

Stephen looked curiously at the old man as he talked on, but he seemed to be content to let David do what he was obviously trying to do. Now and then the boy stared curiously out the window. Nancy could almost read his mind as Stephen recognized, first, snow on the other side of one knife-edged ravine—snow in Hawaii!—and then gazed down with dawning understanding at the whiteness that filled another ravine that was not snow at all, but a cloud. The *top* of a cloud. Seen from above!

"We're pretty nearly there," said David Yanami, catching the boy's concern. "Now, at the top there are four or five really large telescopes in their domes—optical, infrared, all sorts of instruments—"

"Nearly there" was optimistic, but it was true that they were very high on the mountain. At eleven thousand feet the air became distinctly colder, and one of the clouds that hung around the mountain passed over them, turning into a pelting, gray, opaque storm of slanting, falling drops. Nancy Chee suddenly thought that she had not remembered to call on the radio to let them know where she was; but it was too late to think of that just then, because the Datsun took both hands and all her attention. Its engine labored and gasped. It had no power at all. It was, after all, deprived of forty percent of its oxygen, up more than two miles above the ground level, as though the carburetor had been choked off . . .

And then they were there.

The road broadened. Up ahead loomed a round white

dome, half obscured in the passing cloud. There was a second dome behind the first, just visible through the windshield wipers; that was as far as Nancy could see.

Of the police cars she had expected to find there there was no sign.

As David Yanami struggled his huge body out of the car he was aware of the policewoman, still at the wheel, raising her radio microphone to her lips. He didn't wait to hear what might be said. He was out of the car, running ponderously through the sandblasting sleet toward the nearest dome, and Stephen was close behind him.

David had not allowed himself to dwell on what they might find on the peak of Mauna Kea, but none of the images that had flashed through his mind had been anything like the fact. There were no police cars. There were no armed terrorists in sight. There was nothing. No one. No sign that anyone had ever been here, except for a couple of parked vehicles, dimly visible through the sleet, with no one near them.

Even in that moment David was aware of an incongruity: there was a light burning over the door at the base of the nearest observatory dome. A light! A major reason for putting telescopes on remote mountains was to get away from light of any kind; even Palomar was being poisoned by the lights of filling stations and hamburger stands creeping up the mountain. It made sense to have a light over any door in the world—except the door to an astronomical observatory.

Which said something about the kind of weather that might be expected here from time to time. Such a light could not be meant for use at night.

It also did not mean that the dome was occupied, it turned out. The door was locked. There was no bell. Hammering on the door as hard as he could, David could get no answer— could hardly hear the sound of his own knocking over the noise of the hurricane wind. Now it was thrusting irregularly, and the sleety precipitation was melting inside David's collar and coat, as the setting sun began to poke its way through the fringes of the moving cloud.

They *had* to be here somewhere. It was impossible that anyone could have left the peak without passing them on the way down—almost impossible that anyone could have passed, for that matter, on that narrow and treacherous road. David snapped to the boy, "We'll try the next dome!"—and he was turned to run toward it when he felt the boy dragging at his arm.

"No!" Stephen yelled, pointing. "Sergeant Chee's calling us back!"

Even though the sun had begun to shine from one quarter of the sky, the sleet was still falling from another. Its icy wetness almost blinded them as they ran back to the car. Nancy Chee was leaning out and shouting, "We're not supposed to be here! The city police were called back so a team of special Navy experts could come in first!"

"Experts!" snarled David. "Trained to do what?"

"That was an order!" said Nancy Chee. "Get in! We've got to go back down, at least to that wide place at the last curve—"

"Hell," said David, "that's my grandmother they've got there!"

And Stephen added:

"And that's my mother!"

"But we can't stay here," Nancy Chee began.

And indeed they couldn't. Something *splat-spinged* off the hood of the Datsun.

Chee reacted at once. She shoved the car into reverse and backed at high speed behind the nearby dome, David and Stephen running to follow. She gestured them down and was out of the car in an instant, quick and efficient, her police .38 already in her hand, ducking down behind the hood of the car, peering cautiously around it. The others followed her example . . .

And waited.

At the cracked-open doorway of the next dome, peering past the huge bulk of the terrorist Kanaloa, Kushi saw the car vanish. She had her arm around Rachel. It was interesting, she thought with approval, that the little haole woman was not shaking with fear. There was plenty of reason to be scared, all right. Not just for Rachel, but for Kushi herself and for the people in the other car. Not to mention the man with the gunshot wound in his shoulder—Plitt? something like that—who had seemed to have something to do with the radio Kanaloa had been sweating over and cursing at, until he took time out to try to kill her grandkid. She had got to the door too late to do anything about that, but the ugly one had obviously missed anyway.

In the quick glimpse she had had through the narrow opening and the thinning sleet, she was sure she had recognized David. She was almost as sure of the pretty pak policewoman, even almost sure of Rachel's son. It was brave of them all to be there, she thought. That too deserved approval. But why had they not come with fifty policemen with rapid-fire weapons?

The huge terrorist whirled from the door to confront her, his Uzi leveled at her belly. "You lied to me," he snarled, like the rumbling of a great cat. "You told them you were following us!"

Kushi released Rachel and gently pushed her away; no use involving her in this matter. "You crazy, you Kanaloa," she observed. It did not come out as an insult. It was simply a statement of conviction.

The big man gazed at her, eye to eye. Then he turned away as the other haole woman, the one who had the insane effrontery to call herself "Pele," cried, "What are we going to do, Kanaloa?"

Kanaloa looked her up and down. "Take that stupid thing off your head," he purred. Hastily Meg Barnhart reached up to the askew blonde wig and threw it to the floor. Since the crisis no longer seemed immediate, Kushi reached out for Rachel again. It was a pity, she thought, that the terrorists had all the weapons. Barehanded, she would have been willing to chance a fight. She would certainly lose, one on one against Kanaloa. But she would also certainly hurt him a lot in the process. Rachel no doubt could take care of the mainland bitch, and, even with his shoulder wound, the man named Plitt could perhaps handle her great-grandson Lono—Kushi sighed hugely. She did not like thinking about her great-grandson Lono. Even he had a gun now, a little foreign pistol of some kind, and though he returned her stare boldly when she looked straight at him, she could also see that his eyes were clouded and worried when he thought no one saw.

"What we will do," said Kanaloa's deep voice, "is kill them. Lono will take the Uzi and go around the dome to the left. I'll come from the right and draw fire from the woman. Whichever one of us hears a shot first runs around and catches her from behind. Do you understand?"

Lono locked eyes with him. He said clearly, "That's a mistake. We're blown, Kanaloa. We need them for hostages."

"But we already have six hostages," Kanaloa said pleasantly.

Lono looked startled for a moment. He glanced toward the bodies at the back, the other radio specialist and the two security guards who had been with him when the terrorists stormed the dome. "Three of them are dead," he pointed out.

"But no one knows they're dead but us," smiled Kanaloa, negligently shifting position as he cradled the Uzi in his hand.

"It won't work," Lono said doggedly.

"It will. Only the woman has a gun, I think."

"You think!"

"Oh, yes," said the giant. "I think that. I also think that you don't want to kill your uncle, but you have no choice."

"Do it, Lono!" cried the woman, Pele. Still the boy hesitated. "Do it now, before somebody else comes here!"

Lono stared at her. His face was like carved wood, hard, drained of emotion. Whatever his thoughts were, his expression showed none of them. He looked at his great-grandmother with the same total blankness, then at Rachel.

Then, to Kushi's surprise, he leaned to kiss Rachel full on the lips. He turned from her to Kanaloa. "We only kill the policewoman," he said definitely, took the Uzi from the giant and walked out into the clearing dusk.

Pele said nervously, "Give him time to get around behind her."

Kanaloa gave her a look of disdain, but all he said was, "Give me the carbine." He took it to the door, checking the action.

And Kushi, with a deep, soundless sigh, let go of Rachel again.

Over against the wall of the entry cubicle Plitt, the wounded radio man, was holding his shoulder in silence; but his eyes had been watching everything. Kushi glanced at him, then at Pele. Whether he understood her or not she could not say; but past Kanaloa in the doorway she had seen someone peeping incautiously out from behind the dome of the Canadian-French telescope. It must have been the pak girl. Kanaloa would look that way in a minute—unless she prevented it.

"You, Kanaloa," she said conversationally, walking toward him. "You radio"—hum—"sound busted to me."

Kanaloa glanced at the abandoned radio, whistling faintly to itself just as he had left it. Then, understanding, he began to turn back to the doorway.

Kushi moved.

Kushi was no more in the habit of moving fast than an elephant, for the same reasons. But, like an elephant, when she had to hurry she could be very quick indeed. Kanaloa was big. Kushi was, if anything, a dozen pounds or more bigger. She made no attempt to hit him. She simply reached her huge arms out to his shoulders and fell on him. Off balance, he toppled, all her weight crushing him, trying at the last minute to turn on her.

He did not entirely fail. The gun turned.

Kushi felt the .44 slug enter her body with surprise and almost amusement. What joke! All these years, you only die if somebody shoots you in belly!

She heard a scream from inside the dome—the man Plitt, doing something to the woman, Pele, no doubt; and two more shots from inside told her that he had not succeeded. That was too bad. It was too bad, too, that underneath her Kanaloa was writhing to throw her off. The breath was knocked out of him, but he was big enough and strong enough to get free. Kushi made his job harder. With the strength left to her she brought her huge knee up, hard, into his groin. He grunted in pain; but the advantage was not Kushi's. She felt something tear inside her with the effort, and a sudden, agonizing rush of blood. Outside, she saw her great-grandson, Lono, turn in astonishment, and then, belatedly, whirl back to a new danger.

He was too late.

Two four-wheel Navy Jeepsters roared into the parking lot. Six men fanned out of each. Even before the first of them was out of the vehicle some had fired, and Lono went down in a fusillade of fire, his chest torn to ribbons.

Kushi sighed from the bottom of her lungs—almost a wail; and the pain was not only from the savaged cat's-meat inside her body.

She saw the men racing toward the dome where she lay, and behind them her grandson and Rachel's son and the pak policewoman racing toward her; and then her vision blurred.

When it cleared again, David was bending over her. "You David!" she said strongly. "You take care of Rach' and Rach' kid, okay?"

He looked startled, then almost embarrassed. But what he mostly looked was worried. "Don't talk now, Kushi," he begged. "You'll be all right. We'll get doctors, we'll get you to the hospital—"

"Not true, David," she scolded gently, and pushed him a little away so that she could see better. Two of the men from the Jeepsters were dragging the limping Kanaloa to the edge of the parking lot, their guns drawn, while another dragged the haole woman terrorist after him. That was quite strange, Kushi thought.

And, even stranger, the rest of the men from the Navy vehicles were standing watching, with their guns ready. When the men scattered away from the terrorists, the others all opened fire at once.

The two terrorists were dead before they hit the ground.

"Why they do that?" Kushi croaked incredulously.

And then was more incredulous still, as she saw that the firing squad had turned. Their guns were now pointed at David, at Stephen, at the policewoman, even at Rachel and herself.

"Crazy," moaned Kushi regretfully.

But it was no longer her problem. The men did not fire. They simply stood there, waiting, some of them glancing up toward a distant noise.

With the last of her sight Kushi saw something fluttering through the scattering clouds toward the mountaintop, bobbing dangerously in the violent drafts around the peak. It could have been a helicopter . . . or it could have been something else.

"You kick all their asses good, Pele," Kushi ordered, but

could not wait to see if it were done.

She felt a sudden final gush of blood and raised her eyes to her grandson. Good-by, David, you good kid, she said—or thought she said. Good-by, Rach', Stephen. Good-by, Lono. Too bad you went lousy but it too late for you now . . .

And then it was also too late for Kushi, ever.

26

Considered as a laboratory problem in physical chemistry, the planet Earth is in a puzzling state. There's too much oxygen in the air, and too little salt in the sea; the whole planet is in a low-entropy condition.

"Entropy" is one of those terms which is easy to observe but not very easy to understand. It means the tendency of closed systems to go from order to disorder. If you have an ice cube and a cup of hot tea, that is an ordered, or low-entropy, system: one thing is quite cold, another is quite hot, and that is a kind of order. If you then put the ice cube into the hot tea, before long you have lukewarm and weaker tea. There is less order in the system; entropy has become higher.

Are there systems which maintain low entropy for long periods of time?

Yes. There are organized structures with low entropy, which maintain that structure by throughputs of energy. Erwin Schroedinger defined these structures in 1944. They are what is called "life."

That particular trait of living things which tries to keep order high and entropy low has a name, too. It is called "homeostasis." The planet Earth (or at least that part of it which lies between the crust of the planet and, say, the ozone layer high in the atmosphere) seems to be homeostatic. For example: If you put a sample of the Earth's atmosphere in a bell jar, along with a sample of wood from a forest, and ignite them, they will burn. They will go on burning until either the amount of oxygen in the air or the amount of carbon in the wood is reduced to a level too low to support burning.

But outside the bell jar it is quite different. The air is there, with its oxygen. The wood is there, in the form of forests. The ignition is there, if from nothing else, then now and then from lightning striking a tall tree. Combustion begins, just as in the bell jar. But long before it reaches depletion of either the oxygen or the carbon, it stops; usually, a rainstorm puts it out. There is *always* available carbon on the surface and available oxygen in the air. The reaction never goes all the way. Moreover, once the forest fire is over, new growth begins, and before long the carbon/oxygen relationship is back to its starting point . . . which is homeostasis.

It is not an accident that that part of the Earth between crust and ozone layer is called the "biosphere," because it meets Schroedinger's definition of a living thing. Forests regenerate after a fire. New forms of life evolve and expand to repopulate the Earth after an extinction. With the aid of the "throughput of energy" (which comes almost entirely from the radiation of the sun), the structure maintains its low-entropy state.

This is not simply to say that there are living things in the biosphere; that's obvious. It is to say that all these living things taken together—insects and elephants, microorganisms and redwoods, cabbages and kings—constitute a sort of single, collective, unitary living entity.

In 1974 James Lovelock and some other scientists, first at the Jet Propulsion Laboratories, more recently at the Marine Biological Laboratory in Plymouth, England, gave a name to this entity. They call it "Gaia."

The Gaia hypothesis states that life on Earth (taken collectively) not only endeavors to stay alive and to reproduce, but even takes steps to make sure that life on Earth will remain possible forever.

It is a comforting kind of scientific hypothesis. It may even be a true one.

The Gaia hypothesis takes cognizance of the facts that there is too much oxygen in the air and too little salt in the sea.

If the oxygen were to be removed from the air, every animal on the face of the Earth would die at once. So, somewhat later, would every animal in the oceans, because what supports them is the oxygen in the sea that dissolves out of the air. How does the oxygen to support living things get in the air? Why, living things create it. Plants take solar energy, reduce carbon dioxide to its elements, use the carbon for their own purposes and release the oxygen.

The salt in the sea is a more serious problem.

The way salt gets into the sea (most of it, anyway) is from rain. Water drops fall on the land, form rivers, descend to rejoin the sea. As they go, they leach salts out of the land and carry the salt burden with them. Then those same water molecules evaporate from the surface of the sea as the sun warms it, to form rain clouds and repeat the process. As they evaporate they leave the salts behind them. Therefore, little by little, as the ages progress, the sea gets saltier and saltier.

Only it doesn't.

Calculation shows that, starting from oceans of chemically pure, salt-free water, the amount of salt deposited every year would bring the seas to their present salt content in only the twinkling of an eye—well, some sixty million years.

But the oceans have been on the Earth for far more than sixty million years. They have been around for more than three *billion* years, and all the evidence of fossil sea life and deposited marine sediments indicates that the salt content has been just about what it is now for all that time.

By now the seas should be a sludgy brine, so saline that none of the sea creatures could survive. The osmotic pressure of the salts in a living system would not be great enough to expel wastes from their bodies. The oceans would be dead and therefore so would the land before long, since it is ocean plants that keep the land animals alive.

We even know where the salt goes. Shallow seas dry up and leave huge lenses of pure crystal salts; then these are covered over by the bottoms of later seas (a race between deposition of sediment and dissolving of the great salt masses, usually won by the sediments) or are left more or less open to the sky in salt licks in desert areas.

But we don't know *how* this happens—so uniformly and consistently, over billions of years. Lovelock's Gaia hypothesis, even, doesn't give an answer. But Lovelock asks a question—perhaps more than half in jest: "Is it possible that the Great Barrier Reef . . . is the partly finished project for an evaporation lagoon?"

Or, less fancifully, is it that life somehow continually modifies the oceans themselves, as life is known to have modified the atmosphere, for the general good and welfare of life?

If the Gaia hypothesis is true, there is reason to hope that life on Earth will survive almost any catastrophe, at least until the planet itself dies.

There is nothing in the Gaia hypothesis, however, that says that any of that surviving life must be human beings.

27

Bouncing down the mountain was even scarier than coming up, because the sun had set. Most of the road was in deep shadow. Stephen Chindler had not clung to his mother in more than a dozen years, but he clung to her now. Not for his sake. For hers. "It's all right, Mom," he whispered in her ear, pressing close against her as the Jeepster slid and slithered around the slippery roadway.

"It's not," she said definitely. She didn't look at him. Of course, that was true. Stephen looked over his mother's head to the old Hawaiian dude on the other side. David Yanami shrugged, as though to say, she's right, you know. She was. Nothing was all right when there was a man in the front seat watching them, with a machine-pistol in his hand. He had taken off the riot helmet, and the face underneath was a young black man's—not a terrible one like Mr. T, maybe even a friendly one like Eddie Murphy—but he hadn't put the gun down.

And, especially, nothing was all right when they had just seen five people die.

It was too many, really. Sure, some of them deserved it— the big guy with the wicked eyes and the skinny lady; you could understand that. You sort of expected that, Stephen thought. When the lawmen came in to clean out the saloon, the rustlers got perforated in the shoot-out. But the old Jap lady wasn't a rustler. She was an *old lady*! And the man named Plitt had only been doing his job—and what about the three others that the big mean guy had killed before they got there?

And what about the tall, kind of Puerto Rican–looking kid? If he had been a bad guy, it was funny, Stephen thought, that his mother had cried over the body.

What a mess!

The Jeepster slammed on its brakes and skidded to a stop at the one and only level place on the downhill road, barely missing the big white helicopter that was waiting there with its rotor turning over. "Watch what you're doing!" Stephen said belligerently to the black guy with the machine-pistol as their captors invited them out—no, *pulled* them out. The man didn't answer. He only looked at Stephen with a kind of disgusted expression, as though Stephen had made a terrible gaffe, like farting in public. "Get into the chopper," he ordered, and he gave Stephen another push.

Under other circumstances that trip would have been pretty neat. The helicopter was a great Sikorsky Sea Rescue craft, big enough to hold them all. When they were inside and strapped down it hopped into the air, bounced around in the turbulence and straightened out to head south. Stephen had never been in a helicopter before. It wasn't at all like a DC-10. He twisted around in the bucket seat to see what was below—it was so *close!*—and saw the Mauna Kea slopes fall away beneath them and the helicopter dodge around Mauna Loa, swing back south and east over the bare lava decline south of Volcano National Park, out over the dark sea. He could hear David Yanami talking quietly to his mother, so she was all right —right now, anyway—

Stephen did not think past right now. He didn't have the knowledge to form any theories about what would happen next. What he had thought he knew had turned out to be wrong. The script in his head had called for rescuing his mother from the terrorists, no doubt with a lot of people in uniform shooting a lot of guns—yes, that part was all right; check. But it hadn't said a word about being whisked away as prisoners! Where were the TV cameras and the publishers' reps offering book contracts? When did they hear from the Johnny Carson show and "Good Morning, America?" Was any of that going to happen?

It didn't look that way. Stephen's dream script had not included landing on a ship's deck in the middle of the whole damned Pacific Ocean and being ordered at gun point down into what they called a wardroom. It was all so wrong that he didn't even enjoy the wonder of being there. For one thing, he was tired. By St. Louis time he should have been asleep hours ago, not made to sit down on a hard metal chair in a room with armed guards at the door. This time when he jumped to be next to his mother it was as much for his own sake as hers.

From the other side of her, the old professor was staring at a mousy little man who sat primly erect against a wall. "I know you," David Yanami cried. "I saw you in the men's room on New Year's Eve."

The man said with great displeasure, "Indeed you did, Dr. Yanami, very unfortunately for both of us." And, standing by the head of the table, thumbing through papers, a man in sports clothes looked up to twinkle:

"I'm afraid he's right, Dr. Yanami. It's a pity you had to become involved. You see, you've all now become national assets."

Stephen Chindler gripped his mother's hand fiercely. He did not like that man in the hundred-dollar pullover and the snow-white Adidas. He did not like, or understand, any part of what was going on, and least of all did he like, or understand, the look on his mother's face, half a smile, half teary-eyed, when she whispered to him, "Oh, hon, I'm so *tired* of being somebody's asset."

Arkady Bor, on the other hand, understood very well what was happening. If he didn't exactly like it, at least it was a change. From the bottom one can go in only one direction. For Bor it seemed that perhaps the worst had passed. He did not allow himself to hope for any happy ending for him. Happy endings were for children's stories. It was far too early to risk that, and the evidence far too slim.

Still, there was evidence of an upturn. He had not been returned to his cell. He had even been permitted—or was it ordered?—to stay with General Danforth and Jameson Burford for most of the last hour, not counting, of course, the time when that other general, the starrier one named Brandywine, had flown in from Sandia and disappeared with the others for a short, serious talk in private. Burford had come out of that meeting looking hangdog and worried, and that was a very good thing in itself for Arkady Bor.

So perhaps, Bor reflected comfortably, he was not a prisoner anymore, but simply an internee. For someone who had been a guest of the Chekists that was nothing at all! Moreover, now he had all these others to share his confinement. The KGB woman still languished in the brig, he supposed, or at least he did not see her now, but there were new additions to his little party all the time. First the man named Frank Morford, bitterly protesting the invasion of his personal liberties when he was taken from wherever he had been and flown to Vulcan. Now more. As they were waiting for the helicopter to land from Mauna Kea, standing in the brisk wind under the darkening Pacific sky, Bor had even dared to call to General Danforth, "This should clear up any remaining security problems, eh, general?"

But it had been General Brandywine who answered, three stars asserting priority over two. "There are no security problems on Project Vulcan, Dr. Bor," he smiled, watching the helicopter lower itself delicately to the pad. "I do not allow them." And General Danforth himself, though not speaking, had given Bor a long, calculating look.

So when they were all in the wardroom, Bor refused himself the risky luxury of hope of any kind. He simply studied his companions, the survivors of that violent massacre on the peak of Mauna Kea of which he had heard only fragments. The American woman, her son, the old Oriental—they did not seem the right people to be in such violence. But then, who was? Not Bor himself, to be sure! All he asked was a quiet life, the respect of those around him—and, of course, yes, the freedom to conduct a personal life with other persons who shared his interests. And he had been torn away from peaceful pursuits to such terrible ordeals!

At least, he thought bitterly, he had the excuse that he could not help himself. Why hadn't the Americans fought back? Their laws guaranteed them all sorts of freedoms. Why did they not demand them? Yet they had all come so easily, just like a Moscow householder who hears the 3 A.M. knock on the door. Why were they so passive?

Bor had no answer, never having heard of the Stockholm syndrome.

When the stewards had passed coffee around and disappeared, General Brandywine stood up. "With your permission, Jacob," he said politely to the other general, the one in the sports shorts, "I'd like to explain some background to our guests. You are on a vessel of the United States Navy, engaged in an essential defense operation called 'Project Vulcan.' I must apologize to you all for the inconveniences that entails. More than that," he went on, his voice taking on the tones of a minister preaching the eulogy for a deceased he had never met, "I ask you, Professor Yanami, to accept our deep sympathy for the death of your grandmother. I am sure you take pride in the fact that she gave her life willingly, fighting against terrorists. But I know she was a wonderful woman, whose loss is greatly felt." David Yanami didn't reply. He was not even looking at the general; all his attention seemed to be on Rachel Chindler. The general nodded as though he had been thanked and went on.

"I cannot at present tell you any details about Project Vulcan, except to say that I believe it is absolutely essential to the survival of the United States and all of the free world. Like any military man, my deepest desire is peace. Project Vulcan offers us the prospect of world peace, forever. I think all of us share that goal—that dream, I would have said not long ago. But Vulcan can make that dream real!" He glanced casually at Arkady Bor, but Bor was ready for it. His face was impassive.

"However," General Brandywine said, "like any wea—like any device, the Vulcan technology can be used for destructive purposes. The terrorist gang you three have just escaped from nearly caused a serious incident. One element of the device was emplaced on Mauna Kea. Four of our personnel were there, conducting tests, when they were attacked, and three of them were killed, by the terrorists. The fourth was Commander William Plitt, who himself was wounded and later killed. Our losses, too, are great, you see," he added somberly. "It is a harsh world we live in. From time to time we are all reminded of that fact. I wish I could promise you that the difficulties are over. Unfortunately, they can't be, as yet."

He paused, as though for questions. David Yanami spoke up at once, though the question was unrelated to anything the general had said. "What have you done with Nancy Chee?" he demanded.

The general was unfazed. "Sergeant Chee is a police officer. She is at present no doubt in her headquarters in Hilo, being debriefed. It is possible she will join us here later."

"Why?" asked David, and simultaneously Frank Morford blustered: "I don't belong here, either! What are you going to do with me?"

The general said soberly, "You all present a serious problem in security. I regret to say that you are all going to be required to stay here, or at some other restricted area, for a period of time. It may be quite long. I don't think it is possible that it will be less than the best part of a year."

Frank Morford glared. David Yanami started up from his seat. But Stephen was ahead of all of them. "You can't do that!" he yelled. "It's illegal!"

"Watch your mouth," snapped General Danforth, but his senior shook his head at him. He addressed himself to Stephen.

"I certainly would not break the law," said General Brandywine earnestly. "The law gives us this right, son. In several ways. First, this is a matter of national security; certain ordinary laws simply don't apply. Second, I'm afraid that some of you—not you, young man, but all of the rest of you—have been guilty in one degree or another of illegal acts. Some of you might even be charged as co-conspirators, or accessories after the fact, in acts of terrorism. But that legal point doesn't have to bother any of you," he said pleasantly, "because there are some hard realities here. You know things that you can't be allowed to communicate. If you did pass that sort of information on, you would be shot for treason. It is to your own interest that we make sure you don't do that."

For the first time in many days Arkady Bor laughed out loud. It started out as a laugh, anyway; he changed it into a racking cough as he felt the general's eyes on him. Bor bent over, his hand spread over his face. But inside he was still laughing. These Americans! The looks on their faces! So at last they could learn what the world was like! Such words as "freedom" and "democracy" were truly pretty words, to be sure, but could be taken seriously only when times were good and problems small.

Bor straightened up, patting his mouth with a pocket hand-kerchief, nodding apologetically to the others as he resumed watching the performance. How well General Brandywine handled this situation! Even the Chekists would have admired it, Bor thought, as the general said easily, "Of course, none of you are going to be shot or sent to jail, and do you know why? Because we aren't going to force you into anything at all. We won't have to. I know that every one of you is a loyal Ameri-can. When you have had a chance to understand the position, I am sure that you will be as determined as any of us here at Project Vulcan to make sure that our work succeeds."

Morford looked truculent, but it was David Yanami who spoke. "I don't think I can be made to understand cold-blooded murder, General Brandywine."

The general nodded seriously. "You are referring to the shooting of Murray Pereira and Margaret Barnhart, of course. Pereira was part of a group who deliberately and as you say cold-bloodedly killed a whole planeload of innocent tourists—among other things. Barnhart was a member of the Weather Underground and a number of other groups in America—on the mainland, that is," he corrected himself, almost with a smile. "She is known to have killed at least twice, in person, before coming back to Hawaii."

He glanced over at the other general, who had been listening with stern agreement. "The photograph, Jacob?" he asked politely.

"Yes, sir," said General Danforth, hurriedly passing over a small envelope to his superior. Brandywine pulled a photograph out and displayed it to Rachel. "There is also this man," he said. "Do you recognize him?"

Rachel glanced at it quickly, then away. The face was unmistakable. What was also unmistakable was that the photograph had been taken after his death. "He's the one they called 'Ku,'" she said. "I think his real name was Oscar Mariguchi. I saw him shoot my friend Esther in the airplane."

"Exactly," nodded General Brandywine, admiring the photograph for a moment before returning it to General Danforth. "He was shot while attempting to escape. So you see, they're all dead. And no loss to the world."

"I don't doubt that's true, general," said David, "but they didn't get a trial."

"You didn't *see* a trial," the general corrected. "In time of war there isn't always time for a civilian-style hearing. That's a matter of law, professor. The court-martial is an accepted fact of military jurisprudence in all nations. Please remember, we are not vigilantes! We do only what we have to do as a wartime necessity, under the wartime rules of law. Of course," he added, conceding the point, "you could argue whether or not we are in a state of war at this time. But that isn't your decision to make. It's the President's. He has authorized what we are doing."

"Did he authorize employing terrorists?" Morford put in waspishly.

The general looked surprised. "Do you mean the Kamehameha Korps? But we didn't employ them; we *subverted* them. Some of them. That's a very legitimate ruse de guerre. Even in time of peace, law-enforcement agencies are always allowed to infiltrate criminal conspiracies; how else could they be kept from succeeding? In any case, the results of all this will be worth any temporary sacrifice. Not just for us. For the entire human race. Once Project Vulcan is in place the Russians would never dare attack the United States with nuclear weapons, because it would be the end of their life as a nation. But that's not all."

He gazed earnestly around at them, his hands clasped before him almost as though in prayer. "You see," he said, "once Vulcan is operational and certain other preparations are complete—perhaps by next winter—the President will announce it. At the same time, he will call for complete, worldwide nuclear disarmament, to be enforced by inspection. This won't be a plea. It will be an order, for if it doesn't happen we will set off Vulcan. America," he beamed, "will indeed be the policeman of the world, from then on, and we will use our power wisely. *No more war*. The fifty thousand nuclear warheads in the world will never go off. The human race will be free of fear again, for the first time in more than forty years."

He looked around benignly, then clapped his hands. At

once the door opened and a pair of messboys came in to lay a table. "Now," he said, "General Danforth and I have some matters to attend to, and I know you all must be hungry. So enjoy a dinner while you think over what I have just said, and we'll see you again after your meal."

Dinner was steaks, and out of General Danforth's private freezer, Arkady Bor was sure; they were thick, juicy and tender. He ate with a good appetite, even the ubiquitous french fries and the green beans that went with them. It had after all been quite a long time since he had had a decent meal! It did not in the least deter him that none of the others did more than pick at their food, not counting, of course, Rachel's son, who matched Bor forkful for forkful and managed to drink three cans of Pepsi-Cola as well. It was only natural that the others should have no appetites. They had not known what the world was like before.

It was enjoyable to watch them learn.

They were rather slow about it, he thought critically, rapping his water glass for a refill from the messman. True, Frank Morford had offered, early on, "I suppose, in a way, in time of war everybody is supposed to get behind the country." No one had responded. After a minute Stephen had begun to question his mother about her ordeal. No one addressed Bor, except for an occasional "Please pass the salt." He was content merely to listen. It was interesting, he thought, that this Chindler woman seemed to gloss over some parts of her adventure, especially the first night of her captivity. But about her conversations with the terrorists she was very articulate. She did not seem at all upset when she said that the boy, Lono, had admitted from the first that they might well murder her. The others had made it definite. "They offered me a chance," she said. "They said I could join them—like Patty Hearst, when she took the name of Tania and helped hold up banks." She sliced a piece off her cooling steak and chewed it for a moment. "I didn't know about the note they'd sent the authorities until David told me. But I didn't expect to get away alive."

Arkady Bor pushed his plate away. "Coffee now," he said to the messman who came to take it, and studied the cart that was being pushed through the door. It contained sliced melons and pineapple on trays in beds of ice, and the lower tier held two kinds of pie. There was no cheese, of course, and certainly no liqueur. Philosophically Bor accepted a piece of some sort of berry pie and a few slices of honeydew melon. One ate when one could in a camp, and what else was this ship now?

He shut his ears to the others' conversation and appraised them in a different way. Would he spend the next part of his life with these people? Did they present any interesting possibilities? The woman was not a hopelessly unattractive prospect, though a little older than Bor preferred; but from the way David Yanami hovered over her there would be competition. Frank Morford was also rather old. But the boy—he was quite a good-looking boy, Bor thought, and not a bit too old. No doubt there would be risks if Bor were to make any advances—

He almost laughed. Imagine worrying about risks now! In what way could he now do himself any real harm?

He realized the others were looking at him. "Oh," he said, "sorry. I was thinking only that we all may be together for quite a long time."

None of them seemed to enjoy that thought. The boy, Stephen, asked, "Will we stay on a ship like this?"

"Oh, I think not," said Bor politely. "There are many useful islands, after all. Ascension. Kwajalein. Perhaps one of the little islands near Puerto Rico—excuse me, I do not know much about your American colonies, but there must be many under military control. Of course, you will all be asked to write letters to your relatives to say that you are there of your own free will and such other lies. And, of course, the letters will be censored. Do not try any silliness with codes for, I assure you, the censors are quite astute."

He helped himself to more of the pie, quite enjoying the looks the others turned on him. Yes, he thought, he could do worse than remain with this group for the next part of his life. They would come to realize that his experience made him their natural leader. The boy in particular would learn to respect Bor, and with respect, who knew what else might come? They would be held for at least the rest of this year, he calculated. Much would depend on the summer's harvest in America. If the granaries were full, that would be the time to do the job.

First to increase pressure all around the globe—aid to rebels, intervention in local wars, raising the temperature all around until the Soviet Union was on the edge of some boldness of its own—then the announcement.

But not without full granaries; the Americans themselves would not want to be hungry. So the timetable might be delayed for a year, even for two. But they might not be bad years. "We must insist on a stipend," he announced out loud. "It will be useful to order things from stores in the cities. We can make our lives quite enjoyable, I think."

They were all looking at him again. "How do you know so much about it?" Stephen asked.

Bor smiled. Already the beginnings of respect! "It is much the same all around the world," he said. "Trust me, I will show you how to make it all tolerable. Ah, here come our hosts once more!"

And General Brandywine was actually smiling as he came in, the kind of Christmas Eve smile that promises a pleasant surprise to come. "I have good news," he announced. "While Jacob and I were in conference, I sent a message to Washington, and I got an affirmative answer. There is a way out for you. For some of you. Perhaps."

He gazed benignly around the table, his eyes resting on Stephen. "For a bright young man like you," he added, "it may even be just the career you are looking for."

Stephen scowled, pressing his mother's arm. "What kind of career?"

"Intelligence, son," General Brandywine chuckled. "It can take care of your education; it can give you training that will be worth a fortune, it can give you the kind of life work that any decent American would jump at. Besides," he added, the smile broadening, "remember the old motto. 'If you can't beat 'em, join 'em.' And you certainly can't beat us, can you? As to you, Dr. Morford, you're already cleared; there would be no problem in putting you on staff. It's a little more difficult for you, Mrs. Chindler and Dr. Yanami; you'd have to go through a thorough security check. But we do have some information about you both, and there's nothing that looks troublesome."

Morford said interestedly, "What would we have to do?"

"Work for us," the general said promptly. "If you pass security, we'll find jobs for you—in your own specialty, Mrs. Chindler. We have a constant need for data-retrieval people. And I'm sure your technical background could be used, Dr. Yanami. Of course, you then would be subject to very serious penalties if you passed on any classified information—"

"*No*," David Yanami said strongly.

The general blinked at him. "I beg your pardon."

"No, I won't make a deal with you," David said. "That's terrorism too, isn't it? Taking the whole Earth hostage?"

"Developing a new weapon to insure permanent peace," General Brandywine corrected.

"No, general," David sighed. "I don't buy that. I've been hearing all my life that the next new weapon would bring peace, and all they ever brought were new weapons."

General Brandywine said mildly, "I'm sorry you feel that way, but of course it's your decision. How about you, Mrs. Chindler? Will you be more reasonable?"

Rachel shook her head. "I'm sorry. I won't be your Tania, either."

General Danforth was quicker on the uptake than this superior. "How dare you?" he blazed. "How can you compare your own government with a bunch of revolutionary terrorists like the Symbionese Liberation Army?"

But General Brandywine put his hand on the other man's shoulder. "Let it go, Jacob," he advised. "Mrs. Chindler is naturally upset—this has been quite an ordeal for her, you know! Maybe she'll change her mind later on . . . after all, she'll have plenty of time."

General Brandywine smiled benignly at Rachel, supremely confident that what he had said would be true, because it almost always had been. But the general had not yet seen the next day's newspapers.

28

On one of the little islands off the northern coast of Hokkaido, Japan, a policeman named Totsi Kameguchi was interrupted at his noonday sushi. "Hush, you," he growled at the teenage girl who burst into his home. "What can be so important that it cannot wait ten minutes?"

"It is important, sensei," she begged. "Please! Come to the crab dock! It is Russians, I think!"

Russians! What a bore! But a bore which, nevertheless, must be attended to at once. "Go to the school and get the Russian teacher," he ordered. "Tell her to come at once!"

He did not wait to see if the child obeyed his orders but adjusted his cap, picked up his baton, glanced regretfully at the finest slice of tuna he had tasted in weeks and mounted his bicycle for the ride through town. The dock was full of fishermen and dealers and hangers-on. Kameguchi ordered them out of the way, holding his cap tightly against the gusty wind that smelled of sea and spoiled fish, and confronted the two soaked, dirty, unshaven men who sat uncomfortably on the floor at the end of the dock. Even before the teacher arrived he managed to understand that, yes, as he had guessed, they were defectors again. It was not hard to find a fisherman who understood the language all too well. Kameguchi ordered the defectors off the pier, away from the boxes of writhing, clicking crabs. He sat the men down on one of the few Western-style benches the little port possessed until the teacher arrived. "Well, then," he demanded. "What do you want?"

"We have come to seek asylum," said one through the teacher.

"Oh, yes, I had guessed that," said the policeman sarcastically. "You think that now you are in the Free World you have no more problems. Well, understand that here you must work for a living. What can you do?"

The men glanced at each other. "We are drilling experts," said one.

Kameguchi scowled. The wind had picked up, and a misty, sleety rain was falling, very cold. "We have all the drilling experts we need," he said.

The men sat up straighter. A fisherman plucked at the policeman's sleeve. "I think you should talk to them more gently, sensei," he whispered. "They have something important to tell." The policeman gave him a glare. This was one of the Russian-speaking fishermen, the kind who traded bits of information to the Russians for the right to enter the Kuriles' twelve-mile limit unmolested—as many did, for the islands the Japanese had lost to the Russians after World War II included some of their best fishing grounds. Kameguchi did not like the man; but he could not deny that the man might know what he was talking about.

"Tell me, then," he said, the sarcasm muted.

The Russian said: "We are from Kamchatka. What we have been working on is a dreadful plan, involving a nuclear bomb and a volcano. Take us at once, please, to the nearest newspaper or television station."

"For what?" Kameguchi demanded.

"So that we may tell the world! So that everyone may judge of what wickedness is taking place in our country. So that you people in the free and democratic West may know at last what true evil is! It must be stopped at once—for," said the man, beginning to cry, "a weapon that will freeze half the world and doom billions to starvation—no! We beg you to tell the world that we will not be parties to such villainy!"